Praise for Rupture

'Lelic's first novel is impressive in its scope and structural daring . . . [He] superbly captures the wildly different vocabularies and rhythms of speech of parents, teachers and pupils. This is a superior detective novel, proof that crime fiction can break free of the bounds of the genre into something much more complex' *Daily Telegraph*

'Arresting debut . . . Lelic has an exceptional talent for voice . . . The pace is as ferocious as the subject, and some characters . . . are expertly grotesque. Lelic's novel may be his first, but you wouldn't know it; it is so controlled, yet confidently reckless' *Independent*

'Absorbing, convincing and truly frightening . . . Lelic's novel fuses the police procedural and school genres, twisting many familiar situations and characters into the stuff of chillingly realistic nightmares' *The Times*

'Simon Lelic's impressive and fast-paced debut borrows its structure from a standard police procedural, with a fish-out-of-water cop at its centre . . . What slowly emerges, however, is something more nuanced, as Lelic explores themes of bullying and complicity . . . An artful study of what theologians might term "the sin of omission", *Rupture* keeps readers guessing until the end' *Financial Times*

RUPTURE

Simon Lelic has worked as a journalist
and currently runs his own business.
He was born in Brighton in 1976
and recently returned with his family
to live there. *Rupture* is his first novel.

SIMON LELIC

RUPTURE

PICADOR

First published 2010 by Picador

First published in paperback 2010 by Picador
an imprint of Pan Macmillan, a division of Macmillan Publishers Limited
Pan Macmillan, 20 New Wharf Road, London N1 9RR
Basingstoke and Oxford
Associated companies throughout the world
www.panmacmillan.com

ISBN 978-0-330-50768-4

9 8 7 6 5 4 3 2 1

A CIP catalogue record for this book is available from
the British Library.

Printed in the UK by CPI Mackays, Chatham ME5 8TD

Visit www.picador.com to read more about all our books
and to buy them. You will also find features, author interviews and
news of any author events, and you can sign up for e-newsletters
so that you're always first to hear about our new releases.

For Sarah, Barnaby and Joseph

rupture [noun]: *an instance
of breaking or bursting
suddenly and completely*

I wasn't there. I didn't see it. Me and Banks were down by the ponds, pissing about with this Sainsbury's trolley we found on the common. We were late already so we decided to ditch. Get in, Banks says. You get in, I say. In the end, I get in. I'm always the one getting in. He pushes me for a bit over the field but the wheels keep seizing up, even though the grass is short and it hasn't rained in a month. Sainsbury's trolleys are shit. There's a Waitrose just opened up where the Safeway used to be and their trolleys are built like Volkswagens. Sainsbury's get theirs from France or Italy or Korea or something. They're like Daewoos. Although Ming says Daewoo means fuck yourself in Chinese, which is the only reason I'd ever buy one.

How many was it in the end? I heard thirty. Willis said sixty but you can't trust Willis. He reckons his uncle played for Spurs, years ago, in the eighties or something, and that he can get tickets whenever he likes. He never can though. I've asked him like four times but he always comes up with some excuse. Not cup games, he says. He can't get tickets for cup games. Or I asked too late. Says I have to tell him weeks in advance. Months.

Not the day before, even though it wasn't the day before, it was a Monday or a Tuesday or something and the game wasn't till Saturday.

So how many was it?

Oh. Really? Oh.

Just five?

Oh.

Well, anyway. That's where we were when we heard: down by the ponds. There's this track that runs round the edge. It's made of planks. There are gaps where the wheels can get wedged and it feels like you're off-roading in a Skoda but you can get up some speed. You have to watch the flowerpots. They stick out into the path and you can't move em cos the council have nailed em to the floor. I dunno why they bothered. They're full of Coke cans now, not flowers.

When I say we heard, I don't mean we heard it happen. School was half a mile away, back across the railway tracks. But these year eights turn up just as Banks decides to have a go in the trolley. He gets his foot caught and sort of falls, not arse over gob but enough to make me laugh. I shouldn't of. He gets pissed and starts having a go. And then the year eights turn up and even though they haven't seen him trip, Banks decides to have a go at them.

It was weird though. They're crying, the year eights. Two of em are, any rate. The other one just kind of stares. Not at anything in particular. Like he's watching TV on the inside of his glasses.

So anyway, Banks starts having a go but the year eights just kind of let him. They don't run or mouth off or try to fight or anything. I recognise one of em. Ambrose, his name is. My sister, she's in year eight too, she knows him and says he's okay so I ask him what's going on. He can't speak. His words come out all squashed and stuck together. Banks turns on him but I tell him to leave it. In the end one of the others tells us. I don't remember his name. Spotty kid. Normally I'd say shut the fuck up but he's the only one making any sense.

Banks wants to take the trolley with us but I tell him there'll be police and that there so he shoves it in a bush and says to the year eights if they take it he'll shit in their mouths. They don't look much interested in the trolley, to be fair. The spotty kid nods just the same, all wide-eyed like, but the other two don't look like they've even noticed the trolley.

I've never run to school in my life. Neither's Banks, I guess. I remember we were laughing, not cos it was funny, just cos it was something, you know?

I say to Banks, who do you think did it?

Jones, Banks says. It was Jones, I know it.

How do you know it?

I just do. He was pissed all last week after Bickle made him sing on his own in assembly.

Bickle, that's Mr Travis, the headmaster. That's what we call him cos basically he's mental.

You won't tell him I said that, will you?

Anyway, I don't say anything for a moment. Then I say, I bet it was one of them Goths. One of them kids with the hair and the jeans and the boots they wear in the summer.

Banks sort of scrunches his nose, like he doesn't want to admit it but he thinks I'm probably right.

Have you seen *Taxi Driver*, by the way?

You should.

We hear the sirens before we see the school. We've heard em already I expect but we haven't noticed em. And when we get there I count ten police cars at least. Shitty ones, Fiestas and that, but they're everywhere, all with their lights going. But I guess you know that. You were there, right?

But you got there later?

Thought so. Cos it's your case, right? You're in charge.

Sort of? What does that mean?

Well, anyway, there are ambulances there too and a fire engine for some reason. Some are still moving, just arriving I guess. The rest are all across the street and halfway up the pavement like someone's asked my mum to park em.

I'm sweating and I stop and I hear Banks panting beside me. We aren't laughing any more.

Everyone's going the opposite way. They're leaving the building, any rate. At the pavement everyone's sort of gathered, hanging together in groups. There are some year sevens near the teachers, just outside the gates. The sixth-formers are furthest away, across the road on the edge of the common and just along from me and Banks. I can't see any of our lot but people keep blocking my view. It's like three-thirty or parents' night or a fire drill or something, or all of them things at once.

Check it out, says Banks and he's pointing at Miss Hobbs. She's carrying some kid in her arms, crossing the playground towards the gates. There's blood on em but I can't tell whose.

Are you sure it was only five?

Well, whatever. So Miss Hobbs is crossing the playground,

wobbling and swaying and looking like she's about to drop this kid but no one helps her, not till she reaches the gates. All around her kids are buzzing about and the police, they're going the other way, into the school. Then Miss Hobbs yells, she's got quite a yell I can tell you, like the time she yelled at Banks for flicking his sandwich crusts at Stacie Crump, and one of the ambulance men spots her and legs it over with a stretcher. They disappear after that, behind the ambulance, and that's when I see Jenkins with the others by the lights.

I tug at Banks and I point and we weave in and out the cars and over to the crossing.

Where you been? says Jenkins.

What's happening? I ask him.

Someone went loony tunes. In assembly. Shot the whole place up.

What, with a gun? I say and right away wish I hadn't of.

Jenkins looks at me. Either a gun, he says, or a fifty-litre bottle of ketchup.

Who? says Banks. Who did it?

Dunno. Couldn't see. People were up and running and that before we knew what was happening. Someone said it was Bum-fluff but it couldn't of been, could it?

Then Banks says, where's Jones?

Didn't I say? says Terry, who's standing right beside Jenkins. Didn't I tell you it was Jones?

Jenkins gives Terry a punch on the arm. Banks doesn't know it was Jones, does he? He was just asking where he was.

Well, where is he? Terry says but Banks is already moving away.

Where you going? I say but he ignores me. I run to catch up and hear Jenkins behind me. You won't get in, he says but Banks doesn't even look back.

We try the main gates first but there's these policemen there dressed in yellow, they look like stewards at White Hart Lane. They turn us back. Banks tries again and has to scarper when one of the policemen shouts at him and tries to grab him. We go round the back instead, to the side gate by the kitchens, and there's a policeman there as well but he's talking to a woman with a pushchair, pointing at something across the street. He doesn't see us.

I've never been in the kitchens before. I've seen em from the other side, from the counter, but only the main bit and even then you can barely see past the dinner ladies, they're like sumo wrestlers in a scrum. Not that you'd want to. It's fucking disgusting. The main bit, where they serve the food, it's not too bad but in the back, with the cookers and the bins, it's rank. I see what I had for lunch the day before, a pile of pork all glistening with fat like it's been run over by a herd of slugs, just left on a tray in the sink. And there's stuff all over the floor, lettuce gone soggy and brown, and peas with their guts splattered and smeared all over the tiles. I almost throw up. I have to swallow it back down. But I'd rather eat vomit than eat in the canteen again, I swear. Banks, though, he doesn't hardly notice. He lives in a council. I live in a council too but a better one.

We're trapped in there for a bit. We can't find a way out cept for the way we've just come in. In the end we jump up over the counter. I kick at a tray of glasses with my foot, not on purpose, but some of the glasses fall and they break. Banks starts having a go, tells me to be quiet, but no one hears. No one would of cared.

From the canteen we go out into the passageway and along into the entrance hall and that brings us right up to the main doors and there's a crowd there and who should we run into but Michael Jones himself. And we know just by looking at him that it can't of been Jones.

He spots us but doesn't say anything and he's as pale as a custard cream. He's trying to get out by the looks of him but he's stuck behind a wall of sixth-formers. The sixth-formers, they're standing there, waving their arms about and bossing people where to go but it seems to me like they're only making things worse. Bickle's there too, Mr Travis, he's standing by the doors, telling the kids to keep moving to settle down to maintain order to move along. That's one of his phrases that: maintain order. As in, I'm sitting in on this class today to help *maintain order*. Or he'll be marching the corridors, whacking kids on the head, yelling, order children, *maintain order*. He calls us children even though we're like thirteen. The sixth-formers are eighteen some of em. Anyway, it should be our school motto – *maintain order* – not that thing we have in Latin. Something about helping yourself or helping others or doing one but not the other. Something like that.

Bickle spots us too and he looks like he's about to collar us but he's distracted, there's kids pushing past him, banging against him, on purpose some of em I bet, and Banks and me slip past and into the main corridor, the one that leads to the stairs and the classrooms and at the bottom, at the end, the hall, the assembly hall. That's where it all happened, right? The assembly hall.

We almost make it. We almost see it. The whadyacallit. The aftermath. I'm glad we didn't. Banks wanted to but I think I'm glad we didn't. Do you know what I mean?

It's a woman that nabs us in the end, a policewoman and they're the worst. All bossy and up themselves.

Oh.

No offence.

But anyway, we're halfway down the corridor and we can see the doors into the hall and we can see there are people inside, police and that mainly, and we don't see her reach for us. She was in one of the classrooms, I guess. She saw us pass and must of figured what we were doing, where we were going, and she doesn't shout or anything, she just comes up behind us and she nails us. Banks yells at her to geroff but in the end we can't really do anything, I mean what can we do? And she marches us up the corridor, back into the hallway, through the doors past Bickle, who just kind of glares, and all the way to the gates. And then she gives us a shove.

Banks tried to get back in after that but I'm pretty sure he didn't make it. By the time we get outside there's tape and more police and TV cameras and everything's being organised. The teachers, they're calling register and forming lines and that sort of thing. I stand on my own, to one side. I sit on the kerb. Then, I dunno. I just watch, like everyone else.

So that's it, I guess. I told you, I don't know anything really. I wasn't even there when it happened.

This time she started where he had started.

There was nothing in the room that gave notice of the violence it had begotten. Several coats on the rack, though not many. There was one overcoat, on a hanger, a relic presumably of the winter. Otherwise just jackets, lightweight, inexpensive, the one on top with an arm turned inside out. There were coffee mugs on the table, the one nearest to her drained completely, the rest finished with but not emptied, milk curdling on the surface of the liquid. On the arm of one of the chairs, an open packet of digestives, and crumbs on the rest of the seats. The seats themselves were stained, ripped in places, comfortable looking.

Lucia May moved from the seating area towards the kitchenette. She opened the door of the microwave and then shut what she found back inside. The smell escaped, though – sweet, artificial, she thought, low calorie. A packet of Marlboro lay next to a yellow Clipper on the worktop. She did not look at them directly. The cupboard next to the sink served as a makeshift noticeboard. There was a Garfield strip bemoaning

Mondays cut neatly from a newspaper and a 'Now wash your hands' sticker and a handwritten note reminding people to please rinse out their cups. The word people was underlined, as well as the word cups. Four mugs sat festering in the basin. The basin smelt of drains.

He would have left this room alone. He would have waited until he was the last.

Lucia drifted back towards the seats and out of the door and into the corridor. Opposite her was the noticeboard proper, half the size of a snooker table and almost the same shade of green. It displayed fire-drill instructions, medical procedures, assembly rosters, break-time regulations. Nothing else. The notices were attached to the board with colour-matched pins, all red on one sheet of paper, all yellow on the next, four pins to a page. She felt an urge to shuffle the pins, to remove a notice and reattach it at a less regimented angle.

She turned to her left and moved along the passageway, down the short flight of stairs and into the entrance hall. She paused, wondering whether he had done the same. She glanced right, towards the canteen, and then the other way, towards the doors. Through the glass she saw two uniforms, and beyond them the playground, and beyond that the road. The policemen were watching her, their arms folded and their eyes shaded by the brims of their helmets.

There was blood on the floor. She had known it was there and she had meant to ignore it because the blood had come after, during, not before. She looked at it anyway. The girl whose blood it was had still been alive when she had shed it. It had run down her arm and to her hand and from her fingers as the teacher had carried her out. It lay in drops and in several places it was smeared, as if by a toe or a heel or a knee where someone had stumbled.

He would not have stopped, Lucia was sure, and so she carried on, not walking on the blood but not not walking on the blood.

The assembly hall was some distance from the staffroom. The walk would have allowed him plenty of time to think, to reconsider, to change his mind and then back again. Somehow she knew that he had not thought. He had focused on not thinking.

As she paced the length of the corridor she passed classrooms with their doors open and a series of recessed stairwells. She glanced through each doorway and up each flight of stairs, sure that he would have done the same. In her school, she recalled, there had been pupils' work displayed along the corridors: geography projects or charity work or photos from the year-end musical. The walls she passed were bare, breeze-block grey. The only markings were from the paint, a darker grey, that the caretaker had used to conceal graffiti. After every other door there was an alarm switch and at the far end of the hall the alarm itself, higher up and encased in wire.

There was tape across the doors that led into the assembly hall. The doors themselves were locked. Lucia took a key from her pocket, turned it in the padlock and opened one of the doors. She ducked under the tape and stepped inside.

It smelt of plimsolls. Rubbery, sweaty, the yield of scores of scrabbling feet. The assembly hall, she knew, doubled as the gym. There were climbing frames, folded to the walls and locked in place.

She shut the door behind her, just as he had done. He would have looked to the front, she assumed, at the stage and whomever had been speaking. The headmaster. Travis. Lucia's eyes, though, caught on the climbing frame opposite her, on the ropes that bisected the rows of bars. One of the victims had hauled themselves upright, had used a rope to try and help them escape the onrush of bodies. There was blood on the knot at the bottom and at intervals for several feet up. At head height the blood marks stopped.

The hall was as it had been all week. Nothing had been moved, other perhaps than by the faltering feet of a photographer. It would have been hard not to bump into something. There was no clear pathway to the stage, nor to the side of the hall across from her. From the rear wall to the podium, chairs lay on their backs, on their sides, any way but the right way up. Many were still laced together so that where one chair had fallen the rest had fallen too, transforming the row into a barrier, the legs of the chairs into barbs. Lucia was reminded of an image of Verdun, of the land and the barricades between the trenches. She imagined children, their eyes bleeding fear, tripping and becoming entangled and then trampled by those behind. She imagined the impact of one of the upended chair legs against a stomach, a cheek, a temple.

On the chairs and under them were jumpers, some books, the contents of children's pockets. A set of keys here, attached to a chain attached to a belt loop torn from someone's trousers. An iPod, black, with its headphones still plugged in and its screen cracked. Mobile phones. And shoes. There was a surprising number of shoes. Girls' shoes mainly but also trainers and boots. To one side a single brogue, size ten or eleven. A pair of glasses, the lenses intact but one arm snapped off. A handkerchief, white.

She tried to ignore the state of the hall and to picture it as he would have seen it: every seat full, the children silent for once given the circumstances of the assembly, some of them crying and trying not to. The teachers seated in rows flanking the headmaster, jaws tense, eyes downcast or fixed on the head-master himself. Travis at the lectern, his hands on the corners furthest away from him and his elbows locked, his eyes commanding the attention of his audience, his speechifying relentless despite the late arrival to the hall. Travis would have seen him walk through the doors of course. Some of the teachers would have too, though they could not have made out what he was carrying. Children in the back row may have turned, may even have noticed the gun, but they would have assumed, surely, that it was a prop, that his late entrance was staged to coincide with some aspect of Travis's address. The gun was in keeping with the theme of the headmaster's sermon after all. Violence was the theme of the day.

She traced his steps as best she could, moving across the rear of the hall and then turning at the corner towards the stage. Halfway along the side wall Lucia stopped and faced inwards, in the direction of where the pupils would have been sitting.

He would have had no skill with a gun. His aim was poor and his prey would have started moving and the gun itself did not fire straight. So Sarah Kingsley, aged eleven, was the first to be shot. As it turned out, she was also the last to die. Lucia wondered if it had registered, his mistake, after he had squeezed the trigger. Whether he had even noticed. Sarah's blood was at her feet. It was Sarah's blood, mainly, that she had followed along the corridor. It was Sarah's blood on the rope.

The first report would have impacted like a brick through glass. The stillness in the hall would have shattered and been displaced by a jagged, piercing panic. The children would have scattered, they would have screamed. He would have tried to remain still, to stand unyielding against the thrashing bodies, to find his aim again. Once more he had fired and once more he had missed his target. Felix Abe, aged twelve, had died instead.

Two from two. The weapon was a museum piece, not a semi-automatic. It was in poor condition. That he killed five, five with six bullets, was in a way a minor miracle. It was the worst kind of luck.

The teachers would have been standing by now, fixated and immobile, like theatre-goers trapped in the circle as chaos consumes the stalls. They would have seen him fire for a third time and they would have seen the third child fall. When he fired again – his fourth bullet, the second one to hit Donovan Stanley, aged fifteen – they might have understood. When he had then looked to them and taken his first step towards the stage, they might finally have run themselves.

Lucia moved to where the final victim – Veronica Staples, the teacher – had fallen, at the base of the steps leading away from the stage. There were more shoes gathered here, piled almost neatly at the bottom step. There was a handbag too, its contents spilled and scattered: a lipgloss with its case cracked; receipts and scraps of paper, marked and muddied by frantic feet; a pen; a whistle threaded with pink ribbon; half a packet of Polo mints.

She turned, checking the ground around her as she did so, and saw where he had fired the sixth round, the last bullet in the barrel, and where his blood had splattered the wall. The plaster, once yellow, was pitted by bullet and bone. There were strands of hair too, clumps of it, where his head had impacted against the wall and slid towards the skirting. She crouched and imagined herself level with him, looking at him, watching the carnage he had created reflected back at her by his unseeing eyes.

Finally she reversed the order, moving to the point where Sarah, the first victim, had been shot. In her mind, the scene unfolded like a DVD playing in reverse. The bullets retreated, the chairs toppled upright, the blood flowed to the place it belonged. Children found their seats, teachers lowered their gaze and Samuel Szajkowski walked backwards and out of the room.

It was warmer outside than in. Stepping out into the playground was like stepping on to a runway in the tropics. The policemen, tall and overweight both, were red cheeked and sweating. They had been chatting, making jokes, and they were grinning as she came through the doors.

'Find what you were looking for, Inspector?'

Every day the same question. A different uniform but the same question. They thought Lucia enjoyed being here. They thought that was why she kept coming back. But they were asking the wrong thing. She had found what she was looking for – she had found what she had been sent to discover – but she had found out more besides. The question was what to do about it. The question was whether to do anything at all.

Do you have any idea, Detective Inspector May, of the crisis the teaching of mathematics is facing in this country?

Of course not. Why would you?

Do you have a pension, Inspector? Do you have a mortgage? You pay rent, though. Money comes in and money goes out. More out than in, I'd warrant. I do not mean to pass judgement, Inspector, but that tends to be the way. And do you know why? I'll tell you why. Because most of the adult population in this country can barely count their own toes, assuming for a moment that they can see beyond their bellies to locate them. It has been true since the 1960s and it will remain true for as long as you care to consider.

Calculators, mobile telephones, personal computers, electronic chips in the brain or whatever technological so-called advancement is foisted upon us next: they are eroding the human being's capacity to think. And mathematics – addition, subtraction, multiplication, long division – has been the first to suffer. Children don't want to study it. The government doesn't want to fund it. Teachers don't want to teach it. What is the point? they say. There is no glamour in mathematics, Inspector. There is no sex. Children don't care about pensions. They will be young forever, didn't you know? Ministers don't care about numeracy. They care about trees and recycling and structural employment for the poor. And teachers. Well. Teachers, I am afraid, care about nothing beyond themselves.

The young, the graduates, they have a chance to make a difference. They have the opportunity to teach a subject from which the children will actually learn. But if they don't understand it, how can they teach it? And if no one else can be bothered to do it, why should they? It is too hard. It is too challenging. The mathematics teacher, as a consequence, is a dying breed, an endangered species that no one cares enough about to try and save. Mr Boardman has been teaching mathematics at this school for twenty-seven years. Twenty-seven years, Inspector. Can you imagine anyone under forty contemplating pursuing anything for more than twenty-seven minutes? Present company excluded, I hope. And when Mr Boardman retires, as one day he surely shall, who will I find to replace him? A Chinaman perhaps. A Ukrainian, if I'm lucky.

Instead, I get history teachers. History. The study of swords and stupidity and scandal. Just what a teenager needs to prepare himself for a life of fiscal and behavioural responsibility. If it were up to me we would not offer it. We would teach mathematics and grammar and physics and chemistry and economics. But the parents want it. The government demands it. They impose on us their curriculum and they instruct us to teach history and geography and biology and sociology. They instruct us to teach humanities.

I ask you.

You would not have attended university, I assume?

Well. I stand corrected. And what, pray tell, did you read? No, don't tell me. It is clear from your expression. And in a way, my dear, you are a case in point. Where has your history degree got you if not further back than where you began? You are, how old? Thirty.

Thirty-two then. If you had joined the police force when you were sixteen you might be a chief inspector by now. Superintendent.

But I digress. My point is that when Amelia Evans left us – and not before time, let me tell you – we had no choice. We needed a teacher who could recount in order the wives of Henry VIII, who could point on a map to the fields of Bosworth and who could recall the date of Queen Elizabeth's coronation. The first Queen Elizabeth, that is. Heaven forbid we teach them anything of relevance to the age in which they actually live.

It was the name that drew me to him. Russian, I assumed. Eastern European. Of a country that still recognises the educational import of the third of the three Rs. That's what I have resorted to, Inspector. Scouring the international backwaters for someone to help me safeguard the future of this nation.

It was a mistake. Naturally it was a mistake given what has happened but it was a mistake a priori. I am a man who owns up to his mistakes, Inspector, and I can but admit to one here. I misjudged the man. I prejudged him. I willed him to correspond with a template I had envisaged and when he did not I adjusted the template to fit.

Although, having said that, I knew from the start that there was something about him amiss. One just knows, don't you find? He seemed the decent type, isn't that what they always say? Quiet, kept himself to himself. 'Never harmed nobody.' Well, he was quiet certainly. An introvert and I do not trust introverts. I do not trust extroverts either. One needs balance, Inspector, I am sure you agree. In your profession as much as anyone's, words must be followed by action, compassion reinforced with resolve. Good cop, bad cop, am I right?

He had a beard, wispy and ill-considered. He was average in height, average in build, averagely turned out in every aspect of his dress. Distinctly unimpressive in other words but not offensively lacklustre either. He looked, Inspector, like a teacher of history.

He sat where you are sitting. He waited to be asked. He did not smile as he took my hand and he gripped only the tips of my fingers. It was a woman's handshake, Inspector, and that I would say is when I knew.

Yes, I know. I hired him. You may voice what you are thinking. Yes, I hired him and as I have said it was a mistake. Believe me, it has shaken my self-belief. My ability to judge a character is something in which I take pride. Well, you know what they say about pride. Next time I will trust my instincts. I questioned myself, that was the problem. We needed a teacher and Samuel Szajkowski was the least underqualified of a less than inspiring lot.

What else? Lots of little things. His attempts at humour for instance.

How do you pronounce this? I asked him, gesturing at the name on his CV.

It's shy-kov-skee, he says and I ask him where it is from.

It's Polish. My grandfather was Polish.

I see. And do you speak it?

No, not really.

Not really.

I know words. Some useful, most less so. I can't spell any of them.

You see what I mean? He was making a joke of his inadequacy. At an interview, for pity's sake. I did not laugh and we carried on.

Why teaching, Mr Szajkowski? What has motivated you to become a teacher?

Szajkowski nods and for a moment appears to contemplate. I can think of nothing more worthwhile, Mr Travis. My father practised medicine and my mother worked in a bank. Neither profession made them happy.

They are noble professions, young man. They are significant professions.

Oh I quite agree. But so is teaching. It doesn't pay particularly well but can you think of anything more rewarding? Again he ponders. I think the word I'm looking for is meaning, he says. Teaching to my mind has meaning. Genuine meaning.

I did not appreciate that answer either. It seemed pompous and it seemed calculated. He might have read that answer in a book.

He asks for a glass of water. I have not offered but he asks for one anyway. I have Janet bring one in and he thanks her, rather obsequiously. He takes a swig and then seems unsure what to do with the glass. He makes a motion towards my desk but then changes his mind. In the end he just clutches it in his lap. I can tell he regrets having asked for it but I do not offer to take it from him. I do not see why I should have to.

In an ideal world, I tell him, we would have you teaching just the younger pupils. Years seven, eight, nine, ten. But this is not an ideal world, Mr Szajkowski, and we are short-staffed.

Szajkowski nods, gives the impression that he understands. I am not at all sure that he does.

You would be teaching students in their exam years, I say. GCSE, even A-level. And not just history, Mr Szajkowski. Teachers get ill. I do not encourage illness but it happens. It is a fact of life. And when teachers get ill, other teachers need to cover their classes.

I would be happy to, Mr Travis. I'm more than willing to do my bit.

It is a permanent state of affairs, Mr Szajkowski. There will be no respite while you are employed here, I can assure you of that. Assuming of course that we decide to employ you in the first place.

Of course, he says and again he nods gravely. I appreciate the warning, just as I would appreciate the opportunity. I am sure the situation here is not unusual. I would imagine the demands would be similar in just about any state-run school.

Again a hint of arrogance, like he is in a position to lecture me about the condition of education in this country. But I let the matter drop. He will, I tell myself, come to terms with his inexperience soon enough.

Before he leaves – just before he walks out of my office still clutching that infernal glass – I ask him one more thing. I ask him what he thinks of history. I ask him what he thinks history is.

He says, have I read Carr, is that what you're asking me?

I admit I am taken aback. E. H. Carr, Inspector. There is a copy on the shelf beside you. A moronic work. Lucid enough but entirely misguided. A history teacher who has not read it, however, may as well be replaced by a book.

And what did you make of Mr Carr's hypothesis?

I agreed with parts, he says. But in general I found his arguments overblown. A bit too self-important. History is what it is. It can't predict the future but it can help us understand who we are, where we're from. History is all about context, he says, and without context all meaning is lost.

That impressed me, I will admit. He had some intellectual backbone even if he lacked any in his demeanour. His qualifications, indeed, were never in doubt. Good school, venerable university – not one of these self-aggrandising polytechnics – and solid grades. An A-level in mathematics, if you please. He was bright. Green but bright, and because he was green he was cheap.

We have targets now, Inspector. Targets to meet and books to balance. You raise an eyebrow at me but I cannot ignore the cost of the capital in which we invest, human or otherwise. Believe me, I would like to. The handling of currency sullies one's soul as much as one's fingertips. Book-keeping can be a sordid business. But it is a necessary one, and one I would rather deal with myself than leave to bureaucrats who have no facility with the workings of a school.

There were aspects to Szajkowski's candidacy then that

would have made it difficult not to employ him. His references were positively glowing; his CV proved accurate to a fault. There was no trace of delinquency in his past nor half a hint of what he would ultimately prove capable of doing. Any school in our position would have acted as we did, Inspector, and anyone who tells you otherwise is either a fool or an outright liar.

But you asked me what was different about him. You asked me why I had my doubts.

His handshake then, and his demeanour. His attempt at humour, though this he did not repeat. He did not seem nervous, which I am not used to, because I am aware that I make people nervous. He was aloof, rather, and somewhat arrogant. He was in many ways exactly as I hoped he would not be.

All very subjective, I realise. All very ambiguous. But as I say, Inspector, I am talking about instinct more than anything else. Nothing particularly tangible for you to go on and nothing that I could have used to justify a decision not to hire him. But that's the problem with gut feelings, isn't it? They can be powerful, overwhelming even, and yet without any foundation. They are illogical, unscientific and imprecise. And yet they are so often correct.

Such a waste. Such a waste of young lives. Sarah Kingsley, we had high hopes for her. Felix had his problems and Donovan was no end of trouble. Maddeningly bright but no end of trouble. But Sarah. Sarah might have gone to Oxford, Inspector. She was just the calibre of pupil we have been looking to bring to this school. She was precisely the calibre.

Now then. Another cup of tea? Shall I have Janet bring in some biscuits?

'It's dragging on, Lucia.'

'It's been a week.'

Cole nodded. He sat with his elbows on the desk, his fingertips pressed together, his knuckles slightly bent. 'It's been a week.'

'I don't know what you expect me to say, sir, but—'

'You're giving me cold sores, Inspector.'

'Cold sores?'

'Look here,' said Cole. He leant forwards, pointing towards his chin. 'And here. I get them when I'm stressed. My wife says they make me look like a teenager. A teenager with acne or a drug habit or something.'

'I don't think you look like a teenager, sir.' The detective chief inspector was bald on top and where he was not bald his hair was grey. He wheezed when he walked and perspired even when it was cold. Just as Lucia's grandfather had, he wore button-down short-sleeved shirts in the summer. He was wearing one now.

'Have you ever had a cold sore, Lucia?'

She shook her head.

'They hurt. They tingle for a while and then they burn and then they sting like Lord knows what. I don't like them.'

'I can appreciate that. I don't think I'd like them either.'

'What's the hold-up, Inspector? Why is this taking so long?' Lucia shuffled. She opened her notebook on her lap.

'Don't look in there. Look at me.'

'Five people died, sir. That's four murders and a suicide. What do you want me to say?'

The chief inspector rolled his eyes. He levered himself from his chair and creaked until he was standing. He plucked a cup from the stack beside the cooler and drew himself some water. He took a sip, winced as the cold bit his teeth and then settled himself on the edge of the desk.

'Five people died. All right then. Where did they die?' He looked at Lucia but did not wait for her to answer. 'In the same room. And how? By the same gun, at the hands of the same gunman. You have a murder weapon, a motive, a room full of witnesses.' DCI Cole looked at his watch. 'I've got an hour before I'm due to go home. I could write your report and still knock off twenty minutes early.'

Lucia was looking up at him now. She tried to nudge her chair backwards an inch but the front legs just lifted from the floor. 'I have a motive. What motive do you think I have?'

'He was whacko. A nutcase. Depressed, schizophrenic, abused, I don't care. Why else would he shoot up a school?'

'He was depressed. That's enough for you? He was depressed.'

'Jesus Christ, Lucia, what does it matter? He's dead. He's not going to be doing it again.'

'We're talking about a shooting in a school, Guv. In a school.'

'So we are. What's your point?'

Lucia could smell coffee on the chief inspector's breath. She could feel heat leaking through his pores. She tried moving her chair backwards once more but the legs snagged against the pile of the carpet. She got up. 'I'm going to let in some air.' She slid past her boss towards the window and reached through the blind to find the latch.

'It doesn't open. It's never opened.'

Lucia tried twisting the latch anyway but it had long since gummed itself shut. She turned and leant back against the sill. Her fingertips were sticky with grime.

'There's something you're not telling me.'

'No there isn't.'

'There is. There's something you're not telling me. Look, this guy, this Szajkowski—' he pronounced it saj-cow-skee '—no one knew about him, right? He wasn't on any lists.'

'He wasn't on any lists.'

'So no one messed up. No one could have predicted it, which means no one could have stopped it.'

'I suppose so.'

'So why won't you let this thing go?'

Lucia picked at the dirt on her fingers.

'These things happen, Lucia. Sometimes these things happen. It's shitty but it's life. Our job is to catch the bad guys. In this case, the bad guy's dead. All the rest – the accusations, the recriminations, the lessons fucking learnt – leave that to the politicians.'

'I want more time.'

'Why?'

'I need more time.'

'Then tell me why.'

It was one of those thick summer days when the sun seems to exhale over the city so that by the afternoon the whole of London is consumed by its hazy, sticky breath. Though the brightness had faded, the temperature if anything had increased. Lucia stuck out her lower lip and blew air across her brow. She tugged at the underarms of her blouse.

'What if there was more than one bad guy?' she said. 'What if not all of the bad guys are dead?'

'Five hundred people saw Szajkowski pull the trigger. You're not telling me that all of them are wrong.'

'No, I'm not. That's not what I'm saying. But you don't have to be the one to pull the trigger to deserve a portion of the blame.'

The DCI shook his head. He was shaking it still as he lowered himself into his seat.

'I can feel another cold sore coming, Lucia. I can feel a bastard lawsuit coming.'

'Just give me a week.'

'No.'

'Just one more week, sir. Please.'

Cole was shuffling paperwork on his desk. He answered without looking up. 'Can't do it.'

Lucia tapped her notebook against her thigh. She looked out of the window and down into the car park and then back at her superior. 'Why not?' she said. 'Why the urgency?'

He met her gaze. 'I like things neat,' he said. 'I like things tidy. I don't like things dragging on. Besides—' the chief inspector again located a page on his desk that seemed to catch his interest '—you said it yourself. We're talking about a shooting in a school. The longer we leave it . . . Well. It makes people nervous, let's put it like that.'

'What people?'

'Don't be naive, Inspector. People. Just people.'

They heard a jubilant holler from the open-plan office outside. They heard clapping. Lucia and her boss looked towards the sound but their view was obscured by the smoked-glass wall.

'How long are you giving me?'

'You've got until Monday. I need your report before lunchtime.'

'So one day. Effectively you're giving me one day.'

'It's Thursday. You've got this evening and you've got Friday and you've got the weekend.'

'I have plans for the weekend.'

'Then prioritise, Lucia. You can give me the report right now if you'd prefer.'

Lucia folded her arms. 'Prioritise.'

Cole nodded, almost smiled.

'Thank you, sir. I appreciate your advice.'

Walter called out to her as she strode past his desk. She ignored him, carried on walking, but Harry was blocking her path. He was on one knee clutching a fistful of paper towels. There was a puddle of liquid and a cracked coffee pot beside him. The spilt coffee had been the source of the applause, Lucia realised. It would have been Walter who had cried out with glee.

'Here,' she said and she bent to Harry's side.

'Goddammit,' Harry muttered, relinquishing the paper towels to Lucia. There was a welt on the side of his hand. He raised the mark to his mouth and sucked.

'What happened?'

'I dropped it. Goddammit.' He inspected the burn on his hand.

'When you're done on the floor with Harry, Lulu, I'll be waiting for you on my desk.'

Lucia did not turn around. 'You should put something on that hand,' she said.

'It's okay.' Harry stood and shoved the burnt hand into his pocket. The broken pot dangled from his left. 'I'd better do something with this.'

Lucia got up. She threw the paper towels into the bin by Walter's desk and made to follow Harry.

'Don't do that, Lulu. Don't give me the silent treatment.'

She should have kept walking. She should have left Walter in the arms of his ego. Yet she could sense his leer even with her back to him, could picture him reclining in his chair. The others would be watching too – willing her to retort but just as ready to laugh if she stayed silent.

She turned. 'What's your problem, Walter? What is it that you want to say?'

'It's our problem, Lulu. Yours and mine. It's my girlfriend,' he said. 'I think she knows.'

'Your girlfriend?' said Lucia. 'Didn't she burst?'

There was laughter. Heads in the office poked above partitions. Phones were cradled or receivers covered with palms.

Walter's leer was contagious. It had contaminated the entire department.

'I'm serious, Lulu. We're going to have to call this thing off. We're going to have to call it a day.'

'You're breaking my heart, Walter. Truly, you're breaking my heart.'

'But listen.' He glanced at the faces around him and then at the office Lucia had just left. 'Cole'll be gone by six. What say you and I sneak into his office, turn down the lights and say one last goodbye on his couch.'

Lucia looked at Walter's smirk, at the blotched skin on his jowls and at his thighs too fat for his suit, and all she could do was shake her head. And then, willing herself not to but unable to resist, she voiced the only retort that came to mind.

'You're a prick, Walter. A fucking prick.'

She got home and she opened the door and she wished she had a dog.

She thought perhaps she might get one. Nothing too big but not a ratty dog either. A spaniel, maybe. A beagle. She would call it Howard and she would feed it from her plate and let it sleep on one side of her bed. She would teach it to attack fat men called Walter and chief inspectors with halitosis but Walters before chief inspectors.

The flat was hot. The air felt recycled, as though it had been warmed and sucked free of oxygen by a hundred pairs of lungs, and then exhaled and sealed into the box that she still could not think of as home.

She hung her bag by the door. She checked the phone, washed

her hands, splashed her face. There was an apple in the fridge and she ate it, ignoring the bruises but cringing at the texture. She took two slices of bread from the freezer and dropped them into the toaster but while she stared at a wall and thought of nothing, the toast burnt. She threw it away and poured some red wine into a whisky glass instead.

In the living room she opened the window. There was no breeze; the temperature was the same outside as it was in. She had a fan somewhere but wherever it was it was broken. She had a hairdryer. Set to low it would feel about the same.

The living room was the only room of the flat she liked. The kitchen was poky, the bathroom full of mould and the bedroom dark and a mess. The living room was bright all day and it was comfortable. There was a rug and her TV and a view, if she leant right out of the sash window, of a corner of the common. The sofa, underneath the throws, was a disturbing shade of green but its embrace was perfectly judged – an arm around the shoulder rather than a full-bodied hug. Although sometimes, on days like today for instance, the hug would have been welcome too.

It was in the living room that she kept her books. She read a lot. Novels mainly; history books if she felt she had been gorging on Rebus. The books filled the shelves the landlord had left for her, as well as her IKEA bookcase. She liked to let her eyes graze upon the spines. She liked being able to identify a book without being close enough to read its title. The battered corners, the creases on each cover – they were a mark of familiarity. They were a comfort.

Tonight she did not read. The book she had started lay where she had left it the night before the shooting. She had snapped its spine and placed it face down upon the floor, as though such treatment might render it more compliant, more accessible, less determined to make hard work of itself. It was about Stalingrad: the battle, the siege. It was never going to make for an easy read. The problem was she had read too much to give up but not enough to start counting down towards the end. She had reached page one hundred and forty-three and it had not even started snowing.

She picked up the television remote control. She put it down again. She always checked the listings but there was never anything on that she felt the urge to watch. Someone had told her to get Sky, to get a Freeview box at least, and she had agreed that it would probably be worth it, which was as far as she had got.

She stood up and wandered to the window. She looked out at the common and she knelt with her chin on her hands on the sill and then she got up and poured herself some more wine. In the end she gathered her case notes from her desk and returned with them to the sofa. From the pile she plucked a transcript at random. It was an interview with one of the kids. Not one of hers. A DC had taken this one. She had read it before and though she did not remember it, she knew that it said nothing. Nothing. It spoke of pain and grief and shock and more pain but from her perspective, her professional perspective, that was nothing.

She picked up the remote control again and this time flicked on the television. She hit mute and stared at the images as she thought about Szajkowski and about the children and about the upturned chairs in the hall. Then she willed herself not to. She willed herself to think about something else. For a while nothing came to her, until she remembered what she had said to the DCI, about the weekend, about her plans, and she wondered whether he had believed her.

We didn't get on. So what? It wasn't a secret. It's hardly a crime. Turns out I had him down pretty good, wouldn't you say?

Physical education, since you ask. I have a degree in sport and leisure studies from the University of Loughborough. It's the best course of its kind in the country. Tough to get on. Even tougher to complete. Hardest damn thing I've ever done and I used to compete. Triathlons, Ironman, marathons sometimes. My knees put me out. My knees and my ankle.

Physical education: it's a science. When we were at school it meant a cross-country run in our underwear. A game of rugby for the boys, hockey for the girls. No discipline, no organisation and no specialisation. Our headmaster used to take us. He would chuck us out a football and sit refereeing from the window of his office. Refereeing. Hah. He used to read the paper. He would look up if he heard a holler but otherwise he left us to it. When you fouled someone you had to foul them quietly. You had to wind them so they couldn't yell.

There's something to be said for it. The Darwinian approach to sport. You know Darwin, right? But you wouldn't get away with that now. Like I say, it's a science these days. It's become a science. We teach them sportsmanship and skills – transferable skills, we call them – and nutrition and stuff like that. Just last week we had an hour on callisthenics. I can never say that word. Callisthenics. Callisthenics.

People assume it must be easy. There's a lot of prejudice that surrounds my job. Szajkowski, he's a perfect example.

We have a week, before the start of term. The headmaster's there and all the teachers are there and we have to do this training, attend these sessions. It's bullshit most of it, a waste of time. But part of it is a social thing. You know, everyone getting reacquainted, meeting the newbies, that sort of thing.

Anyway. So there were two new teachers last term. One of them's Matilda Moore, she teaches chemistry. Quiet girl but nice enough. Not much into sport but she's not ignorant about it. She's not arrogant. The other one of course is Sam Szajkowski. Sam 'Call me Samuel' Szajkowski.

So it's the end of the day and we're in the hall and the headmaster's laid on a spread. You know, sandwiches with their crusts chopped off, mini sausage rolls, crisps. We're drinking wine or fruit juice or whatever and everyone's having a nice enough time. The headmaster's standing here, Matilda's over there, we're all dotted about in groups. All a bit low key for my tastes, not particularly lively, but you just get on with it, don't you?

So I see Szajkowski on his own and though the headmaster has introduced him to everyone, I haven't said hello myself. So I do. He's new here, I'm thinking. The guy's on his own. I should make an effort to make him feel welcome.

Now I realise me and him aren't exactly alike. He's about half my size and pasty and he looks a bit like Woody Allen but with a scraggly black beard and without the glasses and not as old or into sex. Or maybe he was, who the fuck knows? But just because we're not alike doesn't mean we can't get on. Like George. George Roth. He teaches RE and we're about the least similar people you can imagine. I mean, I've never set foot in a church, let alone a mosque or a temple or a Jew hall, but we get on well enough, we get along. We talk about football and he tells me football is a type of religion and I don't suppose he's wrong. Which would make Pelé God, right? Or Matt Le Tissier, depending on where you're from.

But Szajkowski: right away we're on the wrong foot. I say hi and pleased to meet you. I tell him my name and tell him to call me TJ, because everyone else does, even the kids.

He says, hello TJ. I'm Samuel. Samuel Szajkowski.

Samuel, I say. So Sam, is it? I guess people call you Sam?

And he gives this little shake of his head and kind of smiles and says, no, they call me Samuel.

And his handshake. Did I mention his handshake? You can tell a lot about a man from his handshake. You can tell a lot about a woman too. Like you. You've got a firm shake, a strong grip. That tells me what. It tells me that you're a woman in a man's job and that you can't afford to take any shit. You've got cold hands, though, did you know that? It's roasting in here but you've got cold hands.

Szajkowski's grip was as limp as his . . . I mean, it was a faggot's handshake. That's just an expression, by the way. It's not derogatory. You know exactly what I mean, don't you?

It was like this. Here, hold out your hand. Just hold it out. So I'm Szajkowski and I do this.

You see what I mean?

So after that he's kind of got my back up already but I don't show it. I'm just thinking what I'm thinking about the bloke and I'm thinking, you never know I might be wrong. Turns out I wasn't, didn't it, but that's another story.

So I stick with it, I say, okay, Samuel. It's a pleasure to meet you, Samuel.

Jesus Christ though. I mean, who calls themselves Samuel when that's their name? It takes so bloody long. Sam. I would have liked the guy a whole lot better if he'd just let me call him Sam.

I'm sorry but that kind of thing just pisses me off.

Where was I?

Right. So we're chatting and it gets to the point where he asks me what I teach. And I just know right away that he's gonna have some attitude about it when I tell him. I mean, with him you can tell just by looking at him that he's never run a yard or kicked a ball or even taken his top off in the sun in the whole of his entire life. He's what my old man would have called an intellectual, which is fine, it's not a crime, but it seems to me that he's also a foot and a half up his own arse.

So maybe I get a bit defensive. Not aggressive or anything but I'm thinking, what right has he got to feel superior? And I think, okay, let's see. How about a little test? And rather than tell him, I decide to let him guess.

You tell me, I say.

Sorry, he says, acting all confused.

Go on, have a guess. What do you think I teach?

Oh. I see. Let's see.

And I'm watching him and I'm smiling and he's smiling and we both know that he knows but he's afraid to say.

Well, if I had to guess . . .

Go on, I say. Just have a guess.

If I had to guess . . .

Just say it. You know. I know you know.

If I had to guess, I would say . . . No, I'm going to go for . . . Yes. That's it. TJ, you teach physics.

Cunt.

I mean, excuse the French, but seriously, what a cunt. I should have thumped him one right there. And he looked like he expected me to, that's the thing. Looked like he almost wanted me to. My face, he must have been able to tell, but he didn't flinch. He watched me, still sort of smiling, like he was just waiting for me to twat him.

But I take a breath. I put down my glass of OJ. I edge forwards a little, just a little, and I say to him, I say, are you trying to be funny?

And he's all, no, no, I didn't mean anything by it, but he did, we both know he did.

I say, listen, Sam. I call him Sam, just to make a point. I say, listen, Sam. Don't get smart. Don't get above yourself. I've been teaching five, six years. You've been teaching, how many? I hold up a fist – you know, zero fingers – but also it's a fist, which is the second point I'm making. And you'd think he'd get it, wouldn't you? The point, I mean. You'd think he'd get it. But guess what he says next. Go on, have a guess.

Latin, he says. You teach Latin, don't you.

I tell you, if it wasn't for Bartholomew Travis that would have been the end of Sam-Samuel Szajkowski right there. And look what trouble it would have saved.

He was watching, I suppose. I spoke to Travis yesterday and that was the first thing he said to me, he said, I knew it, I knew there was something wrong with that boy. Said he's had his eye on Szajkowski from the start but I don't know about that. He certainly wasn't watching him at the end, was he? But maybe he was at the beginning and maybe that's why he saw our little tête on tête and maybe that's why he got to us in time to rescue Szajkowski's face.

I raised my voice at that point. Possibly I swore. Nothing bad. Not the c-word. Maybe the f-word. But like I said to the rest of them afterwards, he was the aggressive one, not me.

What's going on here? says Travis. What's all this fuss?

And Sam Szajkowski starts bleating, starts playing the gentle lamb. Headmaster, he says, I'm not sure what I said but clearly I've caused TJ here some offence.

And I'm like, fucking right you've caused me some offence you little cocksucker, you know perfectly well what you said.

And Travis is like, calm down, Terence. He calls me Terence. I've asked him not to but he still does. So he's like, calm down, Terence, and, what did you say, Samuel? And he's like, I don't know, Headmaster, I don't know.

And then they look at me and I'm still about ready to punch someone and the headmaster asks me instead. What did he say, Terence? What did he say to cause you such offence?

And obviously this has worked out pretty well for Szajkowski because now I'm the one who's going to look like the knob. He's watching me and he's not smiling but I know that, just below the surface, he is. And what can I do but answer because when Travis asks you a question you have to answer, you just do. I mean the kids are terrified of him and us teachers, well. I mean, I'm not scared of anyone but let's just say there's a reason that Travis is headmaster.

So I tell him. I say, it's not what he said, Headmaster. It's the way he said it.

The way he said what? says Travis. What did he say?

He said . . . He said I taught physics, Headmaster. He said I teach Latin.

And Travis looks at me like I'm some kind of retard, like I'm that kid with special needs in class C. I try to explain and I say to Szajkowski, you know what you meant by it, you know exactly what you meant by it, don't try and act all innocent.

Everyone's watching by now of course. Not that I'm worried, I mean they know me these people, they know the kind of person I am. They know exactly what's going on, I'm certain of it. Except for Maggie. She's looking at me like I'm a pubic hair in her cornflakes. And you know what pisses me off? This whole little episode: it's what got the two of them going. That's what pisses me off. She felt sorry for him, Maggie did. All the stuff that followed, their little romance, all of it was bullshit because all of it was based on a lie. Szajkowski's lie.

And that was that really. The headmaster, he says maybe I've had enough to drink and I say, I'm drinking orange juice, I'm drinking fucking orange juice, and the headmaster says, yes, well, nevertheless, and mutters some crap about sugar. And he leads me away. And I leave.

So that was it. That was the first time me and Szajkowski met. After that, things just kind of went downhill.

'He won't talk to you.'

'Does he know what's happened? Has anyone told him?'

'You're not listening to me, Inspector. He won't talk to you. He doesn't talk. He doesn't even talk to his parents.'

'And you're not answering my question, Doctor. Does he know?'

The doctor beat his leg with his clipboard. He removed his glasses. 'I believe he knows, yes. His parents and I discussed it. We agreed it might be beneficial if he were told. We agreed that it would do no harm.'

'Beneficial?' Lucia peered through the safety glass and into the ward. She could see only an empty bed. 'You mean you thought it might make him say something. The shock might make him say something.'

The doctor did not flinch. 'That's right.'

'But it didn't.'

'No. It didn't.'

Lucia nodded. She looked again through the glass, angling herself backwards slightly. She still could not make out the boy. 'I'd like to see him,' she said.

'He won't—'

'Talk to me, I know. But I'd like to see him.'

The doctor was tall, dark and strange looking. When he tightened his jaw, his cheeks bulged in two sharp points just below his ears, as though he were attempting to swallow a screwdriver sideways.

'Please be quick.'

'Yes, Doctor.'

'And remember what he has been through.'

'Yes, Doctor.'

'He is still recovering. He needs his rest.'

'I understand.'

The doctor held open the door and allowed Lucia to slip inside. She entered the room and listened for the sound of the door closing behind her. When it did not come, she turned and thanked the doctor and waited for him to retreat.

She thought at first that she was the only person in the room. There were four beds and all were empty. But the fourth bed, the one in the corner furthest from her, had been slept in. The curtain was halfway drawn and there was a glass and a jug of water on the side table. The glass was empty and the jug was full.

'Elliot?'

Lucia tried to step softly but the soles of her shoes slapped against the vinyl-clad floor.

'Elliot, my name's Lucia. Lucia May. I'm a policewoman.'

She crossed the room and stopped at the foot of the un-made bed. She saw a head, level with the mattress. She saw hair, rather. Short and blond, verging on being ginger. It was lighter in colour than Lucia's hair but similar; less obviously red but perhaps only because of its length.

Lucia took another step and the rest of the boy came into view. He was sitting on the floor, behind the bed and against the wall. Lucia noticed Elliot's birthmark before she noticed anything else about him. It covered the left side of his face, the side Lucia could see, stretching from his ear to the corner of his mouth. The effect was as though Elliot had been slapped – hard, more than once – or held against something hot.

After the birthmark she noticed the stitches – a jagged line from the midpoint of his eyebrows extending across his nose and to his jawline. The doctor had told her that Elliot's right ear was also damaged but from where she was standing she could not see the wound. The doctor said the ear had been torn. He said that it had been bitten.

She sought the boy's eyes, which were focused on the book he held resting on the peak of his drawn-up knees. 'Elliot?' she said again. She had been told he would not answer but she hoped he would nonetheless.

'What are you reading?' she asked and when, again, the boy did not respond she edged forwards and bent to read the title from the cover. The words, though, were obscured by the boy's index and middle fingers, which were crossed, Lucia noticed, as though he were wishing for a happy ending as he read.

Elliot turned a page. He had to unfold his fingers to do so and Lucia caught a surname, a fragment of the title: *The Book of* something by someone Alexander.

'Can I sit? Do you mind if I sit?' She perched on the edge of the bed, facing the wall. 'Dr Stein says you're almost better. He says you're almost ready to go home.'

The boy turned another page. Lucia watched his eyes. They drifted from one page to the next and settled somewhere in between. For a moment Lucia did not speak. She looked at her feet and behind her and at the boy again. He turned another page.

'Is it good? Your book. What's it about?'

Slowly, as though hoping she might not detect the gradual movement, Elliot allowed the book to slide from his knees until it was resting, hidden, against his thighs. His eyes did not stray from the pages in front of him.

'You don't have to talk to me,' Lucia said. 'I just wanted to see you. I just wanted to check that you were all right.' It surprised her, as she said this, that what she was saying was true. What had happened to the boy was not part of her investigation so technically she had no business here. The doctor could have denied her entry. The parents could arrive and ask her to leave and she would have no choice but to do so.

She glanced across her shoulder. The door was still closed, the rest of the room still empty. She did not know how strict the hospital was about visiting hours but she was taking a chance that Elliot's parents would not arrive until the allotted period began.

'You're a quick healer,' Lucia said. She focused again on his stitches. She tried to count them. 'It must have hurt, what they did to you.'

The boy turned a page.

'You're very brave, Elliot.' She said this in almost a whisper, though she had not meant to speak so softly. She cleared her throat. 'You're very brave.'

She could not find it in the bookshop.

A cardboard Harry Potter tracked her steps and threatened her with a wand and did not back down when she scowled at him. After checking in the children's section, she ceded her ground. She wove her way to the general-fiction aisle but could not find it there either.

The shop was empty but for Lucia, the boy wizard and, at the cash register, a sales assistant who looked like she should have been in school. The sales assistant was on the phone, to a friend it seemed; a boyfriend. Lucia lingered by the till for a moment. She pretended to be interested in a stack of Moleskine notebooks. Finally, she rested her wrists on the counter and smiled at the girl.

'Hi,' she mouthed.

The sales assistant ducked away and muttered something into the mouthpiece. She turned back to Lucia with the receiver cradled between her chin and her shoulder. 'Hi,' she said. Lucia could not tell whether her eyebrows were raised or whether they had been plucked and painted that way.

'I'm looking for a children's book,' Lucia said. She gave the girl the fragments of information she had glimpsed between Elliot's fingers.

The girl frowned and turned to her computer. She spoke to her boyfriend over the clicking of her nails on the keys. There was to be a party, Lucia learnt. Someone who was supposed to be going wasn't and someone who wasn't supposed to be going was.

'Lloyd Alexander,' said the girl after a moment. 'Try children's classics. No, not you,' she said into the mouthpiece and, looking at Lucia, gestured to the rear of the shop with her chin.

It was fantasy. Escapism. Not a genre with which Lucia was particularly familiar but she could imagine its appeal to a boy for whom reality offered no refuge. *The Book of Three* had first been published before Lucia was born. Even on the copy she found, the edges of the pages were a greyish yellow, discoloured like a smoker's fingers. She replaced the book and scanned the shelves, noticing as she did so authors' names she had worshipped once but long forgotten. Blume, Blyton, Byars. Milne, Montgomery, Murphy. The books she had read, though, would be of no interest to him. She neared the end of the section and almost gave up looking but before she could turn away a title caught her attention. With her index finger she prised the book free. The jacket design was new but the image it presented was familiar. Lucia smiled and flicked backwards through the pages, pausing every so often to read a sentence, a fragment of speech, a chapter heading. She carried her selection to the counter.

Lucia had a retort prepared but Walter was not at his desk. The department was virtually empty.

'Where is everyone?' She allowed only her head to enter the DCI's office.

'He's in court,' Cole said. He was poking at his upper lip, frowning into a mirror propped almost flat on his desk.

'Who is? What?'

'Your fiancé. He's in court.' The chief inspector glanced at Lucia before returning his attention to himself. 'What did the kid say?'

He wanted her to ask him how he knew where she had been. She wanted to ask too. Instead she watched as he prodded and winced. She stepped across the threshold. Her curiosity must have shown on her face.

'One of the uniforms saw you,' said Cole. 'At the hospital. So what did he say?'

'He didn't say anything. He doesn't say anything.'

Cole gave a grunt. 'You know it doesn't matter, don't you? You know it's not part of this case.'

'It's linked.'

'It's not linked.'

'Of course it's linked. Everything's linked.'

'Everything's linked? You've got till Monday, Lucia. Remember you've only got until Monday.'

Lucia checked her watch.

'Have you seen Price?'

'Price? Why do you want to see Price?'

'I don't. I mean, it's nothing. Nothing important.'

'Well I haven't seen him.'

'Never mind.' Lucia was already leaving.

'It's not linked, Lucia.'

She showed him the back of her hand.

Price was smoking. Lucia stood closer to him than she needed to.

'Some weather, huh?' They were on the top floor, on the

terrace behind the canteen. They called it the terrace but really it was a balcony and a bench and an overflowing ashtray. Price gestured to the sky, to the unrelenting blue. 'Thirty-eight at the weekend, that's what they're saying.' He coughed out a laugh and sucked at his cigarette. 'You're lucky you don't have to wear uniform no more. These trousers don't breathe. Might as well be made of rubber.'

Lucia considered her own outfit: dark trousers, white blouse. The only difference between Price's clothes and hers was that she had had to pay for hers herself.

'Tell me about the Samson boy,' said Lucia. 'Elliot Samson.'

Price frowned, puffed smoke from his nostrils. 'Christ, Lucia. It's a nice day. The sun is shining. What do you have to bring that up for?'

Lucia watched Price stub his cigarette against the wall and, ignoring the ashtray beside him, flick the filter towards the city skyline.

'Did he speak to you?' she said. 'Did he say anything?'

Price shook his head. 'He couldn't. His face was too messed up.'

'He was conscious?'

'Yep. Right up until the ambulance took him away. Probably for some time after. He felt every rip, scrape and bite.'

'Who did it? Do you know?'

'Sure I know. Plenty of people seem to know.'

'And?'

'And what? And the kid isn't speaking. And no one saw it happen. And the school doesn't seem to care.' Price took another cigarette from the box in his shirt pocket. 'Same school, right?'

Lucia was looking at the traffic below. A delivery van had pulled up alongside a taxi that had been travelling in the opposite direction. The drivers were leaning out of their windows, waving hands, flicking gestures, ignoring the horns of the cars caught behind them. 'Sorry?' she said.

'Same school. The shooting. The teacher. Same school, right?'

'Same school,' Lucia said. 'Right.'

Did I love him? What a question.

How can I say I loved him after what he did? How can I admit that to myself? I tell myself now that I never loved him and I pray that what I tell myself is true. Otherwise, Inspector, I feel sick. Just the thought of him, after what he did: it makes me want to be sick.

I was fond of him. I can admit that much. I pitied him. I thought that he deserved pity, if you can believe that.

He didn't settle. He didn't fit in. The headmaster didn't like him, TJ didn't like him and because the two of them didn't like him none of the others were anything more than civil to him. Why would they be? TJ can be a nuisance if he feels like you're not on his side – everything with him is sides – and you don't want to upset the headmaster, not in this school. Not in any school, I suppose, but particularly not in this school.

And he didn't help himself. Samuel, I mean. He had his untidy little beard and his scruffy black hair and he always wore one of two suits. One lace was invariably undone, one button on his shirt missing or misaligned. I know, I know: appearances shouldn't matter. But they do, don't they? Everyone knows they do.

He was reticent, stand-offish. He answered, he never asked. I say he answered but he didn't answer how you or I might answer. How are you? someone might say to him. Fine, thank you, he'd reply. And that would be it. Hi Samuel, what are you up to? Reading, he'd say and not look up from his book. He wasn't rude exactly but the others, they didn't like that. They assumed him arrogant. They thought him aloof. Veronica Staples, the woman who died – the woman he killed – she said to me one time, she said, he's like an Oxford don at a children's party, and that about summed him up.

Veronica was a friend of mine, Inspector. She was a friend. She had children, you know. Two children. One of them is a teacher too. Beatrice: she's training to become a teacher. What must they think? What must they be feeling?

No, thank you. I have one in my pocket. I'm fine, honestly. I'm just, I don't know. Just being silly, I suppose. I'm fine.

What was I saying?

Samuel, yes. He was what you might call an outsider. He was an outsider right from the start. It was easier to ignore him than to engage with him. It was easier to laugh at TJ's little pranks than to act like a prude and stand up for him. Him and TJ, they had a little set-to at the start of term. Samuel said something and TJ got upset and I don't really know what happened but it looked like men being men, nothing more. But after that TJ pretty much decided that he and Samuel were mortal enemies and that he would get his revenge one minor humiliation at a time. Pathetic, I know, but harmless enough.

He's just a kid, TJ. He acts like one of the kids. He's always out there with them, playing football, playing basketball. They call him TJ not Mr Jones and the headmaster stands for it because with TJ the kids don't act up. Order: the headmaster demands order and TJ is one of the very few teachers in this school capable of bringing it.

So the first thing TJ does is tell Samuel to turn up one Friday in jeans. Says it's Jeans for Genes day or something and that all the teachers are doing it. This is before Samuel suspects that TJ has a grudge against him. I mean, maybe he suspects but he's still the new bloke, isn't he? He still has to listen to what TJ says. So Samuel does and the headmaster sends him home to change – like he's a kid, he sends him home, because teachers don't wear jeans in this school, oh no, that would not be appropriate at all – and the headmaster has to teach Samuel's morning classes himself. Which he hates doing, particularly a subject like history. The next thing TJ does is leave Samuel a note signed by the headmaster saying his lesson has been moved to a different room, a different floor. So while Samuel is up in the attic – that's what we call it up there, the attic – while he's up there waiting for his class to turn up, his kids are where they should be, shouting, laughing, throwing chairs probably, until one of them ends up with a bloody lip and starts wailing. The headmaster hears all this and he storms into the room and screams at them to be quiet, to maintain order. And naturally he blames Samuel, assumes Samuel was late, and Samuel doesn't say anything because he knows by now what's going on and he knows enough to know that you don't go squealing, you don't go telling tales.

There were other things too. All silly things, childish things, like TJ spilling – tipping – his coffee on to Samuel's lap just before Samuel's sixth-form class. Or the time he stuck an L-plate on Samuel's back and Samuel walked around for half a day before he realised he was wearing it.

I shouldn't laugh. I'm not laughing really. It wasn't funny then and nothing's funny now.

But that's what drew me to him. I felt sorry for him, it was as simple as that. I mean, he wasn't bad looking either. Not good looking, not what most people would describe as handsome, but he seemed sweet. He had nice eyes. They were green, almost grey. He had kind eyes, that's what I thought at the time. What an idiot.

The first time we spoke was after that incident I mentioned, the run-in he had with TJ. The headmaster's leading TJ away and Samuel is left standing there, looking shocked, to be fair, looking dazed. The rest of the room has gone quiet and after TJ and the headmaster have left, people start to clear their throats, to raise their eyebrows, to whisper. No one looks at Samuel but everyone is watching him.

I can't bear it. I feel as awkward as he looks. I mean, he has his glass of wine in his right hand and he swaps it to his left. Then the glass is back where it started and his left hand is twitching at his side. Next he's fiddling with his tie and looking up at the ceiling and then he's wandering along the buffet table, not picking up any food. I meet him by the angel cake.

Don't let him bother you, I tell him and he smiles this curious smile.

That's just what I was telling myself, he says, which makes

me laugh. I laugh a bit too loudly, a bit enthusiastically, and I hear my laugh how the others would have heard it, which you don't often do with your own laugh, do you? It's hideous. I cut myself some cake.

He asks me my name and I say, Maggie. I say, you're Samuel, and he nods. He asks me what I teach and then says, please don't make me guess. I say, sorry, and he says, never mind. Music, I say. I teach music, or try to. He says, oh, and nods.

Do you like music? I ask him because even though I could say a hundred things, it is the only thing I can think of to say.

I do, he says.

What music do you like?

I like the Russians, he says. I don't like Mozart.

You don't like Mozart? Why not?

Too many people like him, he says. Too many people enthuse about how wonderful he is.

Is that a reason not to like him? I ask. I like Mozart, you see, Inspector. I love Mozart. All the more so now.

Yes, he says. I think it is.

And I say nothing because I don't agree with him and I don't want to start another argument. He starts one instead.

You don't agree.

No, I say. It's not that.

You think I'm wrong.

Well, I say. No. I mean, yes, I do think you're wrong but that's fine. You're entitled to your opinion.

I know, he says. What's yours?

I put down my cake. I don't really want it and the piece I've cut is enormous. In my opinion, I say, music shouldn't be constrained by opinion. If music talks to you, you should let it. You shouldn't shut it out just because of what someone else thinks or says or does.

He grunts. He smiles.

What? I say.

You have to say that, he says.

What? I say again. What do I have to say?

What you said. You have to say what you said.

Why? Why do I have to say that?

Because you're a music teacher, says Samuel. You have to pretend to be open minded.

Pretend? You think I'm pretending?

Maybe, he says. And he tears himself a corner from my slice of cake.

That's my cake, I say.

I thought you didn't want it.

When did I say I didn't want it? I do want it.

Here then, he says.

I don't want it now. And when I say this I realise I'm being rude, like the fact that he's touched it has contaminated it somehow.

I think, says Samuel, I think it's time I left. It was nice to meet you.

Yes, I reply. That's all I can say. He leaves and everyone else seems relieved but I just feel like a fool.

The thing with Samuel, you see, is that he had opinions. Have you noticed how these days nobody has an opinion? People say too much and they don't listen but when they speak they talk about nothing. Samuel seemed aloof because he was quiet but if you were ever to talk to him – and I mean talk to him, not chat with him, not try to pass the time – he would talk to you right back. He would listen to what you had to say, genuinely listen, and he would consider it and often dismiss it and he would tell you what he thought himself. And his opinions could seem conceited or misconceived or sometimes a little scary but at least he had an opinion.

Here's what I think, I tell him when I catch up with him in the staffroom on the first day of term. Here's my opinion, since you value opinion so much. Mozart was the second greatest composer who ever lived. He was a genius. Tchaikovsky was a moron and Rachmaninov a sentimental fool.

What about Prokofiev? he says, no hesitation, no surprise in his tone.

Second tier, I say. B list. Also a sentimental fool.

And he nods and I say, just don't tell the kids I said that. If they ask, tell them I said Prokofiev was a genius too.

After that we talked more and more. Never in company. Never if anyone else was around. If we happened to be in the staffroom and someone else walked in, we stopped talking, we just did. I don't know why. I think I assumed he preferred it that way and maybe he assumed that I did too. Maybe he assumed it would be easier for me. You know, because of who he was, because of what the others thought of him. But we were fooling ourselves. Everyone knew. All the teachers knew, the headmaster knew, even the kids knew. Somehow the kids always know.

I was the one to ask him out of course. He would never have asked me. It took some courage, I can tell you. Some courage and, from the bottle we keep hidden under the sink for emergencies, a nip of whisky.

The first time, I ask him to go to the movies with me. There's something European on at the Picturehouse and I think that because it's European he'll like it. I don't know, I just assume that he'll be into foreign films. As it turns out, I love it and he hates it. He calls it pretentious. I think it's exquisite. It's in French and I love French. Such a musical language, so lyrical. I find myself just listening, not following the subtitles, not really knowing what's going on. He takes in every word, I suppose, because afterwards he's all why did they do this, no one would ever do that, who in the world talks like that? So analytical, so overly analytical.

The next time I ask him to an exhibition, to the Caravaggio at the National Gallery. I almost don't but I feel guilty about not asking him out again because I don't really want to, not after the film. So I decide an art gallery will be just the place. You know, quiet, formal, an afternoon not an evening. I'll make it clear that I only want us to be friends.

It's wonderful. I have the most wonderful time. Do you know anything about art, Inspector? I know nothing about art. I know what I like and I admire most things I could never do. Samuel, though – he can paint. Did you know that? He's a painter. What am I saying? He was a painter. He was.

No, I'm fine. Really. I'm not crying because of that. You know, because of him. It's just, I don't know. The whole thing is just—

Well. Anyway. Samuel, he could paint. He said he hadn't for some time but he knew so much about it and he was so enthused, so delighted by the whole thing. Isn't it refreshing to be with someone who has passion? And to be surprised by someone having passion whom you'd assumed had none? Or not none exactly. I mean, I knew about the teaching, I knew how important he thought teaching was but I had no idea there was anything else that inspired that same enthusiasm in him.

We stay in the gallery until it closes. We sit and we walk and we watch the other visitors. Samuel is so funny. He talks about the paintings and he talks about the other people too, making jokes, constructing little caricatures – you know, the pompous art student, the wannabe actor turned tour guide, the philistine American. I thought at the time that he was being funny but maybe, thinking about it now, maybe he was actually being cruel.

We had sex once. Not that day, another day, months later. He wasn't good at it but I didn't mind because I'm hardly an expert myself.

You're recording this. I keep forgetting you're recording this.

What does it matter? We had sex and it was bad. It was awkward before and it was awkward during. I was a little drunk. Samuel was too. He didn't drink much as a rule and neither do I but we'd finished most of a bottle of shiraz. We're at my place and I've made him some dinner and we're watching a film but it isn't very good so I turn it off and I put on the stereo—

You know what? I don't want to talk about this. Can we not talk about this?

We broke up. That's how this ends. I say we broke up but

that sounds so conventional and our relationship was anything but conventional. Apart from that one time, there was no physical involvement. We didn't even kiss. I'm embarrassed to say that, I don't know why. But it's the truth. We didn't kiss, we didn't hug, we didn't even hold hands. Once or twice we held hands but only if we were crossing a road or he was helping me from the bus or something silly like that. And it wasn't just that. In a normal relationship, you don't hide your affection like it's something to be ashamed of, you don't hide your lover from your friends and from your family and from yourself sometimes, even from yourself.

We argued. I suppose in that sense it was a normal relationship. Samuel was having a difficult year. There was the headmaster and there was TJ but also there were the kids. Although with the kids I couldn't help. I didn't try because it was beyond me. What they did – what they would do to Samuel – I just couldn't understand it. I wouldn't have believed it if I hadn't seen it for myself. No, when we argued it was about nothing in particular. It would start off as being about something – about TJ maybe, about his pranks – but in the end it would be about nothing. Nothing and everything.

I would probably have broken up with him sooner had he not been having such a difficult time. There it is again, you see: pity. I'm a hopeless judge of character, Inspector. I must be a hopeless judge of character. Everyone else could see he wasn't normal. Why couldn't I?

No, thank you, I'm fine. Let's just get this finished. Can we please just get this finished?

Was he angry? What makes you say that? He had no reason

to be, if that's what you mean. No reason at all. I mean, he expected it. He must have expected it. He wasn't the easiest of people to read, that was part of the problem, but surely he must have expected it. I don't know though. He didn't seem angry at first but things got bad for him afterwards, which can't have helped. They were bad before but they got worse. So maybe his anger grew. Maybe his bitterness festered. Maybe he talked himself into resenting me because I know one thing for certain, Inspector, I'll tell you one thing. They say he was aiming at TJ when he shot Veronica. That's what everyone thinks. I know better. He wasn't aiming at TJ, Inspector. He was aiming at me. He was aiming at me and Veronica died instead.

The gates were open; the playground had become a car park. It was full of vans: white vans mainly, vans that would have been white had they not been so encrusted with grime. Cleaning contractors, rubbish removers, flooring firms, a plumber. Men in paint-stained clothes sat in the shaded sanctuary of their cabs, the cigarettes that dangled from their sunburnt arms adding to the heat of the engines, the tarmac, the sun. Crumpled Coke cans and tabloid newspapers lined the dashboards that Lucia passed. She caught a headline, something about the weather and the temperature and the beginning of the end of all things.

She ignored the stares. The shadow of the Victorian red-brick loomed and drew her in and all of a sudden she felt chilled. She climbed the stairs to the entrance, passed the uniforms and pushed through the doors.

There was no one she could see. From the assembly hall she heard scraping furniture and baritone voices and the sounds of men at work, disconcertingly jolly given the origins of the mess they were clearing.

She almost left. She had come to the school out of habit. She had come the first day and the second and the third, and after that she had found that she could not not come. But it was Friday and on Friday, she knew, the crime scene was to become a school again.

She almost left but she hesitated long enough for the head-master to spot her. She considered ignoring his call, pretending not to have heard, but he was striding from the assembly hall towards her and covering the ground quickly and if she turned away now it would be too late.

'Detective Inspector May.' His voice held her still. Seconds passed and he was upon her.

'Mr Travis.'

'Inspector.' His smile, as a smile, did not convince. The polo shirt he wore seemed equally ill-fitting, an attempt at smart casual by a man not comfortable dressing down. The collar and sleeves had been pressed, the buttons were fastened to his throat.

'I was just leaving,' said Lucia.

'And I thought you had just arrived,' the headmaster replied. 'I saw you from the window. I saw you cross the courtyard.'

'I forgot the day. I forgot that it was Friday.'

'I almost did myself. It's as if the holidays had started already. Come, let me show you what's been happening.'

'Really—' Lucia began but Travis was already on the march towards the hall. She followed.

'You've been busy, Inspector.' The headmaster moved his chin to his shoulder as he spoke but he did not look at her directly.

'As have you, I'm sure.'

Travis nodded. He turned away from her. 'I wonder what it is that you have discovered.'

Lucia watched the back of the headmaster's head, tracking his over-long neck into the slope of his narrow shoulders. She noticed the surplus skin on his elbows, just visible below the sleeve line of his shirt and, in that one sagging patch, the same shade of grey as his hair.

'Not as much as I would have liked,' Lucia said. They stopped at the doors leading into the hall. 'More than you might imagine.'

'After you, Inspector.'

Lucia tried to slide past the headmaster without making any contact but brushed against the skin of his outstretched arm.

'You're not cold, surely,' Travis said. 'It is difficult to remember the sensation of feeling cold, do you not find?'

The hall had already been cleared, cleaned. The furniture she had heard scraping on the freshly shined floor was of a different kind from the chairs she was used to seeing in the room. The desks that the workmen were setting up in rows folded in on themselves so that they also formed a seat. They did not look like they would stack but they did. They were piled ten high at the back of the hall, though the stacks were diminishing as the workmen surrounded them and plucked at them and bore three units at a time to the opposite side of the room.

'Exams,' Travis said. 'We are two weeks behind as it is.'

Lucia looked across the hall for the rope. It was gone. All the ropes on all the climbing frames were gone. 'Will they not find it difficult to concentrate?' Lucia said. 'Being in here?'

The headmaster acted as though he had not heard. He raised

his voice to a workman, told him not to space the desks so tightly together. He tutted and turned back to Lucia. 'You were telling me what you had uncovered, Inspector. You were telling me what your questioning had revealed.'

'You asked,' Lucia replied. 'That's as far as we had got.'

'It is classified then. You feel I cannot be trusted.'

'No. Not at all. The investigation is still ongoing.'

The headmaster raised one eyebrow. 'That surprises me, Inspector. I was under the impression that your enquiries were now complete.'

'Then you were misinformed, Mr Travis. They are not.'

'Well,' said Travis. 'I shall know next time to talk to you directly. I shall know not to put my faith in the chain of command.'

'The chain of command?'

'I spoke to your superior, Inspector. I spoke to DCI Cole. He telephoned me, in fact. He informed me that your investigation was drawing to a close.'

'He telephoned you? How considerate of him.'

'Indeed,' the headmaster said. 'He seems a considerate man.'

Lucia looked about her. She watched a stack of desks wobble as one of the workmen tugged at the column next to it. It was going to fall and it fell and Lucia flinched at the noise even though she was braced for it. She turned to the headmaster, expecting an outburst, but the headmaster was focused on her.

'We will be having a memorial service,' Travis said. 'On Monday, at ten o'clock. Not in here. Outside. There is an area of the playing field that seems suitable. Perhaps you would be kind enough to join us.'

'Thank you,' Lucia said. 'I won't.'

'You have an investigation to complete.'

She nodded. 'That's right.'

The headmaster smiled. He appeared to contemplate. 'Tell me, Inspector,' he said at last. 'Why are you here?'

'Excuse me?'

'What I mean to say,' the headmaster went on, 'is that it seems as though you have something on your mind.'

Lucia held his eye. She spoke before she could reconsider. 'Elliot Samson,' she said. She watched for some reaction but there was none. 'He was a pupil here, is that right?'

'He is a pupil here, Inspector. He was and he is.'

'Of course. And you know what happened to him, I assume?'

'Naturally I know.'

'Perhaps you could tell me. Perhaps you could tell me your understanding of events.'

There was another noise, another stack felled. Neither the headmaster nor Lucia paid notice.

'He was attacked. He was attacked and he was injured. He is in hospital. From what I understand, he is making a full recovery.'

'He won't speak. Did you know that? His injuries are healed but he won't speak.'

'Forgive me, Inspector. I did not know that you had been charged with investigating the Samson incident as well. You have your plate full. Certainly it explains the delay.'

'I'm not,' said Lucia. 'I haven't been.'

'Then it is connected to the shooting? What happened to Elliot Samson is connected somehow to the shooting?'

'No. Not officially.'

'But unofficially.'

'I am curious, Mr Travis, that's all.'

'I see.' The headmaster nodded. His expression was earnest, his manner perplexed. Lucia imagined herself as a pupil, in his office, explaining some indiscretion that could not be explained. 'And about what, precisely, are you curious?'

'Well,' Lucia said. 'For one thing, I am curious as to your response. As to the school's response.'

'The assembly, Inspector. Our ill-fated assembly. I informed you of the topic of that assembly, did I not?'

'You did, Mr Travis. I wondered, however, what else you had done. What else the school had done.'

'What else would you have me do? Elliot Samson is a pupil here but that is where our involvement stops. If it had occurred within the grounds, then perhaps—'

'It happened on the street. On the street outside your school. And it involved your pupils.'

'You do not know that, Inspector. No one knows that. The Samson boy, as you point out, is not speaking. And unfortunately, there were no witnesses. None that came forward.'

'None that came forward,' Lucia echoed. 'You are sure about that?'

'You would know better than I, Inspector,' the headmaster said. 'But yes, as far as I am aware there were no witnesses. Unless of course your own investigations have uncovered one?'

'No,' said Lucia. 'Not as such.'

Lucia was the only person in London still seated at a desk who did not have to be. She thought about this for a moment. She thought about going to the pub, not doing it, more the concept: going to the pub. She thought about the last time she had gone to the pub in the manner the phrase implied, not as an event she would dither over and dress up for and look forward to. Be let down by.

She thought about calling her father but doubted she had the right number. It was a better excuse than others she had used. She could call her mother. She should call her mother. But the thought of doing so made her feel tired. It made her feel more alone, somehow, than she already felt.

That was unfair. Probably she was being unfair. She was tired already and she was tense and she could hardly blame someone to whom she had not spoken in a month. Talking might help, she told herself. It should help.

She picked up the phone and dialled.

'Mum. Hi.'

'Lucia. It's you. I was thinking it would be your father. This is just the sort of time he would phone.'

'It's late. I'm sorry. I thought you'd be up.'

'I am up. But that's not the point. The point is, he wouldn't care if I were up or not. He'd just call and expect me to answer.'

'I'll call back. I'll call you in the morning.'

'No, no, no. It's you. You're not him. You can call any time, you know that. My, but it is late. What's happened? Has something happened?'

'No, nothing's happened. I'm fine. I just called because, well. It's been a while, that's all.'

'Has it? I suppose it has. But the phone rings these days and it's like someone's jumped out at me from behind the sofa. Because when he's desperate he doesn't let up. He doesn't give me a moment's rest.'

'You know why he does it, Mum. You shouldn't encourage him.'

'I have to give him something just so he'll leave me in peace. If I didn't, he'd end up on my sofa. Or I'd end up on the sofa, more likely, and he'd take over my bed. And then he'd never go. I'd never get rid of him.'

'You can't afford it, Mum. And you shouldn't encourage him.'

'He has a plan, though. He tells me he has a plan. The debt – he says there are no debts. He's starting at zero, he says, but he's looking up now and he just needs something to get him started. A step up.'

'A step up?'

'I'm his stepladder. That's what he says to me. We had thirteen years of marriage and still that's all I am to him. Ironmongery.'

'He hasn't got a plan, Mum. He never has a plan.'

'Talking of marriage, darling, how's David? Is he there? Let me speak to him.'

'Mum. I told you about David.'

'What? What did you tell me?'

'David and I broke up. I told you that.'

'No! When? You didn't tell me. You never tell me these things.'

'I told you. I did.'

'You didn't tell me. What happened? You work too hard, Lucia. You do. The thing with men is, they need to feel wanted. They need attention. They're like poinsettias.'

'It wasn't that, Mum. It wasn't anything like that.'

'Or maybe it's just our lot, Lucia. We're hamsters, that's what we are. They mate once in a while, you know, but they never commit. They cope, though, just like us. We're copers, Lucia. You call yourself a May but really you're a Christie. And Christies cope. We have to.'

Half an hour later, Lucia was still at her desk. She had a report to write. Her hands, though, remained clasped in front of her keyboard. Her eyes focused on the creases on her knuckles.

The sound of voices in the stairwell startled her. Her first instinct was to turn off her lamp, to pretend that she was not there. She forced her fingers on to the keys instead and frowned at her monitor as though it reflected something more involving than an empty page and a blinking cursor. She typed her name, spelled it wrong. She shut down Word and opened a browser window. Her fingers danced in the air for a moment. She typed Samuel Szajkowski into Google and tapped the return key. As the voices grew louder, she studied the results, clicked on a link, hit the back button, clicked on another.

'Give me five minutes,' someone was saying. 'Just fucking two minutes then. Two minutes is all I need.'

She had known it would be him. There had been no possibility that it was not going to be him.

'Settle down you lot. It looks like someone's home.'

Lucia picked up the phone again, realised they would have heard her talking if she had genuinely been using it and put it down. There was an emergency exit behind her. She considered it. She actually considered it.

'Lulu!' His tie was loose and his shirt had escaped his straining belt line. His cheeks were the fat-scarred dappled red of uncooked hamburgers and even from twenty paces she knew that his breath would smell like an ashtray overflowing with beer.

Behind him there was Charlie and there was Rob and there was Harry.

'Walter.'

'Lulu!' he said again. 'You've been waiting up for me!'

'How was court?' Lucia said. She spoke to Harry, who trailed his drinking buddies across the office. Harry hesitated and lost his chance to answer.

'Waste of time,' Walter said. 'Fucking magistrates.'

'Why? What happened?'

'Two dykes and a faggot, that's what happened. But what can you do?' Walter edged closer, rested a buttock on the corner of Lucia's desk. His wallet strained to escape the well-shined fabric of his seat pocket. 'Talking of dykes,' Walter said and he grinned at his tag-along audience. 'What are you doing here, Lulu? You know the weekend's started, don't you? You know Cole isn't here for you to impress.'

'Your flies are undone, Walter. Did you know your flies are undone?'

Walter grinned. He did not even look down. 'Why are you looking at my flies, Lulu?'

'Hey Walter.' It was Harry. 'I'm thirsty. Just get your damn paperwork and let's go, can we?'

'The pub'll still be there, Harry. Don't rush me. I'm chatting with Lulu here.' Walter turned back to Lucia. He slid along the desk, rounded the corner. His thigh was inches from Lucia's mouse hand. She tried to resist withdrawing it but could not. She leant back in her chair and folded her arms.

'Would you look at that?' Walter said. 'My fly is undone. Lulu here's been undressing me with her eyes.'

Charlie laughed. Rob laughed.

'You couldn't do me a favour, could you darling? You couldn't reach over here and zip the little fella back in?'

'I wouldn't worry, Walter. If it happened to fall out, I doubt anyone would notice.'

Charlie laughed. Rob laughed. Harry smiled.

Walter slid closer. His leg touched Lucia's, pressed against it. She could feel the sole of his shoe against her shin and the flesh of his calf against her knee. She could smell the beer now. She could smell his curdling sweat.

'You need a shower, Walter. And you need to get your leg away from mine.'

'Two minutes, you said. Let's go, Walter, come on.'

'You hear that. Now she wants me fully undressed. She wants to see me naked.' He leered at Lucia. 'I'll take a shower, Lulu. Just as long as you bring the soap.'

'Move your leg, Walter.'

'How would you like me to move it? Up?' He slid his leg up. 'Or down?' He slid it down.

'Move your leg. Move your fucking leg.'

'Come on, Walter. Let's go.'

'Harry's right, Walter. It's last orders. It's virtually last orders.'

Walter pressed his leg a little harder against Lucia's. He leant towards her. 'How about a goodnight kiss?' He puckered. He shut his eyes, then he opened them again. 'No tongues, mind,' he said. 'Not this time.' Lucia looked at Harry. Harry was watching over the shoulders of his companions, his hand gripping a chair, his eyes fixed on Walter.

Lucia stood. 'I need some coffee,' she said. She tucked her hair behind her ear and walked the long way around her desk, past Charlie and past Rob and past Harry and she did not look at any of them. She listened to Walter's cackle and she heard Rob and Charlie snigger and she hoped that none of them could see her shaking.

The boys are idiots. They're all of them idiots. And like I know you're not supposed to say this, you're not supposed to speak disapproving of the dead and that but Donovan, Donovan Stanley, he was the biggest idiot of them all.

He wasn't the tallest. He wasn't the strongest. He was the quickest, though. His mouth, I mean, his tongue. He was the quickest. He was the meanest too. He'd say things you couldn't believe and then he'd be saying something else and you'd be there wondering whether you had even heard him right, whether that first thing he'd said had even been said at all. Do you know what I mean?

He was quite good looking. Normally I don't like black hair but I liked it on him. It looked good with his eyes. They were blue, like my little brother's, although my little brother's, they're changing now, they're going brown. Samantha reckons I fancied him but I never did. I was going out with Scott, Scott Davis, at the time so I wouldn't of told anyone even if I had of done. Which I didn't. And anyway, he wasn't interested in girls. He wasn't gay, God, but he wasn't interested in girls as, you know, girlfriends. He'd shag them, I know people who've shagged him, and maybe he'd shag them once or twice but that was as far as it went. I never shagged him. I hope you don't think I would of because I wouldn't of no way.

He was fifteen, same as me. Imagine getting shot at fifteen. Imagine, like, dying. And that girl, Sarah, wasn't she eleven? I didn't know her. I didn't know the black kid either. I only knew Donovan and not that well. He was the oldest of the three of them but he was young enough though, wasn't he? He acted like he was eighteen or something, said he drove his cousin's car, hung out with his cousin in the pub but I don't know if he really did. Imagine dying before you're old enough to learn to drive. Imagine dying before they'll serve you in a pub.

Some kids, though, they'll be glad he's dead. I shouldn't say that either, should I, but it's true. Donovan and the others, they picked on the younger kids mostly, just whoever happened to get in their way. Although one time they beat up this sixth-former. Jason his name was, Jason Bailey. Jason and that, they're playing football and Donovan fouls him, hacks his legs away or something, and Jason calls Donovan a cheat, an effing cheat. Donovan, he was a cheat, he was always fouling someone or mouthing off at them or whatever but you don't go calling him a cheat, no one ever called him that. They used crash helmets, I heard. Donovan and his mates. You know, motorcycle helmets.

He'd never done anything to a teacher though, not before Bumfluff – Mr Szajkowski – not that I'd heard.

Jesus, that sounds weird. What do I call him now? He's not a teacher any more, is he? He's not even Bumfluff any more.

God, that's so weird. It's weird just thinking about it. The whole thing I mean. It feels like some film, like you know when you watch a film and you're half asleep and messed-up things start happening and you don't know if it's in the film or in your head or what. It feels like that. Except I know it's not in my head and it's not in a film and it actually really happened.

Donovan started on Bumfluff right from day one. I'm gonna call him Bumfluff, I think. Is that okay, if I call him Bumfluff?

So it was the first history class of term, double history, and we know Miss Evans has left so we know we're getting a new teacher. So Bumfluff walks in and everyone goes quiet because you never know the first time, do you, you never know what a teacher's gonna be like. So Bumfluff walks in and everyone's quiet and Bumfluff smiles and says, hello everyone, my name's Mr Szajkowski. And Donovan laughs. He had this way of laughing when he wasn't really laughing. He'd kind of press his lips together and sort of hiss and blow a raspberry at the same time. Look, like this. Well, not like that. I can't really do it. Donovan could though and when he did you knew he was about to say something funny. Something funny or something nasty. Usually both.

I'm gonna swear now, just to warn you. Not me, I'm just gonna tell you what Donovan said. Is that okay?

Shitewhatsir? says Donovan. Shite*cough*ski? And in the middle he does this little cough, which really means k'off. You know, fuck off. Anyway, we all know what he means and everyone starts sniggering and one of Donovan's mates, Nigel I think, he does a little cough too and then the sniggering turns to laughing. Bumfluff tries to talk over it but everyone knows by then that this teacher, this tatty little bloke with his proper toff accent, he hasn't got a chance against Donovan.

Szajkowski, Bumfluff says again. He turns and writes it on the board. It's from Poland.

Poland, says Gi. Gi is Donovan's mate. It's short for Gideon, but if you call him Gideon he'll tell everyone that you've got herpes. Poland, says Gi. Does that mean you're one of them plumbers, one of them that are stealing our jobs? My old man reckons all you immigrants should be rounded up and locked away in camps.

What's your name? says Bumfluff. It's going to take me some time to memorise them all but I may as well start with yours.

Horace. My name's Horace.

Horace. Bumfluff checks his list. Horace what?

Horace Morris.

Horace Morris. Really. Well, I don't see it. Are you sure that's your name?

Yes, sir, pretty sure. Horace Morris.

Bumfluff nods. Well, he says. Well, Horace. I'm English. Like you. My father was English. My grandfather was a Pole.

Then Donovan pipes up. He's been wetting himself to, you can tell. Your grandfather was a what, sir?

A Pole. It means he was Polish.

Polish.

Polish, not polish. From Poland.

So that's where it comes from. Shite*cough*ski. It comes from Poland. Shite*cough*ski.

You're not quite saying it right, says Bumfluff. It's Szajkowski.

Shite*cough*ski.

Szajkowski.

Shite*cough*ski.

And this is hilarious because every time Donovan gets to the cough part he does it just a little bit louder, like he's trying really hard to get it right. Bumfluff, he just stops. He stops and he's standing there by the whiteboard and he's still got his brief-case on the desk and he hasn't even had a chance to sit down.

Shite*cough*ski, goes Donovan. Shite*cough*ski. And then the others join in. You know, like they're practising. That's when Donovan drops the ski bit and then he drops the shite part and in the end he's just going cough, cough, koff, k'off, uckoff, fuckoff, fuck off. And the ones who aren't laughing, they're doing it too, and Bumfluff he's just standing there watching.

I felt sorry for him at the time. I was laughing. I could tell you I was laughing just because everyone else was laughing but really I was laughing because it was funny. It was really funny. But I felt sorry for him too. Donovan, he usually leaves me alone. Most people, even his closest mates, all except Gi maybe, they all get it sometimes, they all have to take some grief. So I get it sometimes so I know what it's like. They don't hit the girls or anything but they tease them, they taunt them. Me, it's usu-ally about my hair. It's blonde, right, which isn't so bad but they can make just about anything seem bad, they can turn anything so it's bad. Besides, it's not what they say, is it? It's that they're saying it. And if they're teasing you, everyone else is ignoring you, even your mates, even your best friends, and those days, that term or however long it goes on for, because for some people it never stops, it just goes on and on until God, I don't know, until you leave school I guess, or until Donovan . . . Well.

That whole time, though, you could be surrounded by people, your friends like, people you thought were your friends, and the sun could be shining and there could be a million pounds just lying there in the gutter and still you'd feel like the most miserable, the most unlucky, the most loneliest person in the world. You're a policewoman. I don't suppose anyone ever bullies you. But trust me. Being bullied: it bites.

So I felt sorry for him. Which is weird too now. I felt sorry for him, this bloke who's gone and shot these people, these people who haven't done anything, except Donovan, these people who most of them are still just kids. Even Miss Staples was all right, she was nice. She got some grief about her name too, now I think about it, but she handled it right, she just laughed it off.

Bumfluff, though. He didn't laugh. Even if he had of laughed I don't think it would of helped. Instead of laughing, he did the one thing he never should of done.

But that was later. For a while he kept on going. He's like, okay, yes, thank you, that's enough. And most of the kids stop, the normal kids, but Donovan and his mates carry on, not as loud, not as obvious but they carry on. Bumfluff tries to get them interested, he says to Gi, you know it's funny you should say that, what you said just then about immigrants.

And Gi coughs and says, immigrants aren't funny, sir, immigrants are a serious problem cough. They're a pest. Cough.

No, that's not what I meant. It's funny – it's interesting – because we're going to touch on that subject—

You're not supposed to touch us, sir, says Donovan. It's not legal. Cough.

The subject, says Bumfluff, we're going to talk about that subject, about immigration and how we're all immigrants really, we're all descended from—

Are you calling me a Paki? says Gi and the rest of us are like, shit, you can't say that, and we're looking over at Liyoni because she's from Sri Lanka or Somalia or somewhere but she's not saying anything obviously, she's just staring at her desk.

No, Horace Morris, I'm not. And please don't use that word.

Which word, sir? Cough.

You know which word.

I don't, sir. Honestly. Cough. Tell me, sir. Say it.

I will not say it and neither will you. If I hear you saying it again you'll be explaining your choice of vocabulary in front of the headmaster.

Gi shuts up after that and it's quiet for a minute but then Donovan, he does this cough and his timing is brilliant and he does it really loudly and hardly disguises it at all. It was like . . . Well, I won't do it. But you can imagine it, can't you?

So now Bumfluff sits down and he's got his eyebrows raised and he's got this expression on his face, you know that expression that teachers have, like it's your time you're wasting here not mine. So he's sitting there with his eyebrows and it's not making any difference, the coughing's just getting louder and more and more people are doing it. I did it too. Just once. Samantha, she was sitting next to me, she did it first but she hid her mouth behind her hand. No one would of heard her but me. I did it and I did it properly and Samantha was like Lizzie! and Donovan saw me and he laughed and at the time

I thought it was funny but afterwards, I dunno. Afterwards I wished I hadn't of.

He's sitting there for a while. He's sitting there and it looks for a minute or two like he knows what he's doing, like he thinks he knows what he's doing. But it doesn't stop. The coughing. The normal kids stop but Donovan, Gi, Scott, Nigel and that lot, they don't stop. So Bumfluff gets up after a while and says enough, that's enough, and he's looking at Donovan as he speaks but Donovan just holds out his palms. See, Donovan and Gi are on one side of the room and Scott and Nigel are on the other so when Bumfluff is looking at one pair he can't see what the other pair are doing. He's trying to watch the lot of them but he's like a kid in front of a tennis match who can't keep up with the ball.

Someone throws something. I don't know what it is but it's wet. It's wet and it hits Bumfluff right on the cheek, just above his beard. It makes this sound. Imagine chucking a fistful of mud at a wall. That's the sound it makes.

Bumfluff's reaction: that's what makes it worse. He's shocked, I suppose. You would be shocked, wouldn't you, if someone had chucked something at you and it hit you and you hadn't seen it coming. He gives this yelp. His voice, it's not that deep anyway, but this yelp is like a kid's yelp, it's like a little girl's. I'd be embarrassed if I made that sound, do you know what I mean? I don't even know if I could make that sound. No, it was higher than that. Wait. No, higher than that. See, I can't do it. And as well as yelping, Bumfluff does this spasm, like you see special kids doing sometimes when they can't control their limbs. Like this.

We laugh. Everyone laughs. You would of laughed too, I promise you. You wouldn't of been able to help it.

It must of been quite loud. It must of been loud before then but by now it's been going on for a bit of time. I suppose that's why Miss Hobbs comes in. She knocks and she doesn't wait and she opens the door. She says, Mr Szajkowski, is everything all right in here? We can hear all this commotion two class-rooms away.

I can't really do her voice.

Anyway, Bumfluff, he's Hubba Bubba pink. I don't know if he's angry or embarrassed or hyperventilating or what but even through his beard you can make out the colour of his skin. That's when he leaves. Which is basically the worst thing he could of done. Miss Hobbs is standing there with one hand on the doorframe and one hand holding the door and Bumfluff says, excuse me, and picks up his briefcase and says excuse me again and he's gone. Just like that. And Donovan, I can see the look on his face. And I don't know whether he's been expecting Bumfluff to go but while the rest of us are just sitting there half dumb, Donovan, he gives this little wave.

Bye sir, he says. Right in front of Hobbs and everything.

'**He wasn't the victim, Lucia.** No one is going to accept that he was the victim.' Philip offered her a cigarette. He frowned when she shook her head. 'Since when?'

'Since New Year.'

'You're not jogging as well, are you? You look skinny. I can't stand it when people give up smoking and take up jogging. It's bad for their health. It's bad for the economy.'

'Don't let me stop you,' Lucia said.

'No, I couldn't possibly. I'd feel like I were goading you.'

'Really, it's fine. It doesn't bother me. I'd rather you smoked.'

But Philip put the cigarette case back into the pocket of his shirt. 'You take my point, don't you? This man killed three children. Children, Lucia. He killed their teacher. A mother. Even the *Guardian* had Szajkowski down as a monster.'

'He was not a monster, Philip. It was monstrous, what he did, but he was not a monster. And since when did you start reading the *Guardian*?'

'I don't. One of our paralegals does. Or did, rather. I found a reason to fire him.'

'Then you did him a favour. Probably saved his soul.'

Philip retrieved his cigarettes. 'I just want to hold one. I won't light it, I promise.'

Lucia waved. 'Go ahead.' She watched Philip open the case and prise a cigarette free. He let it nestle in his hand, where it looked as much a part of him as his little finger.

'So maybe he wasn't a monster,' Philip said. 'Maybe he was just crazy. Maybe it was this heat that drove him nuts. Maybe it's the heat that's affecting you.'

The weekend was turning out to be as oppressive as the weathermen had predicted. The sunlight was thin, filtered as it was through the fumes and filth of the city, but the haze was like a blanket piled on bed sheets that were already too thick for the season. There was no natural breeze in Philip's garden. There was no breeze anywhere. Philip, though, had created one. He and Lucia sat under a parasol on his weedless flagstone terrace, on teak furniture that had recently been oiled, with a fan directed at each of them. Lucia had scolded her host for the extravagance when she had arrived but she was relishing his resourcefulness now. For the first time in what seemed like weeks, she felt no compulsion to take a shower, to change her clothes, to shave the hair from her head. She felt comfortable. She felt comfortable and she felt ever so slightly drunk.

'You'll stay for lunch.'

Lucia shook her head. 'I can't. I have to work.'

'You have to decide, you mean.'

'Same thing,' Lucia said. She finished the last of her wine.

'You'll have another drink at least.' He reached for the bottle.

'Don't you have any coffee?'

Philip made to raise his cigarette to his lips. He caught himself, scowled at the unlit tip. 'Who wants to drink coffee in weather like this? Here.' He let the bottle drip into the ice bucket for a moment before offering it across the table.

Lucia placed her hand across the rim of her glass. 'Really. No more. It's not even twelve o'clock.'

'You should get up earlier. On Philip time, it's already the middle of the afternoon.'

'I should be going. I'm sorry. You know, for calling so out of the blue. For dropping by like this.'

'Lucia dear. You're no fun any more. No cigarettes, no alcohol before midday. I mean, really. Is this what they've been teaching you in the Met?'

Lucia stood. 'Your house is lovely. Your garden is lovely.'

'Lucia,' said Philip. He had placed his cigarette in his mouth and was frisking his clothes for a light. He found one. With a guilty shrug aimed at his guest, he struck a match and filled his lungs. 'Lucia, sit down for a moment.' He tilted his head as he exhaled but the fan behind him blew the smoke towards Lucia as though she were drawing it from the air herself.

Lucia sat, breathed in.

'You asked me for my opinion. My professional opinion.'

Lucia nodded. 'And you've given it.'

'Yes but allow me a closing statement. There is no case, Lucia. The CPS won't buy it. Your DCI won't buy it. The pain you would cause would be for nothing, other than to make yourself look like a fool. Which,' he added, flapping at the smoke with his hand, 'is a secret that only you and I know.'

'You're telling me to keep my mouth shut.'

'Au contraire. I wouldn't dream of telling you anything. I'm wondering, that's all.'

'What are you wondering, Philip?' She folded her arms.

'I'm wondering, Lucia, whether this is about what you think it's about. Whether in fact it's about something else.'

'Like what? What else would it be about?'

'Like I don't know. Like maybe you had a dog called Samuel when you were a child. Like maybe you feel some connection with this monster – this man, sorry – just because you read the same books.'

Lucia uncrossed her arms. She dropped her hands into her lap, then tucked them under her armpits once again. 'That's ridiculous. I'm doing it – I'm considering it – because it's my job, that's all. This is my job.'

'Your job, surely, is to do what that boss of yours tells you.'

'You don't think that. I know you don't think that.'

Philip shrugged. 'Maybe not. But I do think you should let this one go.'

Lucia rose once more from her chair. 'Probably I will. I have to think about it but probably I will. Thanks. For the wine and for the advice. I'd better get going.'

As Philip escorted Lucia to the door, he asked after David. Lucia was surprised it had taken him so long. 'He's fine,' she said. 'I'd imagine that he's fine. I'm certain of it, in fact.'

Philip tutted, put his arm round Lucia's shoulder. 'There's someone else though. Tell me that there's somebody else.'

'Why does there need to be somebody else?'

'Because you're too young to be alone.'

'I stopped being young when I turned thirty.'

'Then you're getting too old to be alone.'

'You're old. You're alone.'

'How dare you. I'm not even sixty. Besides, I'm young at heart. And I'm only alone when I choose to be.'

Lucia stopped, kissed her host on the cheek. 'Shame on you, Philip. Corrupting all those young boys.'

'They're solicitors, darling. Barristers. As you so charmingly alluded, they're going to hell as it is.'

It was late in the day when she reached the hospital but earlier than she had planned it to be. From Turnham Green she had taken the tube across London and picked up her car at her flat. She had driven to the school and pulled to the side of the road and for an hour at least she had sat. On her way home again she had stopped at the McDonald's on the Bow Road and ordered French fries and a milkshake at the drive-through. She had parked in the car park and thought about eating but could not. Later, on her way to the hospital, the car had smelt of chip fat, which had made her nauseous but hungry too. She had chewed some chewing gum – soft, flavourless, warm from her pocket – while her stomach had pleaded its case for proper sustenance.

At the door to Elliot's ward, she wished she had accepted Philip's invitation to stay for lunch. She imagined salmon and salads and something with strawberries for dessert. They might still be seated on his terrace, three bottles down, a feverish city sunset tinting their reminiscences with sentiment. But at some point Philip would again have asked about David, and Lucia would have had to relive things she did not have the detachment yet to relive. That and the wine would have turned nostalgia into melancholy and when she thought about that she was glad she had not stayed. She wished instead that she had drunk the chocolate milkshake, maybe eaten a few of the chips.

The security glass was cold against her cheek. She could see Elliot in his bed, sitting upright but with his head bowed. There was a woman perched next to him and she too was staring at her hands. The woman looked like Elliot. No, that was not quite accurate. The woman had the same colour hair as Elliot did. That, and their bearing, was what made them seem so alike. The two of them might have been praying. Perhaps, thought Lucia, that was what they were doing.

She should go, she told herself, but she did not move. She watched the boy. She watched his mouth, as resolutely closed as it had been on the previous occasion that Lucia had visited. They might have stitched it shut when they sealed his wound.

The woman was saying something, Lucia realised. She heard her voice but not her words. Someone else came into view – a pair of shoulders, the back of a head, on Lucia's side of the bed – and Lucia pulled back, out of sight. She should go.

'Detective Inspector May, isn't it?'

She stepped away from the door. 'Doctor,' she said. 'Dr Stein.'

'You're back,' the doctor said. 'I didn't expect to see you back.'

'No, I . . . Yes. I'm back.'

'This is his last day, you know. He'll be leaving us in the morning.' The doctor reached past her. 'After you,' he said and as the door opened and Lucia edged forwards, Elliot's family turned to look.

'Really, I don't want to disturb anyone,' Lucia said. She lingered. She directed a nod into the room. She smiled.

'I'd rather you disturbed my patients during visiting hours. Please.' The doctor gestured her inside. He overtook Lucia as they crossed the room. He was speaking, sounding upbeat, sounding competent, and though Elliot's parents responded to his enquiries, it was Lucia they watched.

She stopped several paces from Elliot's bed. She had meant her expression to seem apologetic, to convey kindness and concern and to let them know she had no desire to intrude but the longer she stood there with her teeth clenched and her lips tight, the more insincere, the more gormless, she realised she must look. She should have said something but she had left it too late. She would have to wait now until they asked her who she was, or until Dr Stein introduced her, which he had no obvious intention of doing.

'Fine,' he was saying. 'All fine. The stitches are doing what they're supposed to but I'm going to have to change this dressing, young man. It may sting, just a fraction.'

Lucia cleared her throat finally and was about to say something but before she could speak the doctor removed the bandage that had been taped across Elliot's ear. For the first time Lucia was able to see the wound. The lobe of Elliot's ear was gone. The boy did not flinch but Lucia did.

'I'm sorry. Who are you?'

It was Elliot's mother who had spoken. Lucia looked at her and then at Elliot's father. She glanced at Elliot and caught him watching her but the boy quickly dropped his gaze.

Dr Stein raised his head. 'I assumed the three of you had met.'

'No,' said Lucia. 'No, we haven't. I'm Lucia. Lucia May. I'm with the Met. The Metropolitan Police.'

'The police?' Elliot's mother turned towards her husband.

'You have some news,' Elliot's father said. 'Do you have some news?'

'No,' Lucia said. 'I'm sorry. That's not why I'm here.'

Elliot's father sought direction from Dr Stein. He got none. 'Then why are you here?'

'I brought something,' Lucia said. She unfurled the carrier bag she was holding and reached inside. 'For your son.'

'What? What have you brought?'

'It's a book, dear.'

'I can see that, Frances. Why have you brought my son a book?' He looked at his son but Elliot sat still. Only the boy's eyes moved as Lucia placed the book on the bed.

'It's *The Hobbit*,' Lucia said. 'You've probably read it. It's just, I thought it might help.'

For a moment no one spoke. Lucia straightened the carrier bag and began to fold it. 'I'm sorry,' she said. 'I didn't mean to interrupt.' She nodded at Elliot's mother but avoided his father's eye. She tucked the carrier into her pocket and made to go. Over the rustle of the bag, she almost failed to hear the sound of Elliot's fragile voice.

'Thanks.'

Lucia turned. The doctor and Elliot's parents were staring at the boy. Elliot had his head down still. The fingers of his right hand were resting on the book.

'You're welcome,' Lucia said. 'I hope you like it. You'll have to tell me whether you like it.'

Elliot's father caught up with her in the corridor. He took hold of her elbow and pulled her around.

'Who are you?' he said. 'Why are you here?'

A nurse squeezed past them. Lucia moved to one side of the hallway. Elliot's father followed.

'Has something happened? Is there something you can tell us?'

Lucia shook her head. 'It's not my case, Mr Samson. I just wanted to give Elliot the book, that's all.'

'Not your case? What do you mean, it's not your case? Why are you bringing my son books if it's not your case? Why are you bringing my son books at all?'

'I heard what happened to him. I . . . I don't know. I thought the book might cheer him up.'

Elliot's father was smiling now but there was no humour in his expression. 'Cheer him up? Do you know what I think might cheer him up? Arresting the kids who did this to him. Locking them away. Making sure they don't have a chance to do this to him again. That might cheer him up.'

'I appreciate what you're saying, Mr Samson, really I do. But it's difficult. From what I understand—'

'Don't tell me that there were no witnesses. I don't want to hear there were no witnesses.'

'Please, Mr Samson. It's not my case. Much as I would like to, I can't help you. Maybe if you spoke to PC Price—'

Elliot's father scoffed. 'Price. Price is a moron. He's an idiot.'

'He's just trying to do his job.'

'Bullshit. As far as I can see, no one here is doing their job. Not one of you. You're spending your time shopping for presents and Price is sitting around contemplating how to get his finger out of his arse.'

'I should go, Mr Samson. I really think I should go.' Lucia backed away. As she turned, she closed her eyes and almost collided with another nurse. Lucia muttered her apologies and slid past.

'Stay away from my son. Do you hear me? The whole damn lot of you. Stay away from my son!'

Lucia focused on the floor. She hurried on.

They shat in his briefcase.

Don't ask me when, don't ask me how. They did it though. I saw it. I wish to God I hadn't but I was sitting right beside him when he found it.

That was the only time I heard him swear. Usually the staffroom's like Bill Nicholson Way on a Saturday. We have a swear box, much good it does. The money's supposed to go to charity, to some hospice or hospital, but I don't think they've ever seen a penny of it. We raid it. The teachers do. You know, for ice creams, biscuits, that sort of thing. I probably shouldn't tell you that, should I? I'll probably get the lot of us thrown in gaol. Janet, the headmaster's secretary, she's the worst. If you're going to arrest anyone, arrest her.

Samuel, though. I'd never heard Samuel swear, not until that day. I won't repeat what he said but you could hardly blame him. Christ knows what the kid must have been eating. I haven't ever seen a turd that colour. I'd be at the doctor's in a jiffy if I had. And the size of it. He must have been saving up for days. I won't mention the smell because you can imagine the smell.

He jumps right up when he sees it, like it's a tarantula in there or something. He jumps and he knocks the table and coffee, people's coffee, it goes everywhere. There are a few of us, you know, scattered around on the chairs, around this big coffee table that we've got in there, and we're marking papers or flicking through *The Times* or the *Sun* or whatever it is we're doing. I was reading a book, this book I got sent from the States. It's about the stock market, stocks and shares. It's called *How to Invest Your Salary and Make Loads of Money and Retire While You've Still Got a Life*. Something like that. My cousin, Frank, he lives in Minnesota, he's the one who sent it to me. Reckons he's made a hundred k in sixteen months. Dollars he's talking about but still. And he's basically a moron and I teach economics, right, so I'm thinking, if he can do it, how hard can it be?

The coffee. It goes everywhere. The others start hollering, moaning at Samuel, saying Jesus Christ this, bloody hell that. But I've seen what he's seen and I'm watching this turd roll on to the floor, under the table, and I'm watching Samuel's face and I can't help but look at this turd. The others can't see it yet but they can smell it. Vicky, Vicky Long, she teaches drama, she's the first. She lifts her chin and flares her nostrils and starts aiming them round the room like the barrels of a shotgun. All very theatrical. She sniffs – rapid fire, sniff sniff sniff. Then the others start doing it. Sniffing. All of them. Sniff sniff sniff. By this time I've got my face tucked into my shirt so as the lot of them are sniffing they also start looking at me. And I'm saying, don't look at me, it's got nothing to do with me, and that's when Samuel picks it up.

He could have used a plate or something. Wrapped it in newspaper. I mean, there was a copy of the *Sun* just lying there and that's about all it's good for, right? But for whatever reason Samuel doesn't feel the need. He just reaches down and picks it up, like maybe he's dropped his pen, like all he's doing is picking up his pen. He holds it up. Everyone can see it now. They can see it but that doesn't explain it. What they're seeing is Samuel Szajkowski, this weird little bloke with his fluffy little beard, standing in the staffroom, holding up a day-old turd.

It was in his case, I say. He found it in his case.

Because if I hadn't said that I don't know what the others would have done. Ran out screaming, half of them. Samuel's not taking any notice though, he's just staring at this thing in his hand. For some reason I think he's going to drop it on me. Throw it to me to catch. I don't know why. He doesn't and he wouldn't have but when someone's standing over you, his fist around a great big turd, you don't want to take any chances, do you?

We watch him, the rest of us. Or I do, Vicky does, Chrissie Hobbs does. Matilda and George, they turn away. They don't want to see it. The rest of us don't want to see it either but, like I said before, your attention's kind of drawn to it.

Chrissie, she's the first to respond. Here, she says. Let me get something.

And Vicky's saying, don't touch it, Samuel, put it down.

It was in his case, I say again. Someone put it in his case.

And Samuel, he doesn't say a word.

He was almost lucky. The people who were there, they were nice people, kind people. I wouldn't call them Samuel's friends.

Samuel didn't really have any friends, except Maggie, although some friend Maggie turned out to be. They weren't his friends but they would have helped him. To clean things up. To sort out his case. They would have helped.

He was almost lucky but then Terence walks in.

I call him Terence. I refuse to call him TJ. I call him TJ to his face because I don't want to make a fuss. It's important to him so I say let him have his little nickname. He might not be so keen on it if he knew what some of the kids say it stands for. Tosser Jones, they say. I hear them and I pretend I don't. Toss Jism. That's why they call him TJ. He thinks it's because they all like him. He thinks I like him too. I don't but what can you do? I work with him. I have to get on with him. It would be awkward for the others if I didn't.

You've met Terence, right? So you've got a fair idea about how he might react. When Terence walks in, Samuel's still standing where he's standing, still holding this thing in his hand. Chrissie is in the kitchen. She's got a carrier bag and the washing-up bowl and she doesn't know which one to bring. I've moved away by now so I'm with the others, on the opposite side of the table. We turn to look at Terence and he sees the expressions on our faces and then the lot of us turn around again to look at Samuel.

Poor bugger.

Poor bugger: what am I talking about? He's a murderer. I keep having to remind myself. He was a murderer. He shot three children. He killed a teacher, an innocent woman. And I'm feeling sorry for the bloke. This psycho nutcase maniac. I'm acting like he deserved compassion.

What's that?

Well, I suppose that doesn't surprise me. If he hadn't done what he did, he might even have deserved it. The sympathy. These people you've talked to showing him pity. But not now.

Terence told everyone. The teachers, yes, but the teachers were always going to hear about it. Terence told the kids. He's friendly with some of them, too friendly if you ask me. He wants to be one of the lads, you know, just a mate, which is not what he's here for, is it? It took him a moment or two to understand, to realise what was going on, because all of us started gabbling at once. But after that he thought it was hilarious. It was like he wished he'd thought of it himself. So he tells his little buddies and his buddies spread the word and in six or seven minutes the story's all over the school. For Donovan it was the perfect result. I mean, no one would have been able to prove it was Donovan but it was, of course it was. Even if it was Gideon who did the deed, it would have been Donovan who had the idea.

I had a word with Samuel after that. Everyone knew the kids were giving him a hard time but there's a line to be drawn somewhere, isn't there? I couldn't tell you where, I couldn't point and say, there, that's the limit. But shitting in a man's briefcase. It's not the kind of thing you stand for. The line, well. It might as well be the horizon.

Go to the headmaster, I say. Tell him what's been going on.

Samuel shakes his head. I've tried, he says. I've tried already.

He makes to move past me but I hold his arm.

When? I say. What did you tell him?

Samuel just sort of shrugs. Not a lot, he says. Nothing

specific. I told him I was finding it hard. I've told him more than once.

And?

And that was as far as we got.

But what did the headmaster say? He must have said something.

He told me it was hard. He told me teaching was hard.

Samuel, I say, that's not good enough. You need to tell him about . . . about this. About everything. He'll do something. He'll have to. I try to make a joke, I say, you've got proof at least now, haven't you? Exhibit number two, your honour.

Samuel seems to consider it. He doesn't laugh of course but he seems to consider it. So I'm thinking he might go and speak to him but in the end he doesn't. In the end I have to force him into it.

We're in the staffroom. This is after lunch one day. I forget when exactly. November maybe? December? It's me and Samuel and George, although George wanders out after a while, which leaves just me and Samuel. And we're both minding our own, both of us just reading, when the headmaster appears at the door.

Janet? he says and takes a step into the room. He looks at me. Have you seen Janet?

I say, no, sorry, I haven't, and he scowls, like he's convinced that actually I have and I'm not telling him just to spite him. He takes another step and peers round the corner into the kitchen. For just a second or two he's got his back to us and I don't even need to think. I give Samuel a dig. I hiss at him. I say, go on, Samuel. Go on. And I give him another prod.

Samuel gets up. He looks at me. He's trying to decide, I can tell, but he's running out of time because the headmaster's finished in the kitchen and he's turning round and he's heading for the door and he's virtually out of the room.

I make a face and Samuel shakes his head. I clear my throat, like I'm about to say something, and I don't know if the noise startles him or what. He says, Headmaster. Like the word was caught between his tongue and his teeth and just needed a jolt to knock it loose. Headmaster, he says again.

The headmaster stops. He turns to look. Meanwhile I get up and I say, excuse me, and I nip between them and into the kitchen like I'm going to make a coffee. Or that's what I'm hoping it looks like. The headmaster, though – either he forgets I'm there or he doesn't particularly care. More likely he doesn't care. I could have settled into one of the armchairs with a Coke and a bucket of popcorn, and I doubt it would have made any difference.

Headmaster, Samuel says again and Travis says, Mr Szajkowski. What is it?

May I have a word? Just for a moment?

A word? says Travis. He checks his watch. He glances towards the door.

It's just, I have a problem. I was hoping . . . I thought perhaps . . . I was hoping that you could help.

Travis sighs. I can't see from where I'm standing but I can just picture him rolling his eyes. A problem, he says. But of course you do. I would hardly have expected anything else.

Samuel hesitates. For a moment he doesn't say anything.

Well, Mr Szajkowski? Please, don't keep me in suspense.

I'm ... I'm having a spot of trouble. With the children.

Again the headmaster sighs. Trouble, he says. What sort of trouble, Mr Szajkowski? With which children?

And Samuel, the silly sod, he thinks he shouldn't name names. It's not important who, I don't expect ...

If it's not important, Mr Szajkowski, then why do you feel so obligated to bring it to my attention? I'm rather busy, as you can imagine.

And for a moment Samuel doesn't know what to say. He looks across the headmaster's shoulder and he catches my eye. I nod at him. I nod twice.

They defecated in my briefcase.

This from Samuel. He just comes out with it, just like that.

They did what?

They defecated. In my briefcase.

Who defecated in your briefcase?

I didn't see anyone do it. But I found it. I still have it, in fact.

You kept it?

No, no, no. I didn't keep it. Christina Hobbs, she took it. She wrapped it up.

Mr Szajkowski. The headmaster's pinching the bridge of his nose now. Mr Szajkowski. Perhaps you would do me the courtesy of starting your story at the customary point of departure.

Which throws Samuel completely.

The beginning. Begin, if you would, at the beginning.

So Samuel does. He tells Travis about the coughing and the swearing and that certain classes of his have become unteachable. He tells Travis that he has been tripped, shoved, abused, hounded, spat at. He tells Travis that his bicycle has been vandalised, his seat stolen, his tyres knifed. He tells Travis about the graffiti he has seen, the notes he has discovered in his pigeonhole, the text messages he has received. He tells Travis again what the kids deposited in his briefcase. And then he drops into a chair like he's physically exhausted and the headmaster's left standing there looking down at him.

How old are you, Mr Szajkowski?

Samuel looks up. I'm twenty-seven. I was twenty-seven just last week.

Well, congratulations. Did you have a party? Was there a cake?

I'm sorry, I'm not sure I—

Never mind. You're twenty-seven. A fair age. Not a mature age but an adult one. You are an adult, Mr Szajkowski?

Yes. Yes, I am an adult.

I am pleased to hear it. And your tormentors. How old are they?

They're year eleven, mainly. Year ten.

Fifteen then. Sixteen perhaps. Fourteen possibly.

That's right. Yes. I would say that's right.

Do you not see a discrepancy somewhere, Mr Szajkowski? Do you not sense something awry?

Samuel nods, he's saying, yes, Headmaster, I do. But they defecated—

In your briefcase. Yes, Mr Szajkowski, you mentioned it. What of it?

Samuel is regretting having sat down, I can tell. The head-master's a tall man anyway and now he's looming right over him.

What of it? Travis says again. What would you have me do? Perhaps I should summon the culprits to my office, make them apologise to you, make them promise in future to play nice. Perhaps, Mr Szajkowski, you would like me to ask them to stop picking on you. Perhaps you think that might help.

No, says Samuel. Of course not. There won't be any need for—

Or perhaps, Mr Szajkowski – now here's an idea – perhaps, Mr Szajkowski, you might consider for a moment your func-tion as an employee of this establishment. You are a teacher, Mr Szajkowski. I have reminded you of that fact before but perhaps you have forgotten it. You are a teacher, which means you teach and you lead and you maintain order. You maintain order, Mr Szajkowski. You effect discipline. You do not allow yourself to become intimidated by a fifteen-year-old boy who in twelve months' time will either be queuing for his dole money or stealing other people's. Do not look so surprised, Mr Szajkowski. You do not name names but you do not have to. I see everything that happens within this institution. I am omniscient. Donovan Stanley is a reprobate. He will be with us only for a few months more. During that time I will not waste time or attention or resources on something as sordid and inconsequential as that boy's *shit*.

And then he leaves. He doesn't look back at Samuel and he doesn't look over at me.

I'm standing there. I've got a teaspoon in my hand and I'm

just standing there. I look at Samuel. I'm watching him. I feel like I should say something but I don't know what. What can I say?

In the end I don't say anything. Samuel doesn't give me the chance. He stands up and he picks up his bag and he packs away his books and he's across the room and without so much as a glance he's out the door and he's gone.

And that, Inspector, was that. That was that and nothing changed. I mean, I assumed that Travis would do something. I told myself that his little speech was for Samuel's benefit. You know, a sergeant major ball-busting one of his troops. But he did nothing. He actually meant what he said. He did nothing and nothing changed.

No, that's not quite right. Things did change. Things got worse. At the time I didn't think it would be possible, but it was, it most definitely was. You heard about the football match, didn't you?

'**It's a joke.** That's what it is. It's a joke report.'

She said nothing. So far she had said nothing.

'Come on, Lucia. Put me out of my misery. Show me the real one. This is hilarious, real comedy stuff, but give me the actual report, the one that says what we all need it to say.'

She could have. The DCI did not know it but she could have. It was at home, on her computer, in the recycle bin. It was in a pile on the side of her desk, sentenced but not yet shredded. It was on the memory stick in her pocket.

'You know the one I mean. The one that says this was a tragedy, that Szajkowski was a lunatic, that guns are a menace to our society.'

She shifted. She sighed. She shifted back.

'Something about social services maybe, something they should've could've might've done.'

She was still. She held herself still.

'The one that's not going to cost me my reputation. The one that's not going to cost you your job.'

There was a fly on his shoulder. She could tell he could not feel it but it was there.

'I'm going to do you a favour, Lucia.' He raised his arm, showed her the folder. The fly leapt free and the folder followed, arching and then tipping into the bin. 'You're early. It's your saving grace. I gave you until lunchtime if you remember. I don't need it until lunchtime.'

'You have it now.'

'My lips are itching, Lucia. My whole jaw: it's itching. It's tingling. It's like I can tell there's bad weather coming, you know, like those guys with their hips in those films. Except the bad weather isn't bad weather. It's a shit storm. That's what's coming: a shit storm.'

'Toothpaste,' Lucia said.

'What?'

'Try toothpaste. On your cold sores. I read about it.'

'What kind of toothpaste?'

'I don't know. It didn't say.'

'There are all kinds of toothpaste.'

'There are. I didn't think about that. But it didn't say.'

'I use whitening toothpaste. My wife buys whitening toothpaste.'

'I wouldn't use that. Or maybe you could. It didn't say.'

The chief inspector watched Lucia for a moment. His eyes did not leave her as his fingers wandered across his desk. They found what they were seeking and Cole broke eye contact long enough to pick up a pen and scribble a note on a scrap of paper. He folded the note and tucked it into his breast pocket.

'All I'm asking,' Lucia said, 'is that you let me talk to them. This doesn't commit us. It doesn't have to go anywhere if we decide it shouldn't.'

'Lucia. I have to make a presentation at three. That's in what. Six hours. Five and a half. The super is going to be there. The commissioner is going to be there. The home secretary might even drop by. Believe me: it commits us.'

'So tell them there's been a delay. Don't tell them anything. Stall.'

The DCI grinned. He grinned and then he winced, raised his fingertips to his jawline. He regarded Lucia as though she were the source of his pain. 'Stall,' he said. 'You want me to stall the home secretary.'

Lucia shrugged. 'Just long enough so I can talk to the CPS. Present the evidence. Convince them that there's a case.'

Cole laughed but this time made no attempt to smile. 'What evidence, Inspector? What case?'

'You've seen the transcripts. You've read what these people have said. Grant, the economics teacher. The secretary – the headmaster's secretary. The kids. You know what happened at that football match.'

Cole tugged at his tie even though it was already loose. He leant forwards on to his elbows and as he did so a slice of sunlight speared his eyes. 'Shut that damn blind,' he said.

Lucia moved to the window and did as he had asked. The chief inspector's desk fell into shadow.

'This bastard sun. This bastard heat. This stuff only ever happens when it's hot. We can't handle it. This country. When it snows, we freeze up. When it gets hot, we boil over.'

'Just let me talk to them. Let me see what they say.'

'I know what they'll say, Inspector. I can tell you what they'll say. They'll say there is no case. They'll say there is no evidence. They'll say they won't go to court and risk their reputation, their career, their conscience by bringing a prosecution against a school.'

'You don't know that.'

'I do, Inspector. I do know that. You've been working in this department for what, eighteen months? I've been here eighteen years. So don't tell me what I do and do not know.'

Lucia's hand was in her pocket, she realised. The memory stick was in her grip. She let go, removed her hand. 'The school could have stopped it,' she said. 'The school should have stopped it.'

'The school is the victim, Lucia. The school is three dead kids and one dead teacher. The school is the grieving parents on pages one to twelve of the *Mail*. The school – and this is quite important, you might want to make a note – the school is the bastard government.'

'The school is an employer. That's all it is. It's accountable. The school is accountable.'

'Who the fuck are you, Lucia? Who the fuck are you to decide who's accountable?'

'That's my job. Isn't it? I thought that was my job.'

'Your job is to pick up the pieces. To tidy them away. Not to chuck them about the room just because your hormones are bubbling over and you're looking for someone to get mad at.'

Lucia folded her arms. She unfolded them, put her hands on her hips. She glared at Cole. Cole glared back.

'So?' he said.

'So? So what?'

'So are you going to rewrite it? Are you going to do this department, me, yourself a favour?'

'No,' Lucia said. 'I'm not going to rewrite it.'

Cole looked at the file in the bin. He shook his head. 'I'm going to ask you one more time, Lucia. I'm only going to ask you one more time.'

'The answer's no,' Lucia said. 'Sir.'

'Then open that door, would you?'

'You want me to leave?'

'I didn't tell you to leave. I told you to open that door.'

Lucia crossed the office and reached for the handle of the door. She looked at Cole.

'Open it.'

She did.

'Walter!' Cole hollered. 'You out there? Walter!'

Lucia was only half concealed by the doorframe. Everyone in the office outside turned towards her. Walter was in his chair, one foot on his desk. He shuffled upright when he heard the chief. He spotted Lucia. He grinned.

'Walter! Get in here. Get your chubby arse in here. Walter! Is he coming?'

Lucia nodded. She watched Walter cross the room. He winked at her as he passed. His elbow trailed. It brushed against her breast and Lucia recoiled. She shut the door and leant against it. She wrapped her arms across her chest.

'What's up, Guv?'

'What's on the board? What have you got on?'

'Nothing much. Me and Harry, we were gonna—'

'Don't. Whatever you were going to do, cancel it.'

'No problemo. What's up?' Walter started to tuck in his shirt where it had come loose. Lucia watched his back, watched him reach below his beltline, watched his trousers ride up from his ankles and reveal his mismatched socks. She looked away, made eye contact with the chief inspector. Her glance rebounded. It settled on a stain on the carpet inches in front of her toes.

'Lucia here has presented me with a problem. She's presented this department with a problem.'

'Oh?'

'I need someone to fix that problem. I need you to fix that problem.' Cole threw out a foot and toppled the waste-paper basket. Lucia's report spilled on to the floor. 'Here,' he said. 'Pick it up. Pick it up, read it, rewrite it. If you can't tell for yourself what needs changing, ask Lucia here to give you some pointers.'

Walter stooped. He shuffled the pages together. He glanced at Lucia before he rose, his teeth showing, his eyes crawling across the bare flesh below her knees. Lucia turned her head away.

'No problemo,' Walter said again. 'How long have I got?'

'Get it back to me by one. And Walter, don't try to impress me. I don't want anything fancy, do you hear me? You know the sort of thing I need.'

'Aye aye, Guv.'

'And you.' The chief inspector looked at Lucia. 'You, take the day off. Take the week off if you want. You blew it. I gave you a chance and you blew it. Now the both of you: get the fuck out of my office.'

She went to the school. She could not think of anywhere she wanted to be so she went there. It was, she knew, the day of the memorial service. They would be starting at ten, Travis had said. A quarter of an hour ago.

The car park was full and the playground was full and the only space she found on the road outside she could not get into. In the end, she parked two streets away. The air conditioning in her Golf was broken and when she stepped on to the pavement she realised her blouse was clinging to her back. She walked slowly to the school. At the gates, she tidied herself. She blew at her brow. There were signs and she followed them, away from the main entrance and down the side of the building on to the playing field.

A man with sunglasses and no hair stopped her. He asked her who she was. She asked him the same.

'Security, madam.'

'Security for whom?'

The man looked over his shoulder, towards the stage. On the platform there were the headmaster and Christina Hobbs and a fat man with a beard who looked shorter than he did on television.

'Busy day for him.'

'Sorry, madam?'

Lucia showed him her identification and he let her pass.

She found a tree and stood next to it. Another goon in a suit watched her for a while before dipping his head and raising a finger to his earpiece. Lucia locked her hands in front of her.

Travis was speaking. He was thanking everyone for coming, thanking his honoured guest, thanking the families of those Szajkowski had murdered, even thanking the reporters, who had been penned in their own section, away from the audience proper. Lucia was standing to the rear and to the left of the main seating area. She could not see the front row but she gathered from the headmaster's bearing that this is where they were sitting: Sarah's parents, Felix's parents, Veronica Staples's husband, her children. Donovan's parents? Lucia doubted it.

Now Travis was praying. Lucia had been scanning the audience, the rows of children and their mothers and fathers. She had not heard him start. She had not noticed that the heads in front of her were bowed. She dropped her chin but did not close her eyes. She tuned out the words. It was not the prayer that she did not wish to hear, rather the voice that was uttering it.

When the prayer was over someone clapped. Others joined in but not many. The applause died of its embarrassment and the audience stood. It stood but remained in ranks. Then the headmaster left the stage and the crowd began to disperse.

Lucia lingered. The children walked quickly away but the adults moved slowly, as though any semblance of speed might be construed as disrespect. It was some time before the field emptied. Lucia heard cars starting up, she heard what had been muttered conversation gain volume, she heard children freed from the bounds of decorum echoing in the building behind her. She made sure there was no one within sight who might recognise her and she stepped out from under the tree.

For a moment she could not work out why something felt wrong. The shade: it had spread from where she had been standing. The ground was one tone, the sky above no longer blue. She saw clouds: proper clouds, colourless but not uniform like the haze that descended late in the day. The sun was gone, not just masked, not like lamplight softened by a veil – it was gone. No corner of the sky was brighter than any other.

'Could be a storm.' It was the goon, the first one. He was beside her, gazing up. He was still wearing his sunglasses.

Lucia looked where he was looking. She shook her head. 'I don't think so,' she said. 'Not yet.'

No, no. I understand. It's your job, Inspector. You're only doing your job.

I'm sorry about my wife.

Yes, I know, but still. It wasn't helpful. It's not helpful. She forgets, I think, that she is not the only person who is suffering. She forgets that I loved Sarah too. I'm her father. Regardless of what Sarah's birth certificate says, I'm her father and I always will be.

Six years. Susan – Sarah's mother – and I have been together these past six years.

Sarah never knew him. He left, went overseas. She was only a month or two old. Not man enough to change a nappy, Susan always says, but she couldn't have stayed with him regardless. No, it's not what you're thinking. It was a mistake, that's all. Their relationship, Susan getting pregnant – it was a mistake. Best mistake she ever made, as it turned out.

Christ. Look at me. I'm worse than Susan. Christ. Yes, sorry, thanks. I don't have one. I should get in the habit of carrying one, shouldn't I?

I have a picture. Here. That's her. We took that in Little-hampton. That's the beach there, you can just about see it. And that ice cream, look. It's bigger than her. It was raining but she insisted on ice cream. This was last summer. It rained from May to September, I don't know if you remember. Nothing like this year. Not at all like this year.

It sounds ridiculous but do you know what I think might help? Rain. I think some rain would help. You know how in books or in films it's always raining when someone's unhappy. Or there's a storm when something awful is about to happen. There's a name for it, isn't there? When they use the weather like that. I think if it rained and if the wind blew and if the sky showed some emotion, I think that would help us. Me and Susan. Because at the moment it's like the world doesn't care. It has no empathy. The sunshine is relentless. It's cruel and it's harsh. And the heat. The heat has no pity. You sit and you think about what's happened and you try to make sense of it but all you can really focus on is the heat, on how hot you are. I think if it rained it would help. It would be like tears.

It's stupid I know. It's not rational. I keep telling myself to be rational. Like the weather. It's not a thing, it's not alive, it's not against us. It just feels like it is. That's what it feels like.

You must be busy. I'm prattling, forgive me.

Well, I appreciate it. I do. Everyone has been very kind. Susan, though, she's finding it hard. She won't talk to anyone. You saw what she's like. She's like that with everyone. With friends, with her family. The press, they've only just left us in peace. I say they've left us in peace. They've left our front garden is what they've done. They're still out there.

That's right. You saw them then. And there's a van parked there sometimes. I think if there's a story that's breaking somewhere else, it gets called away. When it's no longer needed it comes back. Susan, she hasn't been out. She won't go out. She won't even open the curtains in our bedroom. That's where she spends most of her time. In the bedroom. Or in Sarah's room. Sometimes she sits in Sarah's room.

So I'm the one who has to talk to people. You know, deal with things. Not that I mind. I'd rather be doing something. And everyone has been very kind.

The funeral is this weekend. It was difficult because it would have clashed. With the others. So many people wanted to attend them all. Quite a few of the children but also the teachers. It took some co-ordination but they're at different times now. Sarah will be the first. It's called the Islington Crematorium but actually it's in Finchley. Felix, the boy who died, the younger one, his service is happening there too. The other boy, Donovan I think his name was, I think he's being buried. Somewhere south. I don't know about the teacher. Veronica, wasn't it? I don't know about her.

Do you believe in God, Inspector? Don't answer that, I'm sorry. I only ask because I haven't decided myself. I'm forty-seven and I haven't decided. We had to choose, you see. For the service. I wasn't ready for that. My daughter has just been taken from me. She was eleven years old and now she's gone. And I'm trying to arrange things for her funeral and the chap, the funeral director chap, he was a very pleasant chap, I mean it's not his fault at all but he asks me, he has to: are there any cultural or religious requirements of which we should be aware?

Which is like asking me whether I believe in God. Your daughter's just been murdered; do you believe in God? Or maybe it isn't but that's how it struck me. I couldn't answer right away. I'm agnostic – is that the word? I always say one of them when I mean the other. Susan was brought up Catholic. We didn't go to church with Sarah because Susan wanted Sarah to be able to choose. So I couldn't answer. I told him I had to talk it over with my wife.

We're not having a religious theme. That's what we decided. There will be no mention of God.

The music. I'm still not sure about the music. Sarah loved the Beatles. She just adored them. There's a CD she had, a greatest hits it must have been. Maybe there were two CDs. One had a blue cover, I think. One was red. And they were all you would ever hear from her bedroom. The door would be shut but you would hear it through the walls, through the floor. And everyone knows all the songs, don't they, so it didn't matter that you couldn't hear the words. You'd hear the melody and Paul McCartney and you'd find yourself singing along. You could tell what mood she was in by what song she played. If she was miserable, she would play 'Eleanor Rigby', over and over and over. If she was mad at us, at me and Susan, she would play 'Yellow Submarine'. I don't know why. I think it was because she thought we didn't like it. And I don't. I don't know about Susan but I don't. Although I'd like to hear it now.

'Across the Universe'. That's what we're having at her funeral. Does that seem inappropriate to you? 'Across the Universe' and also 'Penny Lane'. 'Penny Lane' was Sarah's favourite.

Will you listen to me? I'm sorry.

No, I'm not being fair. I'll prattle on all day if you let me.

That's kind but there must be something in particular that you wanted to ask me. I'm sure you've not come here just to chat.

No, go ahead. Really, I don't mind.

Well, I don't know what I can tell you. She was only in year seven, she really hadn't been there very long.

No, no trouble. She was very bright. She was very hardworking.

She enjoyed it, yes, I suppose so. As much as any kid enjoys going to school.

No, she never mentioned him. He taught her I suppose. I suppose he must have taught her.

The headmaster, yes, on several occasions. I spoke to him just yesterday, in fact. Something about a memorial service he was planning. He hadn't fixed a date but he wanted to see what I thought. You know, just in principle. I told him I thought it was a fine idea. I don't know though. I mean, I don't know if we shall go. Probably we won't. What with Susan and everything. But I told the headmaster that we would appreciate the gesture even if we didn't actually attend. And that it would help the others. What's that word the Americans use? You know, when you get to that point where you can put things behind you, where you're able to move on.

Yes, that's it. I don't expect we shall ever get there but there's the other children to think about, isn't there? The ones who saw it all happen. The ones who lost their friends.

You've been to the school, I assume?

You've seen the tributes then. The flowers, the notes. The

ribbons too. It's astonishing, isn't it? How many people just one life can touch. That helps sometimes. I feel guilty that it does but it helps: knowing that others are grieving too. In different ways, for different reasons most of them, but they're grieving nonetheless. You know what they say about misery. There's truth in those old sayings, don't you think? Except for that one about healing, the one about time. I can't imagine that there's any truth in that.

But yes, the headmaster. He's always seemed a decent enough fellow. He seems to say the right thing, make the right noises, you know. I don't envy him his job, I can tell you. It can't be easy, even in normal circumstances. He must be doing something right though because they're under such scrutiny these days, aren't they? The school always does well in the tables. It always comes out near the top. That's why we sent Sarah there. That's why we moved here.

No, thank you. I still have this one. I'm okay.

You know, it's interesting that you ask. About the school. Because do you know what a friend of mine said? He said to me – well, actually, it was both of them, him and his wife – they said to me – Susan wasn't there and I'm glad now I think about it that she wasn't – but they said to me: you should sue. The school. Can you believe that? They told me I should sue the school. For hiring him. For putting him in charge of our children, they said. For taking a man at face value, I say. For not knowing what no one could have known.

Because no one could have known, could they? No one could have predicted what would happen. What he would do. You know that better than me, I'd imagine. You have access to his records, don't you, to these lists people have, to these registers. And he was clean, wasn't he? He had no history. The headmaster, he told me all of this. He assured me that there was nothing they could have done. He said this man had a vendetta against one of the children and that Sarah just got in his way. He said it was unfortunate, it was tragic but what happened was a freak, an aberration. He said it was the inscrutable will of God.

I haven't spoken to them since. The friends I mentioned. I'm putting what they said down to shock. I mean, it's everyone's first reaction, isn't it? To look for someone to blame. People say it's an English thing, this need to find fault, to look for scapegoats, but I don't think it's just us. It's human nature. I mean, I can't deny that I have my moments. I can't deny that sometimes I succumb. Do you know what I wish? Obviously you know what I wish but apart from that do you know what I wish? I wish that he weren't dead. So I could talk to him. That's why. Sometimes, that's why. I wish he were alive so I could ask him . . . I'm not sure what I'd ask him. I'd ask him why I suppose. Although I don't know that he would be able to answer. It seems to me if he were rational enough to be able to answer he wouldn't have done what he did in the first place.

Then other times, other times I wish he were alive so I could kill him.

I don't mean that. I don't mean that.

Sometimes I think I do but I don't.

I think what I'm doing is what my friends were doing. It's hard, isn't it? When there's no one to blame when something terrible happens. Or when there's no one left to blame. Do you know what I mean? It's always easier to deal with the pain if you can twist that pain into anger, if you can lash out, if you can blame someone, anyone, even if they don't deserve to be blamed.

Do you know what I mean?

Lucia was right. Though the clouds became bloated, there was no breach. The effect, rather, was like shutting the windows in a room that was already stuffy and overheated. And the clouds lingered. The afternoon was dark long before evening arrived. The evening was sunless, then starless. The night was no cooler than the day.

She did not sleep. Usually, whenever she said she had not slept, she would know that actually she had, in starts, for an hour, perhaps two hours, at a time. But that night, the night following the memorial service, she did not sleep. She lay on sheets that scratched, uncovered but for a corner of a blanket she clutched only because she needed something to clutch, her head perspiring on pillows that felt recently vacated even on their underside. She tried to convince herself that no one in London was sleeping, that the country was awake and uncomfortable and as worn out as she was. She tried but she convinced herself only that she would never sleep again, whereas everyone else, the ones who in the morning would say, no, I didn't sleep a wink, not a wink all night, were in fact sleeping in starts, for an hour, perhaps two hours, at a time.

At the station the next day no one looked as though they had not slept. Her colleagues appeared no more weary, no more dishevelled than usual. Lucia, on the other hand, saw the image reflected by her monitor, by the glass partition of Cole's office, by the mirror in the ladies' toilets as a forgery, painted with mascara and foundation on a canvas that was worn and cracked. She drank coffee though she knew she was drinking too much. She was hot and she was edgy and the coffee made her hotter, more on edge.

And the clouds lingered.

She tried to not think about Szajkowski. She tried to not think about the school, about Travis. She cleared her desk and filed her files. She emptied her inbox and deleted documents from her desktop. But she saw Walter, she heard his guffaw, she smelt his failing deodorant, and the sight, sound, smell of him was more than enough to remind her. She sent Cole an email. She wanted to make sure that the report – the bastardised report, Walter's report – had not been filed in her name. From the moment it occurred to her that it might have been, she became determined to make sure that it was not. She knew it was unimportant but she became determined nonetheless. She blamed the coffee and took another sip.

Cole did not reply and Lucia grew tired of waiting. For the first time since she had joined the police force, she lamented the lack of paperwork awaiting her attention. She craved menial tasks but she had none. When he had first handed her the Szajkowski case, Cole had absolved her of responsibility for anything else. Now Cole had snatched the Szajkowski case back and for the moment Lucia had nothing.

She tried to look busy. It was hard to look busy and at the same time to watch Walter, to listen to his conversations, to angle herself in such a way that she might catch a glimpse of Cole in his office, to walk past the doorway and to linger without seeming to. What she most wanted to do was march in. What she most wanted was to ask and be told what was happening with her case, what the superintendent had said, the commissioner, the home secretary. What she most wanted, seeing as she was playing this game, was to rewind twenty-four hours, forty-eight, and write the report again, write it better, present it again, present it better. Present it later so Cole would not have time to do anything other than accept it.

She pulled out her files again and she read. She read the statements and the more she read the more she felt vindicated, righteous, wronged. She found a highlighter in her drawer, a yellow one, and stole a green one from Harry's desk. As she read she annotated: yellow for the prosecution, green for the defence. She marked yellow, yellow, nothing for a while, then yellow again, more yellow. She drank coffee. Every so often she would pull the lid off the green pen with her teeth and high-light a sentence, a paragraph, not because she felt she really needed to, more to assure herself that she was being fair.

At lunch she bought a sandwich and ate one half of it. She drank water to flush out the coffee but filled her mug as soon as she returned to the office.

The yellow highlighter was running low. She felt like bran-dishing it at Cole, saying, here, look, do you see now? I was right and you were wrong. But it did not run out. She willed it to. She double underlined and scrawled extravagant asterisks in the margins but still it did not run dry. Whenever she was forced to pick up the green pen she left the cap off the yellow. She knew she was breaking the rules she had set but the contest had already become a rout.

Until she reached the end of one statement and realised she had marked it only in green. She read it again with her yellow highlighter poised but found only another section that should probably also have been green. The same thing happened with the next statement, then with a third. And though it was the yellow pen that lay bare on her desk, it was the green one that gave out first. Lucia cursed. She blamed Harry for buying cheap, decided the highlighter must already have been running out, dismissed the game she was playing as void. She gathered the statements in a ragged pile and dropped them into a drawer. She looked for Cole. She looked for Walter.

'Looking for me, sweetheart?'

He was behind her. He was at her shoulder and she had not noticed.

'You wish,' she said. Then, hating herself even before she spoke: 'Walter, wait a minute. What's happening? Do you know what's happening with the case?' She had meant to sound earnest and professional. Her voice was needy and weak. She heard it and Walter heard it. His smile unfurled in stages: first the left corner, then the right, then the hoisting of his upper lip. His mouth parted and his tongue poked through. It twitched and curled upwards, caressing the yellowed enamel of his teeth.

'Never mind,' Lucia said. 'Forget it, never mind.'

She made to spin her chair but Walter stuck out his hand and caught it before she could turn away.

'Lulu, Lulu. Don't be embarrassed. I'll tell you what you want to know.'

'I said forget it, Walter. Forget I mentioned it.'

'I'll tell you what you want to know,' Walter said, 'but first I need you to answer me one question.'

Walter had let go of her chair. She could have turned away but she did not. She folded her arms. She raised her eyebrows.

'Tell me,' Walter said. 'What is it about beards?'

'What are you talking about?'

'Beards. What is it about them? It's the way they tickle, am I right? You like the way beards tickle. Down there.'

'I haven't got time for this, Walter.'

'Because I can grow one. If you'd like me to. If a beard would turn you on.'

Lucia rolled her eyes and twisted away. She clicked her way to her inbox and found it empty. She selected a folder, opened an email at random. She studied it.

'It's the only thing I can think of.' He was addressing the room now. Lucia closed the email and opened another. Without registering who had sent it, she hit reply and started typing. 'The beard, I mean. I can't think of any other reason why you'd have a thing for this Szajkowski.'

'I don't have a thing for him, Walter. Don't be absurd.' She spoke to her screen.

'So what is it, Lulu? If you don't have a thing for him, what's got your knickers up your crack? Why are you so desperate to defend him? To pick on the school instead?' He took hold of her chair again and forced her round. 'Come on, admit it. It's the beard isn't it? Charlie. Hey Charlie! You're in luck my son. Lulu here has a thing for facial pubes.'

Charlie grinned. He licked a finger and ran saliva across his moustache.

'Walter, I'm busy. Let go of my chair.'

'You don't look busy, Lulu. You haven't looked busy all day.' He tightened his grip, leant in close. 'I've seen you watching me. I've seen that hunger in your eyes.'

'Walter, let go.' Lucia wrenched her chair just as Walter removed his hand. She spun and hit her knee against her desk. She bit down on her cry just as it threatened to escape her mouth.

'Walter. Get in here.' It was Cole, watching from the door to his office.

Walter held up a finger.

'Would you shoot me, Lulu? Just because we have our fun. Would you shoot me and say that I deserved it? That I provoked you?'

Lucia held her knee. She did not answer.

'It's the same thing, isn't it? Answer me, Lulu. Would you shoot me?'

Ignoring the pain, she got to her feet. 'No, Walter. I wouldn't shoot you. That would be like admitting that you bothered me.' She bumped shoulders with Walter as she passed him. 'Besides,' she said and she turned. 'A bullet would be too quick. You wouldn't feel it. No, Walter. I'd use something blunt.'

The car park was beneath the building, not quite underground but covered and hemmed in by thick concrete columns. The light was poor. The sun had not yet set, though it was dragging the day with it as it dipped towards the horizon. Lucia peered into her bag for her keys. She gave up and tried rummaging with her hand. She shook the bag, peered in again.

She was late heading home only because she had waited for Cole to leave first. After that she had waited for Walter. She had hoped Cole would tell her something, that Walter might let something slip. Neither one of them had obliged. Instead, she would have to read about it in the papers. She would hear it on the news. It was her case but she would hear what had been decided on the news.

Lucia's Volkswagen was parked in the corner furthest from the stairwell, opposite a line of empty squad cars. She reached it before she had found her keys. The light on the wall was faulty: it buzzed and it fizzed and it flickered on and off. Lucia angled the bag towards it. She cursed, dropped on to the balls of her feet and tipped the contents of the bag on to the floor. She found the car keys immediately. She swore again, scooped up the keys and refilled her bag. With her hands pressing on her unbruised knee, she struggled upright.

Walter had hold of her throat before she realised he was there. The bag dropped and the keys dropped and he had her against the wall. She saw his face in the light and then his silhouette and then his face again and she was thinking, that's twice now, that's twice I didn't hear him coming. She could smell him. She could smell his hair, like hotel pillows beneath their cases; his breath, sour and needing water. She could smell oranges. His fingers across her mouth, they smelt of oranges, as though he had been peeling one while he had been waiting.

'Something blunt. That's what you said, isn't it? Something blunt.' He hissed. As he hissed he spat, he sprayed.

Lucia struggled. She tried swinging an arm but found it pinned. She tried lifting a leg but could barely shift her foot. Walter was against her, his thighs trapping hers, his elbows across her shoulders, his weight keeping her down.

'How's this?' he said and he was wriggling now, the hand on her throat slipping downwards. 'How's this for something blunt?' He shoved her away and she fell, grazing the wall and rebounding from her car. She gagged. She tried to stand and turned her ankle. She tried again. She looked at Walter.

He had his flies open. He had his dick in his hand.

'How's this?' he said again and he moved closer. His crotch was level with Lucia's eyes. 'Is this the sort of thing you had in mind?'

Lucia gagged again. She tried to shout but found herself croaking. 'Get away from me. Get the fuck away from me.' She raised one hand to her throat. She held out the other in front of her, fingers curled, nails at the ready.

Walter stopped inches from Lucia's hand. 'Don't get over-excited,' he said. 'That's as close as I'm going to let you get. I just want to show you what you're missing. What you're missing and what you're lacking.'

Lucia swiped but Walter was ready. 'Whoa! Easy, tiger.' He cackled. He inched forwards again. 'Do you see, Lulu? Do you see what I'm telling you? What I'm showing you? You need one of these to do this job. You need two of these.' He cupped it, thrust towards her with his hips.

Lucia cringed. She withdrew her hand.

'That's your problem. That's why you're in the mess you're

in.' He tucked away the thing he was holding. He bent at the waist and zipped his fly. 'Let me give you some advice, Lulu. Grow some balls. Lose the lip and grow some balls. Because having one and not the other is going to get you into trouble.'

'Is that it?' Lucia wheezed. She was still on the floor, still crouched at Walter's feet. 'Is that all there is?'

Walter grinned. He shrugged. 'It may not look like much, darling. But it's enough to stop me getting weepy about some immigrant kid-killing freak. And if you like—' he reached for his fly again '—if you like I can show you just how big this pal of mine can get.'

'Walter. Hey, Walter!'

Walter turned and Lucia turned. It sounded like Harry but Lucia could see only Walter and concrete and car.

'Everything okay? You lost something?'

'Just helping Lucia here find her keys. She dropped them. Didn't you, sweetheart?' He looked down at her. He held out his hand. Lucia knocked it away. She reached past and used the car to steady herself as she stood.

'Lucia's there?' Harry was closer now, a few cars away. Lucia did not look at him but she nodded. She held out her keys. Got them, she tried to say but the words did not get past her throat.

'Well, that's me for the day. You remember what I said, Lulu. You remember what I showed you.' Walter stepped out from behind the car. He nodded at Harry as he passed him, dropped a palm on to his shoulder. 'Nighty night, ladies.'

Lucia fumbled with the door handle. She jabbed the key at the lock and scraped the paintwork. She tried again. Harry edged towards her.

'Lucia? Is everything okay?'

Still Lucia did not look at him. She held up her palm. She coughed. 'Everything's fine, Harry.' All she could manage was a whisper.

'Are you sure? I mean, you don't sound—'

'It's fine.' The key found the lock and Lucia tugged at the door. 'Goodnight, Harry.'

She slid inside.

She wanted just to sit but she did not let herself. She tripped the ignition and fastened her seat belt. She did not cry.

She put the car into reverse and released the handbrake. She turned in her seat and eased the vehicle backwards. She did not cry.

When she was clear she applied the brake and shoved the gear lever into first. She released the clutch and eased away. She did not cry.

Harry stood aside to let the car pass. He held up a hand but Lucia stared ahead. She passed the squad cars and slowed at the barrier and pulled out into the road. She did not cry.

Fifty yards on she pulled the Volkswagen to the kerb and killed the engine. She closed her eyes and gripped the wheel and allowed her head to slump against it. She coughed. She swallowed. She did not, would not cry.

And yet the tears came. In spite of herself, Lucia cried. And she cried.

What are these things always about, Inspector? Samuel taught history, right? So let's look at history. In all of history, what has been the common motivation in any act of lunacy, of depravity, of desperation? What more than anything else has driven people to steal, to lie, to cheat? To lose their minds sometimes. To kill.

Love, Inspector. Always love. Love of God, love of money, love of power, love of a woman. Of a man too but we're women, we both know history is written by men so invariably it's love of a woman. There's hate of course but hate is just the flip-side of love. Hate is what happens when love turns rotten. Hate comes with betrayal.

I can't say I knew him well but I know the signs. And I know Maggie. She's one of my best friends, in or outside of school. And because she's one of my best friends, I can say what I'm going to say without malice. That's what friends are for, don't you think? To praise you when you deserve it but to be honest about it when you don't. To support you, to be faithful to you but not to lie, not to tell you that you're right when you know that actually you're wrong.

Maggie was wrong. What she did, what she's done: it's wrong. She should have told him. She shouldn't have done it in the first place if you want my opinion but when she did she should have told him. She shouldn't have left him to find out for himself. She shouldn't have left him to find out how he did, when he did, in the way he did. But I suppose that was part of the plan. I'm not saying there was a plan, not a plan as such, because as much as she was fooling Samuel she was fooling herself. But underneath it all, there was a plan. Deep down, she knew what she wanted. Do you see?

You don't. You're lost. I've lost you. Where did I lose you? No, no, no. Since then. Since they broke up.

You mean you don't know? You didn't hear? She didn't tell you, did she? I can't believe she didn't tell you. Although I can of course. Of course I can.

I won't start at the beginning because clearly you know the beginning. I'll start at the end.

They broke up. Samuel and Maggie. You know this. She told you this. It was a long time coming, them breaking up. She probably told you that as well. Samuel had problems, you see. Clearly he had problems but well before all of this happened it was obvious that he wasn't coping. Which, by the way, is why Maggie found herself attracted to him. She's a motherly one, Maggie. I don't know if she's ever been with a man she couldn't mother. They're kids usually. Not literally of course, I don't mean literally, but mentally, they're children. They need protecting. They need looking after. Which shows you how caring Maggie is as a person. Which explains why she's always so generous as a friend. It's a strength of hers definitely but also a frailty.

So Samuel, he didn't settle, he didn't mix and he didn't have any control over his students. I don't know much about his private life but I think that's partly because there was never very much to know. Maggie, it seemed to me, was his private life. She became his private life. Before she asked him out, Maggie was terrified that he would say no. I told her, no way. Don't be ridiculous. I said, he's besotted with you, you can tell. He used to watch her. I used to watch him watching her. Me, I would have found it creepy. Or maybe I wouldn't have. Maybe I'm just saying that because of what he's done. Either way, there was no possibility that he would have turned her down. The only reason he might have done would have been because he was shy, scared, afraid of being with a woman. And at one point it occurred to me that maybe he would say no, precisely for that reason, but it was too late to say anything to Maggie by then and anyway he didn't.

You know all this. She asked him out and he said yes. They went together for a while, a few months, but Samuel had his problems and Maggie couldn't help, that's the gist of it. She tried and all the while she was trying she became more ... more ... what word should I use? I'm not sure she was in love with him. I hope for her sake that she wasn't. But she was fond of him. More than that, she was attached to him. Attached like ... I don't know, like an owner gets to their dog. No, that's awful. What an awful analogy. Like a nurse, say. Like a nurse to a patient, like in *The English Patient*, you know, the film. All I'm trying to say is that even after they split up, Maggie was still involved. Emotionally. She had the sense to break it off with him because it was going nowhere, it was driving her insane, and as I said to her, she was wasting her life. So she broke up with him but not in the sense that really mattered.

This was oh gosh. February. March maybe. The end of February. But that, really, was just the beginning. It was the beginning of a whole other phase.

They broke up and Samuel said nothing. That's what Maggie told me. Literally, he said nothing. Okay so maybe it wasn't a shock but you still might expect a few words. If not of regret then of anger or desperation or misery perhaps, of despair. But Samuel curled up. You know, like spiders do, the way they wrap their legs around themselves whenever they feel threatened. Like that.

And Maggie, she's convinced it's because he didn't care, that he never cared, when of course it's exactly the opposite. Samuel just went on being Samuel, cold, withdrawn, solitary, but his behaviour was so exactly like it had been before that it was obviously just an act. It was obvious to me anyway. Maggie, though, she couldn't see it. And it hurt her. You know how humans are seventy per cent water? Seventy per cent, sixty per cent. Something like that. Maggie is seventy per cent emotion. She cares easily – she can't watch the news, she tells me, because it's worse for her than watching *Casablanca* – and she hurts just as readily too. So Samuel, after they split up, he's treating Maggie like she's just another colleague, like she's me or Matilda or Veronica, which means he's basically in denial about her existence. And Maggie can't stand it, I mean she hides it in front of him, she hides it very well considering, but she's questioning herself, she's questioning her self-worth, she's questioning how she looks, the sound of her voice, the size of her hips, she became obsessed with the size of her hips. We have our little chats, you see. During lunch usually, if neither one of us is on duty. And for several weeks that's all we spoke about: her; Samuel; Samuel and her. I didn't mind. I suppose maybe it was a bit much sometimes. Once or twice I swapped days with George or Vicky just to give myself a break but on the whole I didn't mind.

At first she blamed herself, like I say, then after a while she started to blame Samuel, which was progress, I thought, and closer to the truth of it, more to the point. He's Asperger's, she said. He must be. He can't engage. He won't commit to anything more emotionally demanding than a book. And I don't suppose she'll mind me telling you this but their sex life: it was stillborn. They did it once, she said, and she cried the whole of the next day. She didn't come in to work. She stayed at home and stripped the bed and sat in the bath and ate Quality Street and in the evening she made herself throw up. I don't know what Samuel did. Probably he just went on being Samuel. Probably he assumed it had gone okay. He was a man after all.

So anyway, that's why she did it. She wanted Samuel to show some passion, to show that he had feelings for her. Deep down, that's what she wanted. She told me she was over him. She told me and I suppose I believed her. She had stopped talking about him. Or if she talked about him she also laughed about him. Our little chats went back to how they used to be. I stopped switching rotas. If I switched at all, it was to bring mine into line with Maggie's. I genuinely thought she was over him. Clearly, though, she wasn't. Clearly she wasn't because how else could you possibly explain her decision to go to bed with TJ?

Here's how Samuel found out. This was May probably,

late April, the end of April. Maggie had been going with TJ for about a week or so. Don't ask me how it started. Basically Maggie was lonely and TJ was sweaty and they happened to run into each other when they were both in the mood for sex. End of story. Although it wasn't. It should have been. It should have been just that one time. Guess where they did it by the way. I shouldn't tell you this but guess.

Yes but not just in the school. I'll tell you where they did it. They did it in the boys' changing rooms. Can you believe it? I mean, it's disgusting really. It smells of adolescents in there, of mud and festering towels. But I shouldn't have told you that. Promise me you'll delete that bit. I should have made you stop the tape, shouldn't I?

What was I saying? Oh, I remember. Maggie and TJ. You remember what I was saying about Maggie, about Maggie and men who need mothering, who behave like children. Well, TJ is a case in point. And also there was this thing underneath, this urge to make Samuel jealous. So it should have ended when it started but it didn't. If she had told me right away I would have said something. I would have asked her what on earth she was thinking. TJ is basically a body and a pair of shorts. There's nothing going on upstairs. So one time you could maybe understand. You know, if you were really in the mood and there were no strings attached and you could be sure that no one else would ever find out. But he's not a keeper. Not for someone like Maggie. Except she did keep him and she's still with him, although now it's because she realises what she's done and she can't bring herself to admit it, not even to herself, especially not to herself. She'll be with him for another month, no more than that. Just long enough to hide from herself any association with what's happened.

Samuel found out the same time I did. As we all did. It must have been killing TJ, not telling Samuel. That's the other thing, you see. You have to wonder about TJ's motives too. I mean, Maggie is one of my best friends and she's a wonderful person but she's no Audrey Hepburn. If she could lose some of that weight she's carrying on her hips, maybe shift a bit of that to up top. But I can hardly talk. I'd move it the other way if I could. So you have to wonder, that's all I'm saying. Maggie has asked him to keep quiet, begged him probably, pleaded with him, and for a week or so he's managed. For TJ, that's quite some achievement. Particularly when you consider their history, his and Samuel's. But it's like dieting, isn't it? You starve yourself for as long as you can manage but then someone brings in a tray of Krispy Kremes and there's chocolate glaze and caramel glaze and hundreds and thousands and it's still an hour to go until lunchtime and you've got a fresh cup of coffee and everyone else is having one so you're going to indulge yourself, aren't you?

He slapped her bottom.

In the staffroom, in front of everyone who was in there, which is me, Vicky, George, Janet I think, Matilda was there and Samuel of course. There may have been a few others. And everyone's sitting around the table and we're all talking, just chatting, I can't really remember what we were talking about. Samuel's not chatting but he's following the conversation so when Maggie gets up and says, does anyone want a drink, and TJ reaches over and whacks her on the rump, Samuel sees it just like the rest of us.

The sound of it. That's what reverberates in my mind. He gave her a good old whack did TJ and the sound was like he'd slapped her naked skin. So I remember the sound and I remember Maggie's face. It was like she'd walked into a classroom and suddenly realised she was naked. Which we've all dreamt about, by the way. All of us teachers. We did a poll once and every single one of us said we'd had exactly the same dream. Except Samuel and the headmaster, who didn't take part, and George, who probably had dreamt it but didn't want to admit it, and Janet, although Janet once dreamt that she was naked in front of the headmaster, which for her amounts to the same thing.

TJ's face too. I remember TJ's face. He looked like a kid who'd farted in assembly. Which also happens sometimes and some of them, they know it's foul, but also they think it's hilarious. And just like one of the kids would, TJ brings his fingertips to his lips. You can see he's smiling though. It's obvious to everyone that he's smiling. And he looks at Maggie and Maggie glares at him and both of them turn to look at Samuel.

Samuel's face. I mean at first I'm staring at Maggie and probably I look as shocked as she does but then I realise what's going on, what's been going on, so like them I look at Samuel. And for once Samuel doesn't look away. Normally, if you so much as caught his eye, that's what he would have done. Instead, though, he's sort of frozen, you know like computers sometimes get when you click on too many things at once, when you give them too much to think about, well he's the human equivalent of that. His eyes sort of flick, left right, left right, left right, like he's looking at Maggie, then at TJ, then at Maggie, then at TJ, then at Maggie.

Maggie leaves. She's out of the door. TJ gets up. He makes to follow her but he can't resist another look at Samuel before he goes. I don't watch a lot of western films, they're not really my thing, but my husband does and I've seen those shots they always have, you know those close-ups. Samuel and TJ, their eyes drawn together, it reminded me a bit of that. Like at the end of the film, before the shoot-out, before the showdown, and the goodie's there and the baddie's there and the director, he takes you right in so you can see their eyes. It's cheesy, in the films, but that's what I was reminded of at the time.

After that, TJ gave Maggie a whack every time she and Samuel were both in the room. To the point where Maggie wouldn't get up before TJ did. Although even then TJ would feint or spin or lunge so that he always managed to get a hand to her. She'd shout at him, yell at him to knock it off but it was a game for TJ after that, you see, which means it was a competition, which means he always had to win. And he did win. If you watched Samuel's face when it happened you could see that every time was like another defeat. He didn't react, not outwardly, but that's exactly my point. TJ was taunting him and he thought Maggie was taunting him and he could only put up with it for so long. The Donovan thing, I'm not saying that wasn't part of it, I mean it was hard for Samuel, the entire situation, but the thing with the kids, that was just a fuse. He shot Donovan but only on his way to the stage. He was trying to shoot TJ. TJ or Maggie. Either way, you see my point. Samuel was in love and Samuel was betrayed and Samuel couldn't stand it any more. It's the oldest story in the book.

'I've had enough.'

'Lucia.'

'I've made up my mind.'

'Lucia.'

'I mean it, Philip. I never should have joined in the first place.'

'Then we never would have met. Which means you and Nabokov never would have met. Which means you would still be reading crime novels. Police procedurals. Whodunnits.'

'I still read crime novels.'

'No you don't.'

'I do. I read Ian Rankin and Patricia Cornwell and Colin Dexter and I've even read *The Da Vinci Code.*'

'Lucia!'

'And I enjoyed it too.'

Philip took hold of Lucia's elbow and guided her towards the kerb. 'At least keep your voice down when you talk like that.' He nodded towards the building they were passing. 'I'm known by people in there.'

Lucia read the sign. 'You're known in Sotheby's?'

'Well, no. I'm a barrister not an oil baron. But the security guards have seen me lurking and I would rather their suspicions about me were not confirmed.' He gestured with his chin. 'Down here.'

They turned on to Bond Street and almost immediately Philip jerked to a halt. Lucia had taken two steps on. She stopped when she realised her companion was no longer at her side.

'What's wrong? What are you looking at?'

'That suit.'

'Oh.' Lucia moved closer. 'It's nice.'

'Not that one. The blue one, there.'

'That one's nice too.'

'It's not nice, Lucia. Look at the cut. Look at the cloth. Look at the stitching on the cuff.'

'Why? What's wrong with it?'

'Nothing's wrong with it. It's exquisite. To describe such a thing as nice is like describing the Millennium Star as shiny.'

'It's a suit, Philip. You wear it to work.'

Philip shook his head and turned away from the shop window. 'This is what happens,' he said. 'This is what happens when you forsake literature and take Don Brown to your bedside. Your vocabulary shrinks and your taste buds wither.'

'Dan. It's Dan not Don.'

Philip wafted his hand in the air, as though just the name carried with it a stench. 'Is there something you're not telling me, Lucia?'

'No. What? What do you mean?'

'What's happened? Why are you suddenly talking about resigning?'

Lucia stopped to allow a Japanese man dressed in Burberry to take a photo of his wife at the entrance to the Burberry store. Philip strode through the shot and gestured for Lucia to catch up.

'You know what's happened,' Lucia said. 'What's happened has happened. It's enough.'

'You don't agree with your boss. If that were enough, Lucia, half the workforce would be handing in their notice. It's left here. Not far now.'

'Don't you have people to do this sort of thing for you?'

'Alas,' said Philip. 'None of my people has the same inside leg as I do. A visit to the tailor is something I must endure myself. Although the inside-leg bit I must admit I enjoy.'

Lucia tutted, rolled her eyes, forced a smile. They walked on in silence until Philip once again came to a halt.

'What now?' said Lucia. She turned to the shop they had been passing. In the window were lingerie and ladies' nightwear and several unidentifiables that were predominantly fluffy and pink. 'Or perhaps I don't want to know.'

'Let's find somewhere to sit,' Philip said.

'Sit? What about your suit? Didn't you say you had a meeting to get back to?'

'The suit can wait. The meeting can wait. This way.' He took Lucia's hand and guided her back the way they had come. They crossed Bond Street and passed along a side road lined with art galleries and car showrooms until they came to Berkeley Square. They found a crossing and then a gate into the island park. The grass was yellowed and brittle and strewn with office workers, Starbucks cups and Pret A Manger carrier bags. Most of the benches were similarly occupied but Philip guided Lucia to a seat tucked in a corner and only half decorated by the birds from the trees above.

'Sit,' Philip said.

Lucia sat.

'Talk,' Philip said.

Lucia was silent.

Philip glanced warily at the bird muck. He brushed a palm over the cleanest section of the seat and then checked his hand. He lowered himself close to Lucia. 'Talk,' he said again.

Lucia could feel Philip's leg against her own. His bony shoulder pressed against hers. She shuffled to her right until the arm of the bench poked against her ribs but with a glance at the mess on the bench beside him Philip followed. Lucia thought of Walter and tensed so she would not shudder. She turned her face away and found herself watching a man in a bedraggled black suit sharing crusts of bread with an equally unkempt pigeon. He threw one then ate one, then ate another and threw another.

'It's not me, Philip. I thought it was but it isn't.'

'What isn't you? Which bit?'

'All of it. The people. The work. The choices.'

Philip laughed a weary laugh. 'That's life, Lucia. That's how it is everywhere, with everything. It's not just the police force.'

Lucia shook her head. She sighed and looked up and found herself suddenly irritated by the clouds above. It was hot still, stifling, and the storm that threatened was like a sneeze that would not come. It was all suspense, Lucia thought. All suspense and no release.

'No,' she said. 'It's more than that. I was wrong. About Samuel. About the school, about the headmaster. I think I was wrong.'

'You weren't wrong.'

'I think perhaps I was.'

'You weren't,' Philip said, a conviction in his voice that Lucia craved but no longer felt.

'How would you know, Philip?' Lucia stood. She paced. 'All you know is what I told you.'

Philip nodded. 'That's right.'

'So did it occur to you that I might have left something out? That I might only have told you the evidence that supported the case I was trying to make?'

'Must I keep reminding you, Lucia? I'm a barrister. Of course it occurred to me.'

'Well then. Exactly. So I was wrong. You don't know that I wasn't wrong.'

Philip got up. He flicked a hand across his trouser leg, picked at a speck that was not there. 'You did what we all have to do, Lucia. In any walk of life. Faced with a dilemma, we have to consider the evidence and make a judgement. I know you weren't wrong because I trust your judgement. Perhaps not in novels but in general I trust your judgement.'

With a gesture, Lucia batted away Philip's attempt at humour. 'You shouldn't,' she said. She continued pacing.

'Lucia. I know you. You're only questioning yourself now because it's easier to believe you were wrong than to ignore the fact that you were right.'

'You don't know me, Philip. You're David's friend really, not mine. I've seen you what. Twice in six months.'

'That's twice more than I've seen David. And he was a colleague. He became a friend by default. He became a friend because we became friends.'

Again Lucia shook her head. 'You don't know what I'm thinking. You wouldn't want to know what I've been thinking, why I've been doing what I've been doing.'

'Tell me,' Philip said. 'Tell me why you think you've been doing what you've been doing.'

Lucia stopped. She bit down hard and returned Philip's gaze.

'Tell me,' Philip said again.

'Fine,' said Lucia. 'I will, if you want to know. It's because I feel sorry for him. I feel sorry for the man who murdered three children. I can put myself in his situation and I can imagine doing what he did.'

Philip did not hesitate. 'Nonsense,' he said.

'I told you.' Lucia resumed pacing.

'You feel sorry for him. I can't say I agree but I can empathise. That's all though. That's where it ends. You could never do what he did. None of us could. Maybe one person in a hundred million could do what he did.' Philip took Lucia's shoulder and brought her to a halt. 'Lucia. Listen to me. It's not pity that's guiding your judgement on this. If I know you at all, you came to a decision in spite of how you felt, not because of it. You were right and your boss was wrong. Morally. You were right.'

'He was jilted, Philip. The woman he loved dumped him and started sleeping with the bloke he despised more than anyone. There's your motive. I didn't mention that before, did I?'

'A contributing factor,' Philip said. 'Nothing more. This man, why did Szajkowski despise him? Because he tormented him, am I right? And his affair with this woman. Who's to say it wasn't conceived as part of the same torment?'

Lucia began to move again, three strides one way, three strides back. 'Szajkowski's sister,' she said. 'She told me about Samuel, about how cruel he could be. She told me he was a bully himself.'

'Sibling rivalry,' Philip countered. 'Prejudicial and unsubstantiated and therefore inadmissible. Irrelevant too, probably, because all brothers fight with their sisters. Please, Lucia. Will you please stand still for just a moment?'

Lucia stopped. She allowed Philip to reach for her hands. 'Sarah Kingsley,' she said. 'The girl who died. I spoke to her father. He said something about lashing out. About twisting pain into anger. That's me, Philip. That's how I feel.'

'He was bullied, Lucia. He was being bullied and the school knew about it and the school refused to act. It was negligent. As an employer, as an organisation responsible for the well-being of its staff, the school was negligent. Those are the facts.'

'Didn't you say, Philip? Didn't you tell me that I was wrong? Didn't you tell me to drop the case?'

'I told you to drop the case. I never said that you were wrong.'

'You should be gloating then. You should be telling me you told me so. You should be delighting in the fact that you were right.'

'That's hurtful, Lucia. That's a hurtful thing to say. Besides, I wasn't right. I was telling you to ignore your conscience. Since when could that be considered right?'

Lucia bit her lip, twisted her head away. She felt a tear at the corner of her eye. Before she could free a hand to catch it, the tear was loose and running towards her mouth. She rolled a shoulder across her cheek and then slid past Philip and out of his grip and sat down again on the bench.

'What do I do?' she said. She spoke to her feet. 'What should I do?'

'If you mean should you quit, the answer is no. Not now. Not while you're feeling like this.' Philip rested a hand on the arm of the bench. 'If you mean what should you do about Szajkowski . . . Well.' He exhaled through his nostrils. 'I don't know, Lucia. The honest answer is, I don't know.'

Lucia felt an urge to laugh. She gave in to it but the laugh came out as a sob. She pressed the heels of her hands to her eyes as though to force her tears back inside.

Philip cleared his throat. 'Lucia. Maybe this isn't the best time. It's just, I have a small confession to make.'

'A what?'

'Don't get angry.'

'What? Why?'

'Just don't get angry when I tell you this.'

'What did you do, Philip?'

'I . . . ' Philip coughed again. 'I spoke to David.'

Lucia pulled herself upright. 'You did what?'

'I didn't mention your name.'

'I should hope not!'

'But he guessed anyway.'

'Oh, Philip!'

Philip showed Lucia his palms. 'It's not my field, Lucia. I deal with chief executives. I deal with CFOs, with accountants. What do I know about criminal law?'

'It's not exactly David's field either.'

'It is. Just about. He came to us from the CPS. He deals with civil litigation at the firm he works for now.'

'That's not the point, Philip.' Lucia was shaking her head. She could feel her tears evaporating as her cheeks burnt. 'You know that's not the point.'

'Lucia, please. I thought it would help. I thought David might be able to help. You came to me for legal advice but you may as well have asked your conveyancer.'

Lucia glared at Philip, then turned her face away. After a moment, she allowed her eyes once again to meet his. 'What did he say?'

Philip shrugged a guilty shrug. He winced. 'He said what I said.'

'He said what you said.'

'That's why I almost didn't mention it. He said there was no precedent. He said the only thing that came close was a case a few years back of a pupil suing a school. He said that even if you could find a prosecutor ambitious enough to take it on, it would never come to trial. He reminded me that it was an election year.'

'You sound like Cole. My boss. You could be Cole talking.'

'I don't agree with it, Lucia. I'm just telling you how it is.'

Lucia stood. She wiped her eyes again and adjusted her

blouse. She stepped past Philip and cast around to get her bearings. 'Which way's the tube?'

'Take a cab. I'll expense it.'

Lucia shook her head. 'I'd rather take the tube. I'm sorry, Philip. You're busy and I'm wasting your time. All I'm doing is wasting time.'

'Don't say that. Please don't say that. I just wish there were something more I could do.'

'You've done enough.' Lucia brushed her lips against his cheek. 'Thank you. You've done all you can do.' She made to go.

'Lucia. Wait. There's one more thing. It's not important but I said I'd mention it.'

Lucia waited. She knew what was coming and she knew she should be angry but she was not. 'I'm not going to talk to him, Philip.'

'Just a phone call. You don't have to go and—'

'I'm not going to talk to him, Philip.' She turned and she started walking. She did not know whether Philip could hear her but she said it again anyway. 'I'm not.'

What's your earliest memory?

I'm not sure either. I'm on a boat, I think, and I'm wearing this jumper that I liked. It had a flower on it.

Do you wanna know my earliest memory of Sam?

He's pinching me. I was four, I think, maybe five so he would of been seven, I guess, maybe eight. I'm on my back and he's got his knees on me and I've got one arm free and I'm hitting him but he's ignoring it or not feeling it cos he's focused on my other arm and he's pinching me here, here, here, all the way up and he's pinching me and he's smiling. I remember it clearly. It's like it was on the TV just the other night.

He hated me. I hated him but he hated me first. He resented me. That's what Annie says. She says he didn't hate me he resented me but I looked up the word resent and it basically means that he hated me. I knew what resent meant already by the way. I'm not stupid, I just like to check. I have a dictionary, Annie got it for me, and I like to check what words mean cos sometimes they mean something different from what you think they mean, not a lot always but enough to change what you're saying when you don't want it to. Do you know what I mean?

I'm glad cos not everyone does. Some people use words without even caring what they really mean. They just say em and think about what they're saying after they've finished saying it.

My dad was good at words. He's dead now. He drowned. I was ten. But he used to have these books, they were full of puzzles: crosswords and wordsearches and what are those ones where the letters are all mixed up and you have to put em back in the right order? Like on *Countdown*, at the end, the ones I can never get.

Right. Anagrams. So my dad would sit there every night with one of them books and sometimes he'd let me sit with him, if I was quiet and I didn't wriggle, and I'd help him or I'd try to. I could do the wordsearches, I was good at em, but I don't like crosswords, I never liked crosswords. Sam could do crosswords. Sometimes if Dad got stuck he would ask Sam and Sam would say it's this or it's that or sometimes he would just shrug but most of the time he would know. Sam went to university in the end. Dad said he would and he did. He shouldn't of though, that's what Annie says. He should of stayed with me, that's what Annie says. Annie says that if Sam had stayed it would of been better for everyone: me, she says, Sam, she says, her, she says, them kids. But I'd rather have Annie than him. I'd of run away if they'd of made me live with him.

Annie? Annie's like my mum. She's not my mum but she looks out for me. Ever since they moved me here, Annie stops by and checks up on me. They give her the bus fare, that's what Annie says. For stopping by. Sometimes she comes to the supermarket too. That's where I work. If Annie comes I get an extra break but she doesn't come all that often.

Do you wanna know how my real mum died?

It's okay, I don't mind saying. My brother killed her. Not Sam. My other brother. But he's dead too, he died at the same time. He didn't mean to kill her but he did. He killed her with complications. I was eight.

Do you wanna know what Sam did when she died? He burnt her clothes. Her dresses and her trousers and her jumpers and her skirts. He took em out of her wardrobe and he made a big pile in the garden and he burnt em. My dad and me, we found him. My dad did really but when he started shouting I found the both of em too. When I found em, though, my dad had stopped shouting and he was hugging Sam instead. Sam was crying. I could see he was crying but he was hitting too. He was hitting my dad, on his back and on his arms, but my dad was just hugging him. I watched. The fire went out after a while and Sam stopped hitting but he didn't stop crying. Him and my dad, they just stood there. There was smoke. There was lots of smoke.

After Dad died, we got taken away. They took us from our house and I thought we were coming back but when we left that was it. I had this necklace, it was my mum's, I left it there and they said they'd fetch it but they never did. I cried about that necklace. I cried about that necklace almost as much as I cried about my mum, which is a silly thing to do, I think, that's what Annie would say if I ever told her. Now when I cry I cry about Mum or about Dad, not about the necklace. I don't

back but two years later he was leaving again, this time to university. I didn't care. I did better without him there.

When I turned eighteen they moved me to another place. It was like all the other places really cept they gave me my own room. There was a lock on the door and I had the key. At first I didn't like it there, I couldn't sleep being on my own. But I got used to it. I stayed there a while and then they moved me here cos it's closer to the Tesco where I work. Now I only have to get one bus and in the mornings I can usually get a seat. And I have Annie.

I don't know. I suppose about six weeks ago. He visited, just as though visiting's what he always did. He's at the door and he says, hello Nancy, and I say, it's you. I say, what do you want? He says, nothing, I don't want anything, I just wanted to say hello, and he's smiling and I've never liked his smile. I let him in though. He follows me in here and he sits where you're sat. We're quiet for a while and then he says, do you have any tea, and I say, no. He says, oh. He says, never mind, I'm not actually thirsty. He says, how have you been? I shrug. He says, this is a nice place. I shrug. I nod. He says, do you have any help? I shrug. I say, I have Annie. He says, Annie is it, that's good, is she nice? I shrug. I nod.

What do you want? I say.

I told you, he says. I just wanted to say hello.

Why? I say.

Why? Why do you think? Because you're my sister.

No I ain't, I say. And I'm thinking of Annie and how she's like my mum even though she's a different colour from me and how Sam and me are the same colour and the same blood and the same second name but the truth of it is we're barely brother and sister at all.

Of course you are, says Sam. What do you mean?

You left, I tell him. You left and you didn't call and you acted like I didn't exist.

You could have called. They would have told you where I was.

You left, I say. You're the one who left.

And he just shakes his head. He sits there and he shakes his head. Then he says, you're okay though. Right? You're okay. And I nod and he says, good. Good.

After that he's quiet for a bit. I'm quiet too. I'm just watching him. He's looking at his hands. He says, Nancy, and I say, what? He looks at me. I wanted to say something, he says.

I wait.

I wanted to say something, he says again, about before. About when we were younger.

I wait some more.

About the way I acted sometimes. About how you and me, the way we used to fight . . .

What? I say and he looks at me. He looks at me and then he's looking back down at his hands.

What? I say again cos I'm getting annoyed. He used to do this. He always used to do this. Start saying something and get you interested and then stop before he's said what he was gonna.

Never mind, he says. It doesn't matter. Maybe it doesn't actually matter. Not any more.

And I'm thinking, fine. Whatever. Cos I've fallen for it before and gotten all irritated with him but not this time. That's what I tell myself.

I don't know. It can't of been important though, can it, or otherwise he would have said it. But he didn't. Whatever it was he didn't say it and he didn't really say much else.

He left soon after. I did have tea and I could of made him some but he wouldn't of stayed long enough to finish it even if I had of done.

Oh my gosh. Do you want some tea? I should of offered you, shouldn't I? You'd of finished it by now if I had offered you right away so we could pretend I was offering you another cup. Do you want another cup of tea?

Are you sure? It's no bother. I don't need no help or nothing.

Next time then. I'll make you tea next time. Cross my heart.

So Sam gets up and I get up. He says, maybe I should go, I think it's best that I go. I don't argue. I watch him. I stand apart from him. He walks over to the door and I watch him some more and I follow him. He says, well, goodbye then. He has his hand on the latch. I cross my arms. He says bye again and he opens the door and he leaves. I shut the door behind him and that's the last time I see him till I see his picture on TV.

Lucia parked in a different space. She did not have to; her usual spot was empty. But she parked nearer the entrance, in the only section of the car park that was not covered by the building. She parked and she got out and she made it as far as the stairwell before she turned around and unlocked the car and restarted the engine. She reversed and straightened up and then pressed the accelerator too hard so that as she shot forwards the tyres slipped on the tarmac and yelped. There was no one around but Lucia flushed, feeling foolish, and eased off so much that the car almost stalled. She passed the line of police units and then swung the Volkswagen out wide. With her left arm wrapped around the passenger seat, she backed into the space the entire station thought of as hers.

Fuck it, she told herself. Fuck him.

The stairwell was dark and Lucia hesitated. But only for a moment. She climbed the stairs and she climbed slowly, daring her fears to manifest themselves and God help them if they did. In the lobby she swiped in and nodded at the blokes on the desk. They nodded back. Ahead of her were the double doors that opened into the part of the station that only police-men and prisoners and kids on school visits ever saw. She tapped a code into the keypad below the handle and pulled when the buzzer buzzed. She passed through. There was only one lift in the station. Today it was working and it was wait-ing for Lucia so she took it.

She was the first of the day shift to arrive. She had planned it that way without admitting to herself that she had. But as she passed Walter's desk, she saw there was a mug next to the keyboard, a coat on the back of the chair. She paused, glanced around, until she realised the mug was one the cleaner had missed, the coat part of the department's soft furnishings. She walked on, wary in spite of herself. She poured herself coffee from the pot left over by the night shift. At her desk she clutched her mug in both palms. She sipped. The coffee was burnt but she was not drinking it for the taste. She took another sip and waited for the day to descend.

Cole arrived next, then Charlie, then Rob. Cole said a gruff good morning; Charlie and Rob just nodded at Lucia when they noticed her. At one minute to nine Walter arrived read-ing the back page of the *Mirror*. He held up a palm without looking at anyone, set the polystyrene cup he had been hold-ing on his desk, tucked his newspaper under his arm and disappeared into the men's room. Harry was late. He said, sorry I'm late, and was still panting and wiping at his forehead several minutes after he had taken his seat. When he saw Lucia he said, hey Lucia, and she said, hey Harry, how's it going? Harry said, what happened to you yesterday, and Lucia said, stomach bug. Then the phones began to ring and the board began to fill up and, for all the possibilities that Lucia had imagined for it, the day looked like turning into any other.

Until the call came in.

Lucia answered so it was Lucia's case. That was how it worked. Unless there was some obvious reason to defer to Cole, that was how it had always worked.

'Charlie can take it. I'm giving it to Charlie.'

'Charlie's busy. Charlie's got two missing kids.'

Cole looked at Charlie. Charlie shrugged.

'What about you, Walter? You look like you've got a few calories you could do with expending.'

'Love to, Guv, mainly because Lulu here seems to want it so bad. But I've got court again, remember? This fucking thing's gonna drag on all week.'

Cole exhaled. He looked around him. 'Where the fuck is Harry? And Rob. Where the fuck is Rob?'

'I saw them twenty minutes ago,' Walter said, grinning now. 'They were holding hands and heading for trap three in the men's room. Harry had a hard-on.'

Charlie laughed. Cole swore. He flicked a hand towards Walter. 'Get your goddamn feet off that desk.'

Lucia was moving and Cole spotted her. 'You. Where are you going?'

Lucia picked up her phone, her keys, her notepad. She reached for her mouse and shut down her email. 'There's no one else, Guv. Who else is there?'

Cole held up a finger. 'I'm warning you, Lucia.'

'What?'

'You know what. Don't pretend you don't know what.'

'What?' Lucia said again. 'It could be anyone. How do you know it's not just anyone?'

'What's the address?'

Lucia flicked through her notepad.

'What's the address, Lucia?'

Lucia shut the pad. 'Sycamore Drive. It's Sycamore Drive.'

'That's right around the corner from the school. It's not just anyone. I mean it Lucia, I don't want you—'

'Gotta go, Guv. Taxi's waiting.'

She rode to Sycamore Drive in the back of a squad car. There was no air conditioning in the rear and the windows did not open either, which meant there was no respite from the heat or from the stench of simulated pine. Lucia allowed her lips to part and did her best to breathe in through her mouth. One of the two uniforms up front, the passenger, was talking to her across his shoulder. His voice was overwhelmed by the siren so Lucia just nodded occasionally, raised and dropped her eyebrows. She stared at the city passing by, at the abundance of people on the streets even after nine o'clock on a work day, all rushing it seemed, drained of patience by the heat and the crowds and the sheer effort involved in completing a simple task, a trip, a transaction.

A dead body. A surname. That was all but it was enough.

They drove past the school. There were children in the playground, shouting, screeching, standing in groups around mobile phones, sitting on steps and sharing headphones, others playing video games by the look of them, with friends craning over their shoulders for a glimpse of animated pixels. One group, at one end of the yard, was kicking a ball. They still do that then, Lucia thought and immediately recoiled from her sourness. She was thirty-two. Just thirty-two and yet she felt obsolete, alienated from the generation to which, until recently, she had assumed she still belonged. She had an iPod but she could not use it. She was aware of Facebook but she had heard about it first on Radio 4. Children, when she came into contact with them, referred to her as a woman, as in, why's that woman dressed like a policeman, Mummy? Parents, what was worse, called her a lady: mind the lady, darling, be careful. She had laughed, the first time. The second time she had panicked. When had that happened? When had the world decided – decided and not informed her – that the girl she thought she was had been displaced, disabused, disinvented? When had her peers handed the future to these children who could so readily shrug off violence, who were so inured to hate and brutality that they could laugh and joke and play on ground still stained by blood? And all while a boy of their age, whom they knew and had sat with and had spoken to and had laughed with, some of them, suffered and wept and bled himself.

No. It was a common enough surname. It might not be him. She did not know for certain that it would be him. Not for certain.

They turned into a side street. The driver cancelled the siren but left the lights flashing. A car moved as though to pull out from the kerb in front of them and the policeman at the wheel of the squad car hammered the horn and swerved though he did not really need to. Lucia turned her head as they passed.

She saw a woman's face, her expression teetering between shock and fury. The policeman up front switched the siren back on.

They arrived. They were the first. The car stopped and the siren stopped but Lucia heard its echo. An ambulance, four blocks away perhaps. She got out. The uniforms followed, placing their caps on their heads and trailing Lucia up the path.

The front door was ajar. Lucia rang the bell, knocked, rang the bell again. Without waiting for a reply, she pushed the door wide.

'Mr Samson?'

Immediately she heard sobbing. A woman, upstairs.

'Mrs Samson?' Lucia spoke louder, almost shouting. She said her name. She said, 'It's the police, Mrs Samson. The ambulance is right behind us.' She led the way towards the staircase.

She did not recognise anything and though she could not have expected to, this gave her hope. In the hallway was a coat rack straining with coats and just about clinging to the wall. There were shoes, some placed neatly in a line along the skirting board, others discarded with their laces still tied. There was a child's bike, too small for him, she thought, almost certainly too small for him. They passed the living room and Lucia saw remnants on the coffee table of a breakfast interrupted: toast buttered but naked of jam, juice half drunk from glasses perspiring in the heat. The weather girl on the television grinned and caught Lucia's eye but Lucia's gaze did not settle. She looked for bookcases. In his house she expected bookcases. There were none in the living room and this was a relief, until she saw a set of shelves in the hallway beyond the stairs and another just inside the kitchen door.

She climbed the stairs quickly. Her feet scuffed against the wooden steps but the sound was soon masked by the stomping boots of the uniforms behind her, the crackle of their radios, their open-mouthed breathing at her ear. At the top Lucia hesitated and she sensed the men behind her collide. The sobbing had stopped. The door ahead of her was shut and there was no obvious movement further along the landing. She called aloud once more.

'Here. In here.'

A man's voice: quiet, defeated. It was a voice Lucia recognised. She hurried on, tensing her stomach to catch her falling heart.

She reached the doorway to the bedroom. The door was open, obscuring the main portion of the room. Ahead of her, slumped against a wardrobe, was Elliot's father. His head was bowed. His hands were crimson.

Lucia stepped inside. She watched Elliot's father as she moved. She knew she should turn her head, refocus her eyes but her body no longer felt under her control. Even her feet seemed to be carrying her against her will. She knew what was waiting inside and she did not want to see it. She wanted to back away, to turn, to leave the house. She wanted to rewind and tell Cole, give it to Charlie, give it to Walter even, because then at least she would not have to see it. But the uniforms crowded behind her and her feet kept moving and before she could resist she was in the room.

Elliot's mother was cradling her son's body. The blood was

everywhere: in black puddles on the sand-coloured carpet, in Elliot's hair, on his mother's face and up her arms, on the bed sheets that were still entangled around Elliot's legs, soaking through the strips of linen that were wrapped and knotted about Elliot's wrists. With the blood, the colour had left Elliot's skin. His eyes were closed and his head was tilted backwards and the fingers of his left hand were crumpled against the floor. Beneath the hair that covered her face, Elliot's mother was sobbing still but silently. Her shoulders trembled. Her hands shook. She clung to her son as though willing the warmth of her body to diffuse into his.

Lucia took another step and reached with a hand and all of a sudden she was on her knees, the carpet damp and cold through the fabric of her trousers. She reached again but her hand hovered in the air and fell away. She looked behind her, up at her colleagues. They were staring at the boy. It was all they could do. It was the most that any one of them could do.

Someone told you about that, did they?

Who?

Whoever. Doesn't matter to me.

What did they say?

Whatever. They can say what they like. And anyway I'm glad. I'm glad we did it. I'd do it again if I could. I'd do it even better. I wouldn't get in trouble for it neither. They'd be thanking me. They'd be cheering me. They'd be saying I did em all a favour.

Why do you wanna know?

Why, what does it matter?

Am I gonna get paid for this?

So why should I?

Fuck you. Arrest me for what?

Obstructing. What the fuck am I obstructing? You're the one obstructing me. And anyway, you can't arrest me. I'm too young. You can't do anything to me.

Do me a favour. They only send you to them places if you've killed someone, shagged some tart and she's called it rape. You might get em to give me an asbo but I've always sort of fancied one of them.

Fuck it though. I'll tell you. Doesn't matter now, does it? Like I say, you should be thanking me. The teachers, the parents, your lot: you should be thanking me.

We knew he was a freak from the start, me and Don. It was obvious. You just had to look at him. His beard. I mean, fuck. What was he thinking? Did he look in the mirror in the morning and think, yep, that's the look I'm going for: I want my face to look like an arse. The ladies'll just love it. And his clothes. I never knew it was possible to wear so much brown. His jacket was brown, his shirt was brown, his trousers were brown, his socks were brown. He had brown shoes and brown pants probably, ha, yeah, brown pants. But that's another story innit?

He was an immigrant. That's what he told us. He wasn't ashamed of it neither. He was boasting about it, making out he was better than the rest of us. Teachers aren't supposed to do that, are they? They're not supposed to insult you. Like when I told him my name. He asked me and I told him and he didn't believe me. Said I was a liar. Called me one to my face. Threatened to hit me. Teachers aren't supposed to do that either. Or maybe he said he'd touch me, which when you think about it is even worse. So he was threatening us and insulting us and acting like he was some kind of big shot even though he wasn't no older than a sixth-former.

Do you know what he did? This is funny. His first class, right, and guess what he does. He runs out blubbing. Can you believe it? Although you're a bird so you probably cry all the time. Like my sister, she's always fucking snivelling, saying Gi did this, Gi did that, blah blah blah, blah blah blah.

All right all right. Don't get your tits in a twist. I was coming to that, wasn't I?

The football match.

This is much later though. We did loads of good stuff to him before then. Like the turd, that was funny, and the Guy Fawkes we made of him and set alight on the hockey pitch. And this one time we bought these eggs, right, and pierced em so they'd go off. Then we—

All right, whatever. Your loss. You'll never know now, will you?

The football match. We have this match, right? Once a year. Just before Christmas usually but this time it was afterwards, cos of all the snow and that. It's teachers against the first team. It's Terence's thing, he organises it. Terence. Most people call him TJ. Or Twat Jam. We just call him Terence cos it's Terence he hates the most. So it's Terence's thing, he loves it. You should of seen him when Bickle made him put it on hold. It was like he'd been promised an Action Man for Christmas but got given Fag Hag Barbie instead.

Me and Don, we were in the team. The first team. Don was up front. He was captain. I play midfield. Terence is the coach. He calls himself the coach – no, that's not right, what he calls himself is the manager – but he does fuck-all coaching if you ask me, and fuck-all managing come to that. What he does is he makes the first team play the second team and he makes one player from the first team sit on the bench so that he can take his place. So Terence'll be in defence for five minutes while the defender's off the field, and then he'll swap with a midfielder while the midfielder takes a rest, and then he'll swap with a striker. Mainly he swaps with the strikers. He never goes in goal. There's never anything to do in goal cos the second team are shite. There's no point playing em really. We usually win like eleven-nil. Our record is twenty-four-nil. This was in a sixty-minute game. Ask Terence if you don't believe me. He's always going on about it cos he got a double hat-trick.

Anyway, teachers against the first team. Terence loves it but when it comes to getting a team together he always starts bitching, saying it's hardly fucking fair, what the fuck am I supposed to do with this rabble, I've barely got enough for eleven. Basically, the only teachers who are halfway decent are Grunt and Jesus Roth. And Bickle always refs so that's one less for Terence to choose from, not that Bickle'd be any good, I mean he'd probably have a colonary. So apart from Grunt and Roth there's Terence and Boardman, although Boardman's older than Bickle, and Daniels, he teaches physics right, which just about says it all, and there's . . . oh fuck , I dunno. The point is there's hardly anyone.

So Terence is getting desperate, right? I mean, he's already drafted in the caretaker and the guy who sorts out the DVDs. Mr Pressplay we call him. But he still needs a keeper, right, just someone to stand between the posts.

Wow. That must be why you're a detective. You're like frigging Columbo. Or that bird, ha, yeah, that old biddy who goes around solving murders. Only she was better looking.

Fuck knows how he managed to convince him. Maybe he didn't convince him. Maybe he, I dunno. Made him an offer he couldn't refuse. Whatever. I just remember we're all on the field and it's pissing down and it's fucking freezing and we're like, what the fuck are we doing out here? And Don, right, he goes, fuck this lads, I ain't losing a testicle just so Terence has something else to do but sit at home and play with his. And he starts walking off and the rest of us, we follow. There's a crowd along the touchline, all with umbrellas and that, and the rest of the school's inside, all toasty and smug, watching out through the classroom windows. And everyone starts pointing and someone starts booing and Bickle, he's doing lunges in the centre circle, he stops and he puts his hands on his hips and then he's digging in his pocket for his whistle. He blows. He shouts, he goes, you boys, where the blazes do you think you're going, and Don, he shouts back, he goes, the library, sir, and, just a little bit quieter, where do you fucking think? And we're all looking at Bickle, wondering what he's gonna do after that. But it turns out he doesn't need to do anything cos that's when Manchester United come running out on to the pitch.

They're wearing the strip. All of em. Not just the shirt, I don't mean just the shirt. They were wearing the full kit: black socks, white shorts, red top. And Terence, he's got on green boots. Green ones. Such a cock.

We stop. I mean, us lot, we've got the school kit on, which is blue and white stripes, like Wigan or, I dunno, like Brighton. Cept it's all faded and torn and it stinks of vegetables even when it's just been washed. We've been going on at Terence that we need a new kit and he's always like, you'll get a new kit when you deserve a new kit. And here's him poncing about in a kit so fresh off the boat from India or wherever it's made that you can practically smell the curry.

It would of been annoying if the lot of em didn't look so fucking ridiculous.

Check it out, goes Don and he's pointing at Terence and Roth. It's the Neville brothers! Which one are you, Terence?

And Terence, he checks Bickle isn't looking and he grins at Don and slips him the bird. Then he turns around and points with his thumb at his back. He's wearing number seven and he's got Beckham across his shoulders. Which is funny enough, right, but then Roth turns around and he's wearing a Beckham shirt too. And Boardman is. And Grunt is. And Mr Pressplay is. All of em are. And this is just too much.

They couldn't agree. I found this out later. Terence wanted to be Beckham but so did Boardman. Then Roth, he decides he wants to be Beckham too. And Terence goes, I'm captain so I have to be Beckham, it's obvious. And Boardman goes, maybe if Beckham were still playing for United but he isn't. If you're captain then you have to be Gary Neville. And Terence is like, fuck that, there's no way I'm being Gary Neville. So in the end they order ten identical shirts and all of em get to pretend they're shagging Posh.

But it gets better. Bumfluff, he can't be David Beckham, can he? Bumfluff is playing in goal, which means he gets a costume all of his own.

We hear the cheer before we see him. By this time we're all lined up again cos we're obviously gonna play em now, I mean they look ridiculous already but we also wanna make em look stupid, right? So we're ready and Terence's lot are ready and

Bickle's ready and the only thing missing is Peter Schmeichel. And Terence is looking around, he's like, where the fuck is he, and then we hear this clapping on the sidelines, just quiet at first, down at one end. But then some of the kids pull back and Bumfluff appears and by the time he steps on to the pitch even the teachers are applauding and hollering and whistling, you know like workmen whistle when they see a decent rack.

You know those big foam hands those dickhead Americans wear when they go and watch baseball? Imagine Bumfluff in two of them: at the end of his scrawny arms, his goalie gloves look like that. And his shorts, they're bright yellow and so baggy you could of got two of him standing in each leg. Although you can only really see the bottoms of em cos the rest is somewhere under his shirt, which is yellow too but sort of splattered with black. It's like he's wearing a bumblebee outfit his mum's made him but she's got the measurements all wrong. And maybe he's having trouble walking in it and that's why he's fifty yards behind the rest of em. Or maybe he just wanted to make an entrance. Maybe he wanted to make sure that everyone's eyes would be on him.

I grin at Don and Don grins at me. We don't say anything. We don't need to. But right then: that's when we decide.

Bickle blows and Terence kicks off. He knocks it to Roth and Roth knocks it back and Terence launches one straight at the goal. It's a crap shot. The ball doesn't even reach the keeper. So now we've got it and Scott, he plays in defence, he passes it to me and Terence is behind me but I do this little turn, like this, like imagine the ball's here, right, I do this, and Terence is left standing there and I knock the ball out wide. Micky plays on the right, he's well quick, he picks up the ball and he knocks it on and he's legging it down the wing and he's past Mr Pressplay and he whips in this cross and Don gets a head to it but he puts it inches wide. Bumfluff, he's just standing there. He has no idea what's going on. Terence is shouting at him, telling him to watch his back fucking post, and Bumfluff looks at the goalpost like he's only just noticed it's there. And while Terence and Boardman are arguing about who's gonna take the goal kick, Don goes over to Bumfluff. He says, nice outfit, Mr Shite*cough*ski sir. Did you choose the colour yourself? And Bumfluff sort of looks down at what he's wearing like, what, what's wrong with luminous yellow, and while he's doing that Don brushes past him and lands his studs on Bumfluff's toes.

He squealed. I mean, he actually squealed. We went on this school trip once, to this farm or something, and Scott, he brought his catapult and a bag of carpet tacks. It was well funny. The cows didn't hardly feel anything but the pigs . . . Honestly, it was fucking hilarious.

But you know what a squealing pig sounds like, don't you? You get to hear it all the time.

So Bumfluff squeals and he goes down but nobody's taking any notice cos the ball is back in play. Mr Pressplay's got it. He passes it inside and the caretaker gives it back and then Mr Pressplay knocks one across to Terence. Terence shoots again, from the edge of the area this time. All day long. That's what I say to him. Is that all you've got? And he's jogging towards me and I'm standing there and he dips his shoulder, like this, and it feels like I've run bicep first into a doorframe. And I'm like, fucking hell Terence you cocksucker. And Terence turns and he's like, watch your mouth, boy, I'm still your fucking teacher. And I wanna say something back but Bickle's watching us now so I just hold up my good arm for the ball.

It's out with Micky again. This time he loses it to Mr Pressplay and the ball goes loose and Terence is nearer but I'm quicker. I get it and Terence is behind me and he's expecting me to do the turn, right, the one I showed you before, but instead what I do is—

What? I'm telling you, aren't I?

No you didn't, you said you wanted me to tell you what happened at the match.

Well, you should of fucking said so.

You fucking didn't. Jesus Christ. You're worse than my fucking mum.

All right all right. It wasn't till the second half though. I mean, loads of stuff happened before then, like Don, he scored this blinding volley, right—

Can I at least tell you the score? Are you gonna get your period if I tell you the score?

Four-nil. We were four-nil up at half-time. The teachers, they're fucking shattered. Terence is on his feet but the rest of em haven't got the juice to suck on a piece of orange. Us lot, we're having a brilliant time. Mickey's doing keepy-ups and Don's lighting up a fag and the rest of us are just chatting and messing about. We could of been seven or eight up, easy. I mean, we've won. It's only half-time but basically we've won. So when Bickle blows his whistle and we jog back on to the pitch, that's when Don gives me the nod. The game's over, right? Time for a bit of fun.

Bumfluff is last on again. He's in a state. He hasn't touched the ball all match, cept for when he's been picking it out of the net and rolling it out to Terence, but he's fallen over a fair few times; fallen or been made to fall. So he's covered in mud and he's limping from where Don stamped on him and he's got a bruise across his ribs probably cos that's where I gave him a little dig when I was up on his line for a corner. Oh, I didn't say, did I, I can't believe I didn't say. Don pulled down his shorts. In front of everyone. We were all waiting for a free kick and Terence, he was shouting at Bumfluff, saying, watch it, Sam, don't fucking miss it, here it comes now, and Bumfluff almost looked like he was making an effort. He had his knees bent and he was holding his hands up in front of his chin and his tongue was sticking out between his teeth and just as the ball came over and Bumfluff was about to make this leap into the air, Don crouches down behind him and gives his shorts a tug.

The ball went in. Bumfluff fell over and the ball went in. If someone had been filming it we'd of been, thank you very much: five hundred quid from *You've Been Framed*.

Anyway, the point is that when it comes to the second half Bumfluff is looking a bit sorry for himself, like he'd rather take a kick in the nuts than come back out on to the field. But us lot, we're buzzing, and I know you don't want to hear it all but basically we kick off and pass it around and one thing leads to another and we end up getting a corner. Happy with that or was that too much detail?

So this is it. Micky's taking the corner and Don and me are standing on the edge of the box. Mr Pressplay's got a post and Grunt's come back to pick up Scott and Terence is covering the short one. The caretaker's taking care of me and Don but we make it easy for him cos we don't move. Yet. Bumfluff, he's just standing on his line. He's not even looking at the ball. What he's looking at is the two of us, like he knows what's about to happen. But he can't do anything about it, can he? There's nothing that he can do.

Micky knocks it in. It goes high. Mr Pressplay leaves his post. Scott draws Roth to one side. Don moves. I move. The caretaker doesn't know which way to move. The ball's falling now and Bumfluff's watching it but he's also watching us. He sees us coming. He sees us smiling. The ball finds someone's head but I don't know whose cos I wasn't looking. It bounces in front of us. It bounces in front of Bumfluff. It distracts him, just for a second. He flaps at it. He misses. Don slides and I slide. The ball goes in, I think, but we're still sliding, through the mud and the water and with our feet sticking out in front of us like we're Bruce Lee aiming a kick at some other chink's head. We would of slid for ever if there hadn't been something there to stop us.

Don got his knee. I got his ankle. Not quite simultaneous but near enough. The sound it made was like ice cubes. You know, like when you drop ice cubes in a warm glass of Coke.

I got up. Don got up. Bumfluff stayed down. He was squealing again. Actually, he was screaming. He was on his back and he was writhing. He had one hand on his leg and his other arm across his eyes. The crowd, they were cheering so I suppose the ball must of gone in. But it felt like they were cheering for us.

Grunt was closest. I don't know whether he saw it but he thought he did. He collars us. He's like, you boys, what the hell do you think you're doing? And we're like, what, what, let go you twat, let go. Bickle blows his whistle. He's still blowing it when he reaches us.

What's going on here? Mr Grant. Mr Grant!

And Grunt's shaking us and sort of growling and he's looking at Bumfluff on the floor but it's like he doesn't want to let us go.

I dunno, sir, goes Don. I dunno. And he's holding out his arms, you know, like players do on the telly when they're about to get carded by the ref.

They did it on purpose, goes Grunt. You little thugs. You did it on purpose.

And it's like Bickle notices Bumfluff for the first time, even though he's screaming still and crying probably and making more racket than the crowd.

Did you? he goes. Did you do it on purpose?

And I shake my head and Don's like, course not, sir, we were going for the ball. It was fifty-fifty.

And Bickle looks at Bumfluff and he looks at Grunt and he looks at Bumfluff again. Let them go, he says. Let them go, Mr Grant.

But Mr Travis—

I said let them go. And he sort of turns away but then stops and spins back. And see to Szajkowski, will you? He's making a fool of himself. He's making a mockery of this game.

And we jog away and we pass Terence and he's just fucking smiling. He knows what we've done and he's glad. As far as he's concerned, Bumfluff's lost him the match. Which is bullshit of course, they'd of lost with Gordon Banks in goal, but that's what Terence thinks. So he's smiling and he even gives Don this little wink.

It was that easy. I mean, I couldn't believe it. Don says later, he's like, no sweat, Gi, what could they of done? And he was right I spose but I was still expecting a fuss, like a warning or a detention or even a fucking suspension, I mean we snapped his fucking leg. But we didn't get so much as a yellow. Bumfluff got stretchered off, the caretaker went in goal, Don scored two more goals and in the end we won nine-nil.

So that's it. The end. Can I go now?

we R watchN U. evN f U cnt c us we cn c U

The blind was halfway closed and the overhead lights were off. She almost did not notice him shaking. She stood for a moment by the doorway and then made her way past him to the window.

'Do you mind?' she said. He raised his head and turned to look at her. She waited but he said nothing. She pulled at the cord and the slats of the blind flipped wide. Dust scattered, fleeing the daylight. Elliot's father recoiled.

'Sorry,' said Lucia and she angled the slats so that the light was less obtrusive. 'Are you too hot? Would you like me to open a window?'

Again he did not respond.

'What about a drink? Can I get you some more water?'

This time he croaked a reply. 'I'm fine,' he said. 'Really.'

Lucia nodded. She hesitated, then moved around the table into his eye line. 'May I?' she said and she pulled out a chair. In her hand she held a transparent plastic bag. In the bag was a mobile telephone, a silver Motorola with a colour screen.

Lucia sat down. She placed the phone on the table. Elliot's father looked at it, then looked away.

do aL gingrs smeL of piss?

'I'm sorry,' she said. Her hands were resting on the table in front of her. She pulled back, allowing her hands to drop into her lap. Then she lifted them again and this time placed her elbows on the surface, her chin in the crevice between her thumb and forefinger. Finally, she let her forearms fold downwards and clasped her midriff with her palms. 'I'm sorry,' she said again.

wot hapnd 2 yor fAc? how lng til U dI of cancer??

'Since when?'

'I don't know. Since he started. I don't know.'

'But these were recent. They were sent recently.'

'Maybe he deleted the others. I don't know. Probably he deleted them. Wouldn't you?'

'You didn't suspect, though.'

'We thought he was making friends. We were pleased. We thought . . . I don't know what we thought.'

'He didn't say anything.'

'No. Nothing. They just used to arrive. He would read them and he would look at the screen for a while and then he would put the phone back in his pocket. Until the next one came.'

'Did he reply?'

'Yes. No. I don't know. I thought he did.'

'It doesn't look like he did. Not to these.'

'Then he didn't. I guess he didn't.'

'It looks like they were sent from a website.'

'A website. Which website?'

'There are dozens of them. We're looking into it but we won't find anything. We won't be able to prove who sent them.'

'I see.'

'I'm sorry.'

'You've said that. You've already said that.'

f U dont wash dat tng off yor fAc we R goin 2 cut it off

The room was small but he had wedged his chair under the table and created an area in which to pace. He waved an arm and hit the blind without meaning to. As he spoke he spat.

'They hounded him. They fucking hounded him.'

Lucia watched. She waited.

'It's not bullying. It's worse than bullying. It's mental fucking torture. That's what it is.'

He knocked the blind again and then turned on it, swiping at it this time as though it had goaded him. Something fell on to the floor: the valance. He swore. He picked it up. He stood holding it and he looked at Lucia. There was spittle at the corner of his mouth.

Lucia waited. She watched.

He dropped the valance and he wiped his sleeve across his face. He turned and pressed his forehead against the ragged blind, followed by his palms. The room darkened. Lucia closed her eyes.

f U ask any1 4 hlp we wiL burn yor hows

She pressed the evidence bag smooth against the table. Air

bubbled in a corner as she ran her hand from one side to the other and she was reminded suddenly of skin blistered by the sun. She moved the bag to one side.

There was nowhere else to look so she looked at Elliot's father. He held the mobile phone in front of him, his elbow on the table, his thumb twitching as he scrolled. His other hand was across his mouth. Periodically he muttered, shut his eyes, allowed his hand to drift up to his forehead and down again. He had known what to expect when he had asked to look again at the texts. Like Lucia, he was probably already able to recount them by now in the order in which they had been sent, down to the syntax and the spelling so outlandish to his generation. Looking at the screen, though, he would be able to suffer what his son had suffered. He would be able to suffer and his suffering would for an instant displace his grief.

Njoy yor vzit 2 d hospital. I hOp dey mAk U beta so we cn fck U up agen

Lucia carried in two coffees. 'It's got caffeine in it,' she said. 'That's the best I can say for it.'

Elliot's father took the paper cup that Lucia had brought for him. He muttered his thanks, shook his head when Lucia offered the crumpled packets of sugar she held in her palm.

She sat. She looked at her notes, checked her watch, glanced across. Elliot's father had his hand wrapped around his cup. Lucia's was so hot she could barely hold on to it long enough to lift it to her lips. He was gripping his and he was staring at his fingers.

'I need to ask you something,' Lucia said.

Elliot's father finally withdrew his hand. 'I thought that's what you'd been doing.'

'Something else.' Lucia closed her notebook. 'Something I don't necessarily expect you to answer.'

He shrugged. He took the lid off his coffee and vapour burst from the cup, intensifying the smell within the room of burnt coffee beans. He set the lid upside down on the table.

'Why would you send him back?'

Now he looked at her, his expression rigid.

'I mean, forget about the text messages. You didn't know. But after what happened. After what they did to him. Why would you even consider sending him back?'

For a moment he held her eye. Then he looked again at his coffee, replaced the lid and slid the cup away.

'Do you have children, Inspector?'

Lucia shook her head.

'Brothers with children? Sisters? Do you have friends with children?'

'No. I don't.'

'Then you have no idea.'

It seemed like he would say no more. Lucia lowered her eyes.

'I work here,' Elliot's father said. 'In the City, I mean. My wife, she doesn't work. I earn some but not a lot. More than a police detective, I would imagine, but unlike you I have four mouths to feed.'

'Four?' said Lucia. Elliot's father flinched and Lucia realised the implication of what she had said. 'No, I'm sorry, I didn't mean that . . .'

He looked at the table and rubbed his forehead.

'It's just, I didn't know,' Lucia said. 'I assumed it was just the three of you.'

'We have a daughter,' said Elliot's father.

Lucia recalled the bicycle in the hallway of their house, the one that had seemed too small for Elliot. 'She's younger,' Lucia said. 'How old is she?'

'She's nine.'

'What's her name?'

'Sophie. Her name's Sophie.'

Lucia nodded. She liked the name but she stopped herself from telling him so.

'I was saying,' said Elliot's father, 'that I work here. I have to work here. If we could leave London we would but we can't afford to. And because we can't leave, we have to make the most of where we are.'

'I don't follow.'

'Property. Public services. Schools, Inspector. We don't have a great deal of choice so we do what we can with the choices that we have.' He paused. He sighed. 'It's a good school. The results, the tables: compared to the alternatives it's the best we could manage for him. That's why we bought a house in the catchment area. For Elliot's sake. For Elliot's sake and also for Sophie's.'

'For Sophie? You said she was nine. Isn't that what you said?'

'She's nine but she's getting older. Children do that, Inspector.'

There was scorn in his tone, which Lucia ignored. She tapped a fingernail against the side of her cup.

'It's changing status,' Elliot's father continued, less aggressive now. 'The school is. Did you know that? They're talking about private funding, more autonomy. It's on some government scheme.'

'Scheme?' said Lucia. 'What kind of scheme?'

'A pathfinder scheme, they call it. A public–private partnership. The school: it's one of the first. So it's the best that's available to us and it's going to get better. And it will be more selective. It will be able to pick and choose. If we took Elliot out, there's no guarantee we'd be able to get Sophie in.'

Lucia shook her head. 'I don't understand.'

'They're siblings. If the brother is in already, they have to admit the sister.'

'That's not what I mean,' Lucia said. 'What I mean is, I don't understand why you would want to. Academically, it's a good school. Fine. But your son was attacked. He was beaten and cut and he was bitten. Why would you want to send your daughter there as well?'

Elliot's father raised his hand to the bridge of his nose. She noticed that his eyes, already bloodshot and ringed by shadow, were glistening now. He screwed them tight, then stretched them wide. He brushed away the single tear that escaped.

'We thought . . . ' he said and stopped. He cleared his throat. 'We thought, after what happened. I mean, the boy who died, the boy that teacher killed. He was one of them, wasn't he? I know, I know: no one saw anything. But everyone knew about him, didn't they?'

'Donovan,' Lucia said. 'Donovan Stanley.'

Elliot's father nodded. 'We weren't going to at first. Send him back, I mean. But after what happened . . . We thought that would be the end of it.'

'You thought he would be safe.'

He nodded again, emphatically. 'And when we looked at the alternatives, Inspector. The other schools. Some of them . . . You just wouldn't. You just couldn't. And there was Sophie of course. We had to think of Sophie.'

not a wrd. kEp yor gingr mouf shut

'Cuts. Bruises. Nothing he might not have got from playing football.'

'Did he play football?'

'No. He didn't. But that's not the point.'

'What is the point?'

'The point is, it was nothing serious.'

'So you did nothing?'

'No! Christ. What do you take us for? Of course we did something.'

'What? What did you do?'

'We spoke to Elliot, for one thing. We spoke to the school.'

'What did Elliot say?'

'Nothing. He wouldn't say anything. I mean, he said he fell over.'

'And the school? Who did you speak to at the school?'

'We spoke to the headmaster. I did. I told him what we thought was happening. I asked him to keep an eye on Elliot.'

'And what did the headmaster say?'

'He said I shouldn't worry. He said, in his experience, all kids get into arguments at Elliot's age. All kids have their little scuffles.'

'Scuffles.'

'That's right. But he said he would keep an eye on things. He said he would ask his staff to keep an eye on things.'

'And what happened?'

'I don't know. Not a lot, I guess. Things didn't get much better but they didn't get any worse. They didn't seem to anyway. We didn't know about the text messages.'

'And later? What about later?'

'Later?'

'After Elliot was attacked.'

'I'm not sure I follow.'

'What did the headmaster say then?'

'Nothing really. I mean, what could he say? What could he do? There were no witnesses, Inspector. Remember?'

kill yorself. f U cum bak yor ded NEway

He was on his feet. There was nothing to prevent him leaving yet he lingered. His hands clasped the back of his chair. Lucia noticed the skin around his fingernails. Strips had been gnawed away, leaving tracks of exposed flesh and traces of blood.

'There'll be publicity,' Lucia said. 'The press, the reporters. They'll latch on to this. They'll latch on to you.'

Elliot's father nodded.

'Because of the school mainly,' Lucia said. 'Because of what happened.'

'The teacher. The shooting.'

'That's right. You should warn your wife. Your daughter too.'

'I will,' he said. 'I have.'

Lucia bobbed her head. She waited. Still Elliot's father did not move.

'It will die down eventually,' Lucia said. 'If they can't find an angle, if they can't find a link. They'll move on to something else.'

'Yes. I expect they will.'

'But if I can help. In the meantime. I don't know what exactly. But you know where I am.'

'Thanks. Thank you.'

Lucia stood. 'I'm sorry,' she said. 'Really, I'm most desperately sorry.'

Elliot's father cleared his throat. He patted his pockets. He scanned the table. 'Right then,' he said. And he left.

The room was dark again, this time because the shadow of the building opposite had reached outwards. It had worked its fingers through the gaps in the blind and wrapped the furniture and the floor and the walls in its grip.

we R watchN U. evN f U cnt c us we cn c U

Lucia sat alone. She held out the mobile phone in front of her, her thumbs resting on the keypad. She scrolled.

do aL gingrs smeL of piss?

She imagined Elliot, seated in the same room as his family but wrenched by the words on the screen into a place of loneliness and terror.

wot hapnd 2 yor fAc? how lng til U dI of cancer??

She tried to decide what she would have done in his place. She tried to decide but she realised that in fact she had already decided. Like Elliot, she had chosen to trust in denial, to confide only in herself, to try to cope with what others inflicted upon her without help of any kind.

f U dont wash dat tng off yor fAc we R goin 2 cut it off

And why? Because the help that was on offer was no help at all. Elliot had been wise to the reality in which he was caught. His parents were well meaning but ineffectual. His friends, if he had any, were probably just as well meaning but weak. There was the school of course; just as for Lucia there was the chain of command. But like Lucia, Elliot had known better than to even try.

f U ask any1 4 hlp we wiL burn yor hows

Samuel Szajkowski had tried. He had tried more than once. That he had tried was perhaps the only thing that might have slowed his soul on its descent.

Njoy yor vzit 2 d hospital. I hOp dey mAk U beta so we cn fck U up agen

More than alone, Elliot had been forsaken. Why should he have had to ask for help? Why had help not been forthcoming? It was no secret, after all. Those who had the power to intervene: they knew. Why was the onus always on the weak when it was the strong who had liberty to act? Why were the weak obliged to be so brave when the strong had licence to behave like such cowards?

not a wrd. kEp yor gingr mouf shut

It wasn't over. She would not accept that this was over. Fuck Cole. Fuck Travis and the whole fucking school. It wasn't over.

kill yorself. f U cum bak yor ded NEway

The room was dark but it was not late. There was still time. For what Lucia had in mind, there was still time.

A blog. You know what a blog is, right?

Well my mum doesn't and she must be almost as old as you. She's got no idea. She thinks I'm being foul when I say it. She tells me to chew on soap. I've got one, you see, and I write on it most days. I write about animals mostly. Birds and that. Things I see. I haven't told anyone at school about it though. I don't use my real name either. Jesus. Can you imagine? I call myself Firecrest. It's a bird. It's stupid, I know. Please don't tell anyone, will you?

Anyway, that's what it was. A blog. Supposably it was written by him. Bum— I mean, Mr Szajkowski. They called it the BumLog. You know, like blog but also like Bumfluff.

At first it was pretty funny, what they wrote. It was supposed to be him in hospital – you know, after he broke his leg. You're supposed to imagine him like lying on his bed with his laptop, and his blog is all the stuff he's thinking about and everything that's going on around him. Like day one is him in pain and that but also he's thinking about all the shots he should of saved in the game and worrying cos he wasn't wearing his best pants when Donovan Stanley pulled down his shorts. He's thinking about his girlfriend – you know, Miss Mullan – and he's afraid that she saw his, um, I mean, well, us kids, we call them skid marks. I don't know what the medical word for them is.

Anyway, that's day one. And there's other stuff, like when TJ – Mr Jones – when Mr Jones comes to visit and he's mad cos the teachers got beat and he's taking it out on Bumfluff and whacking his leg and that and trying to pull the plug on his life-support machine.

Which is a bit stupid really cos he wouldn't of had a life-support machine, would he? I mean, thinking about it, he probably wasn't even in hospital for more than a few hours.

But that's not the point. You're not meant to take it seriously. Although this kid I know, Gareth his name is, he read it and he was like, why does Bumfluff call himself Bumfluff, does he not know what it means? And, how does he manage to type if he's all hooked up to a life-support machine? And this other kid I know, David, he's like laughing at Gareth and going, I dunno, Gareth, maybe he dictates. And Gareth is like, oh. Which is like, duh.

So anyway, it was funny at first and everyone was reading it. Miss Parsons, she caught a bunch of us looking at it during ICT and at first she was like, what's that you're looking at, you're supposed to be researching news stories not messing about in the webosphere. She calls it the webosphere. She thinks it makes her sound cool. And she reaches past us and takes the mouse and she's about to close the browser but she sees what we're looking at and starts to read. Us lot, we're sort of hanging back a bit but when we see that she's reading it we crowd in and start reading again too. And Miss Parsons, when she scrolls to this bit about how this nurse is trying to shave Bumfluff but can't find his face cos it looks exactly the same as his arse, she gives this little snort and brings her hand to her mouth. Someone else laughs too, I think it was Owen, and that's when Miss Parsons realises the rest of us are gathered round her. And she's like, right, that's enough, get back to your desks, that's enough now, and she hollers at us all to sit down. But I'm watching her. When she gets back to her computer at the front of the classroom she turns off the overhead projector so none of us can see her screen. She types something in on her keyboard and then she just sits there reading, smiling, shaking her head. When the bell goes, she doesn't barely notice. All she says is, quietly now, keep it down, and still she's staring at her screen. I leave my PE kit behind so I have to come back for it during lunch but Miss Parsons, she won't let me in. She opens the door just a fraction and says, what is it? I tell her and she says, not now. I say, but Miss, I've got PE, and she says, not now! And I don't argue but I know what's going on. I see them. The lot of them. Mr Daniels, Mr Boardman, Miss Hobbs, Mr Jones. They're all in there, reading it just the same as us. And they're laughing. I can hear TJ – sorry, Mr Jones – I can hear him laughing cos he's got this really distinctive laugh. It's like he's choking on a wad of phlegm.

It got nasty though. The blog did. I mean, people still read it and that. I did too. But it wasn't funny. It was gross, really gross. I wouldn't of read it at all but I had to cos everyone else did and you look like an idiot if everyone's talking about it and you can't even go, yeah I know, or, what about that bit, did you read that bit?

I don't want to say.

Please Miss, I really don't want to.

What should I call you then?

Okay but I still don't want to say.

What if I showed you? It's probably still up. I doubt there's anything new on it but it was definitely up three weeks ago cos I heard Tracey Beckeridge tell Gabby Blake that Meg Evans peed in her pants when she read it.

Oh yeah, it's been going on all year. The football match was February, wasn't it, so yeah, three or four months.

Do you want me to then? Do you reckon that computer over there is working? We're not supposed to use the computers without permission so if anyone says anything will you tell them that you said it was okay?

Where's the button?

Oh yeah.

These computers are really slow. They're like jurassic or something.

God. It sounds like it's gonna take off.

My dad's got this brand-new computer and he says it's like the Lambogenie of all computers. It's got this blue light on it, like it's a spaceship or something. He doesn't let me use it.

God, come on.

Come on come on come on come—

Right, here we go.

Look. See, I told you. And it's in the history, which means

someone's been looking at it in here. It would of been a teacher probably. I bet it was a teacher.

This is it. Look, the last post was on 6 June. So that was like what. A week before the shooting.

So if I click here and then here . . .

God it's sooo slow.

Right. Here's the first one. Then you just scroll down. When David reads them out he does this voice, like an accent. It's supposed to be Polish. I mean, Bumfluff, he doesn't have an accent – he didn't – but on the blog he does. So David, he goes like this.

Day 3

Today i think again about game. never should i to be in goal. i am forwardstriker. Back home, in pooland, cats i would chase for food. fast am i. how you say. like thunder. In pooland, in my village, they call me greyhound. they call me other thing too but these word i cannot to repeat.

Terence is to fault. he is stupid man. he is, how you say, a—

When David does it he does the swear words. I won't though. I mean, I would but I won't.

he is, how you say, a something. *Too also, he is gayman. It is true, there cannot be doubt. Always he wears the short's and watches in the mirror. He is like ladywoman. in pooland could he be Happy. in Pooland, he make poolish Man very*

handsome wife. He would to cook and to clean and to have
the bottom sex all the Days long.

I can't really do voices. I can do birds. I've never shown anyone
though. I've shown my mum, that's all. But I can't do voices.
You get the idea though, right? Although not all of the entries
are written like that. With the accent, I mean. Here, like this
one.

Day forteen
Somethinged *myself 2 sleep last nite. Couldnt find my Thing*
at 1st but kept thinking abot Maggie and up it popped. One
day i hope she will let me touch her bottom. Its big and
round and probaly doesnt have much fluff on it at all. Even
if it was fluffy i wouldnt mind. I would stroke it and hold
it and rub my beard against it.

What I think is that Donovan did the ones with the accent.
They're much funnier. The other ones are just stupid really.
Gideon did them I reckon.

God, don't say anything to anyone, will you? Don't say I said
they were stupid. God. He'd murder me.

Look, here's another one with the accent.

Day 37
My heart, it is inoperative! Why my Maggie no visit me in
this place? she be so ashamed of me perhaps. she think i
have some disease. I have no diseases my Maggie, only dis-
ease of lovesickness! also i am Hornyman. To long is it for

*me without the Jiggy Moving. today i try to jiggy move with
pretty nurselady but nurselady she clap my face. She say
"bad Mr Shite, not to touch the nurseladys!". I beg but she
no give up to me. She clap me again but i no feel for beard-
fluff it protect me. I say "bring me my Maggie to me!". I say
"I must with the Jiggy" but she say "jiggy to yourself!2. And
so again must I give reliefs to my own. Oh my Maggie. Why
you no visit me?!*

So anyway, you get the idea. Like I said, it gets worse later
on. There's more swearing and, you know. Other stuff. It gets
more . . . more . . . what's that word when you read something
and you can almost see what's happening in your head?

That's it. Graphic. It gets more graphic. I'll leave this open,
shall I, and if you want to you can see what I mean for yourself.

Oh yeah, he must of done. He must of heard people talking. I mean, all the kids, all the teachers – everyone read it.
After the game, he was only away for about a week. He came
into school on crutches. And during class and that, all the kids
would be dropping hints. You know, going, nice post, sir, or,
how was hospital, sir, or speaking in a Polish accent and repeat-
ing the stuff they'd read. He must of known. If it'd been me I
would of asked one of the other teachers what everyone was
going on about cos all the teachers knew, that's for definite.
Mr Grant, he even tried to stop them. Donovan and Gideon.
This is what I heard from Tracey Beckeridge. Tracey said that
Grant tried to ban them using the computer lab, which I suppose is where they were writing it and uploading it and that,

but Donovan and Gideon went to TJ – Mr Jones – who went
to Bickle – Mr Travis – and Bickle – Mr Travis, I mean – he
said they – Donovan and Gideon – oughtn't to be banned cos
IT skills were fundamental to something-or-other and pupils
shouldn't be discouraged and anyway this school didn't prac-
tise the censorship of expressions. Something like that. That's
what Tracey Beckeridge said anyway. I don't know how she
found out but Tracey always seems to find out everything and
what she says turns out to be true probably half the time at
least.

Do you know what Tracey also said? She said she felt sorry
for him. Bum— I mean, Mr Szajkowski. Which I didn't really
think about till she said it but that's part of the reason I didn't
like looking at the Bumlog later on. Cos you could kind of
imagine what it would be like, being him. He's a teacher and
everything and probably it didn't even bother him but it's not
nice, is it, when it happens to you? That's probably why Tracey
said it. Cos she's a bit of a gossip and that, which sometimes gets
her in trouble herself. You know, picked on. She's got freckles.
They're not too bad, not like on some kids, like on ginger kids,
but she's definitely got them. And last year – this is what Gabby
Blake told me – last year Tracey was getting picked on so much
that for a week she told her mum she was going to school but
really she went and sat all day by the ponds on the common.
And she bought this mirror, like one of those mirrors girls use
for make-up, and she bought a cigarette lighter and she sat on
a bench and put the mirror on her lap and she used the lighter
to try and burn her freckles off. That's what Gabby Blake said.
And I reckon it was true cos when Tracey came back to school

she had like these raw bits all round her nose. She said she got them from being scratched by her uncle's cocker spaniel but it didn't really look like she'd been scratched. I mean, they looked more like blisters that'd been burst, which would make sense if she did what Gabby said she did, wouldn't it? You can still see the marks even now. They're kind of shiny. Sometimes, in a certain light, it makes her look like she's been crying.

No, not that much really, not any more. I mean, I was for ages, for basically my whole first year, but now I only get picked on sometimes and virtually everyone gets picked on sometimes. It's just how it is. Actually I'm lucky cos there's this kid I know, Elliot his name is. He's the year below, year seven. He has this massive birthmark on his face and also he's ginger and also he hasn't really got any friends so he gets picked on most of all. If I stay quiet no one really notices me any more. Also, I have five friends, which helps. Actually, four and a half. No, four. It's actually four. Vince Robins broke my PSP so I'm not friends with him any more.

Four friends isn't that many I suppose. You've probably got loads more than that. Most people have. My sister, she must have like a hundred friends. They're always round our house. It's annoying cos they take over the lounge and I haven't got a telly in my room. It's embarrassing too. They blow kisses and stuff. They put on this voice and they're like Nick-eee, oh Nick-eee. I ignore them or I tell them to shut up. I go upstairs.

So my sister's got hundreds of friends but I only have four. I don't mind though. It's better than how it was. And four is enough for me. When I think about it, four friends is quite a lot. I actually feel pretty lucky. I am pretty lucky, compared to some of the other kids.

Across from the school gates, a pack of journalists lazed in the heat. They could have positioned themselves anywhere but, as hunters with a common prey, they had gravitated together. Lucia recognised some of the faces. Most of the journalists no doubt recognised hers. She approached on the opposite side of the road but still, as she drew near, those who had been sitting got to their feet. Pencils were drawn, lens covers snapped off. Cigarettes were sucked, dropped and ground with rubber soles into the pavement.

'Inspector!' someone called. 'Hey, Inspector!'

'What's the occasion, Inspector? Come on, darling, give us something!'

She would have liked to. In spite of the 'darling', she would have liked to. Yet she strode on. She had almost reached the gates when another voice called out to her.

'Inspector! What's going on, Inspector? The Samson boy. The shooting. Some coincidence, don't you think?'

This time Lucia stopped. She stopped before she could think.

'Come on, Inspector.' The same voice again. 'You can tell us. We can keep a secret.'

There was laughter but a flutter of excitement too. The gap between Lucia and the journalists was closing. One man – the man who had spoken, Lucia assumed – was halfway across the road; his Dictaphone was even closer. He spoke again. 'Off the record? We don't need to use your name.' Like a movie cop surrendering his weapon, he lifted the Dictaphone above his shoulder and made a show of switching it off.

Lucia said nothing. She turned away. She ignored the pleas that sounded behind her, the single profanity too, and continued towards the gates.

The playground was empty but there were eyes, Lucia knew, at every window. As she crossed the playground she felt the building narrow its gaze. The sun was straining through the film of cloud that had settled over the city but as Lucia approached the entrance the day seemed suddenly less bright. Hot still, oppressive still, but gloomier too, though the building today gave no discernible shadow. Lucia climbed the steps. The glass on the doors cast her back at her. No one's home, the building seemed to say. No one's home who wants to talk to you. Lucia pulled one of the doors wide and stepped inside.

Immediately the sensation was dispelled. A group of students trotted across the entrance hall. All girls, they were hunched together and laughing. Either they did not see Lucia or they ignored her. From distant classrooms she heard children's voices and teachers' voices raised over them. She heard the bangs and scrapes of a school in session: chairs sliding, books dropping, doors slamming.

From the corridor a teacher emerged: Matilda Moore, the young chemistry teacher who had started at the school at the same time as Samuel Szajkowski. A staccato of heel-steps escorted her across the parquet floor. She smiled as she drew near. 'It's Detective Inspector May, isn't it?' she said. 'Can I help you, are you waiting for someone?'

'I'm here to see the headmaster.'

'I'll see if he's available, shall I? Is he expecting you?'

'No. He's not expecting me. But don't trouble yourself. I know where to find him.'

The teacher seemed unsure but Lucia simply nodded at her and turned away. She sensed Matilda watching her as she climbed the short flight of steps that led to the administrative area of the building, then heard her footsteps again as she drifted away. Lucia approached the door to the headmaster's office. She reached it and she knocked.

'Enter.'

Lucia did as the voice instructed.

'Inspector. Well, well.' The headmaster peered up from his desk. Janet, the school secretary, stood over him, clutching a stack of papers to her bust. She smiled and nodded at Lucia and seemed surprised when Lucia did not smile back. She made her excuses and scuttled past, heading for the door that linked her office to the headmaster's. It closed noiselessly behind her.

'Inspector,' Travis said again. 'I must say, I wasn't expecting a visit from you.'

'No,' said Lucia. 'I don't suppose you were.' She did not move from her position by the door.

The headmaster waited. He reclined in his chair, rattled the phlegm in his throat. 'Well,' he said at last. 'To what do I owe this pleasure?'

'It's over,' Lucia said. 'The investigation.'

'Yes. I know. I spoke to your superior.'

'You needn't worry,' Lucia continued. 'There'll be nothing that comes out that will cause you any trouble.'

Travis had his elbows on the armrests of his chair. He held an expensive-looking pen in front of him, suspended between the fingertips of each hand. 'If your intention is to discomfit me, Inspector, you will need to be a fraction less equivocal.'

Lucia felt adrenalin constrict her lungs. She willed her heart to slow its pace. 'Discomfit you?' she echoed. 'No, that is not my intention, Mr Travis. I would have hoped, given recent events, that you were quite discomfited enough.'

Travis put down his pen. 'I assume you will not be wanting tea, Inspector May. Would there be any point in asking you to be seated?'

Lucia shook her head.

'No,' Travis said. 'Of course not. Well then. Let's get down to it, shall we? I assume you are referring to the Samson boy. I assume you have some grievance that you wish to express.'

'I am. I do. But I had also hoped that it would not be necessary to spell out what should be as plain to you as it is to me.'

'What?' said Travis. 'Tell me. Spell it out, why don't you.'

Lucia inhaled. 'You are responsible, Mr Travis. You are culpable. You are to blame for that boy's death, just as you were to blame for the blood that was spilled in your assembly hall.'

For a moment the headmaster was still. No emotion was discernible on his face. Until he laughed: a single, contemptuous bark.

'You find it amusing, Mr Travis. Another boy is dead. Another family has lost a child. You find it amusing.'

The headmaster's expression grew stern. 'How dare you?' he said. He stood up. 'I say again: how dare you? If I find anything about this situation comical, Inspector, it is the absurdity – it is the impertinence – of your allegations.'

'I am not one of your pupils, Mr Travis.'

'Meaning what, Inspector?'

'Meaning, do not talk to me as though I were.'

The headmaster laughed again. 'I will talk to you any way I wish, young lady. What right have you to demand otherwise? What right have you to walk so brazenly into my office and make accusations you know perfectly well you cannot substantiate?'

'From a legal standpoint it seems you are right. I cannot substantiate them, not to the satisfaction of those who have the power to decide whether to act on them. But I have seen and heard enough to convince me that they are true.'

The headmaster scoffed. 'Do not put too much faith in what schoolchildren and—' he jerked his head towards the adjoining door '—secretaries tell you, Inspector. Both have notoriously hyperactive imaginations.'

There came a noise from behind the door, something fallen or knocked over, as though Janet had recoiled at what she had overheard and toppled one of the many trinkets Lucia knew she kept on her desk.

'I have drawn my own conclusions, Mr Travis.'

'Have you indeed? Such a shame then that your superiors do not seem to agree with them. What was their reaction when you outlined to them your theory?'

'The Szajkowski case is closed, as you well know. The Samson case will barely be opened. It is a shame, as you say. More than that: it is a disgrace.'

The headmaster smiled. He smirked. 'You call it a disgrace. I call it common sense, a regrettably rare condition among the public servants of this country.' He sat back down and reclined in his chair. 'You single me out, Inspector. Why? Why not the children who tormented the Samson boy? Why not their parents? And Szajkowski. You really hold me more accountable than the man who ended those poor children's lives?'

'There is plenty of blame to go around, Mr Travis. The simple fact is that you could have acted to prevent what happened but you did not. More than that, you were obliged to act. You knew – you know – about the bullying that goes on in this school. You know who the victims are and which children, which teachers, are responsible.' Lucia took a step towards the headmaster's desk. 'You once told Samuel Szajkowski that you were omniscient. Isn't that the word you used? You claimed to know everything that happened within the walls of this building. Even if that were an empty boast, Mr Travis, you are still the head of this institution and therefore accountable.'

The headmaster yawned.

'Am I boring you, Mr Travis?'

'Frankly my dear, yes. You are. I find your arguments moralistic and naive. I find your manner obnoxious and disrespectful.

I find your very presence a distraction from matters that are far more worthy of my attention.'

This time Lucia laughed. She could not stop herself. 'You old fool,' she said. 'You pompous old fool.'

'Name calling. Really, Inspector. There was a time when I would have expected so much more from you.'

'Then I suppose we are both failures in our way,' Lucia said. 'We have both fallen short of expectation.'

Travis rose. He moved from behind his desk towards the door through which Lucia had entered. He opened it and held it wide. 'Thank you for your time, Inspector. I am sorry if it appears to have been wasted. I don't suppose you have considered what you will do now that you have allowed your bitterness to be aired.'

Lucia passed through the doorway. 'As much as it pains me, Mr Travis, I will do the only thing I can do. I will do the same thing you did. I will do nothing. I might sleep a little better, that's all.'

The headmaster smiled. 'My dear,' he said. 'I would not count on that. I would not count on that at all.'

That's a lie.

Please, love. Calm down.

I'm not gonna fucking calm down. How fucking dare she? How dare you? He's dead. My son is dead, murdered by that faggot freak of a teacher, and you expect me just to sit here while you go around pissing on Donnie's grave?

Bollocks. That's not what you said. You weren't asking. You were telling. You were what's the fucking word. Insinuating. That's what you were doing. If Donnie was such a trouble-maker, how come the school never said nothing? My wife, she was at parents' evening what. Just last month.

It was February. It was four months ago.

February then. What does it fucking matter when it was? The point is they never said a word. Not a fucking word.

Barry, please. Language.

Shut up. Just shut up a minute. You. You listen to me. My son was a good lad. He had a mouth on him, I'll grant you. He was sharp too, too sharp for his own good sometimes. But he was never in trouble. No drugs, no booze, nothing like that.

He was smart enough to know what would happen to him if I found him with any. And maybe his grades weren't all that great but he was quick. He was canny. The only stupid thing he ever did was hang around with that loser mate of his. Wassisname. Christ. What was his name?

Gideon. Gi. Gideon.

Gideon. That's it. Waste of fucking space. You come here asking about Donnie causing trouble but this kid Gideon is the one you wanna be talking to. Donnie was always getting blamed for the shit Gideon pulled. I told him, I said, you better be careful, boy, or that loser mate of yours is gonna drag you down with him. And I was right. That's exactly what happened. Gideon got a reputation for being a low-life and Donnie got tarred just the same.

Back me up, Karen. I'm right, aren't I? Tell her I'm right.

He's right.

Of course I'm right. Like last summer. Like what happened last summer with that kid on the bus.

It was November.

It wasn't fucking November. It was summer.

It was November, I'm sure of it. It was dark outside, don't you remember?

It was summer. You, write that down. It was summer.

I don't care if you're recording it, I'm telling you to write it down as well. You're writing other stuff down. Write that down.

So it's summer. I'm eating dinner. I've just sat down. It's been a long day and I'm in a bad mood anyway because the only beer we've got in the house is warm.

I told you, Barry, it's the fridge. It's not been working properly

*for months. And I said I'd run down to the off-licence to get you
some cold ones but you said—*

Jesus H. Christ. Can you not just be quiet for a single minute?
It hardly bloody matters, does it? So the fridge is broken. So
the beer was warm. So fucking what?

What the fuck was I saying? All your fucking interrupting,
I've lost track of what I was saying.

You were eating dinner.

I'm eating dinner. Right. I've barely started. So I'm sitting
there and the sodding doorbell goes. Then, right away after,
there's this knocking. Hammering, more like. You know, like
with the back of someone's fist. And I go to Karen, who the
bloody hell is that? She just shrugs. She's looking at me all
gormless, just like she's looking at me now, and then the doorbell goes again, dingdongdingdongdingdong, like whoever it is
has got their finger held against it. And I'm like, I'll get that,
shall I? Even though Karen here, she's already eaten and Christ
knows she could do with the exercise. So I get up and I'm not
even out of the kitchen when whoever it is starts hammering
again. I yell, I go, there better be something on fire out there,
pal. I'm in the hall and I can see this figure through the glass
– you know, like a shadow, a what's the word, a silhouette –
and I can tell he's got his face pressed against the glass. So he
can see me coming but all the time I'm walking towards him
he's still got his finger on the bell. By this time I don't care
what the hell's on fire. Whatever it is will just have to burn
while I take care of this joker.

I open the door. I've got my left in a fist. But guess what.
It's a woman. Which is lucky for her because if she hadn't of

been the conversation that followed would of ended up a whole lot shorter.

I say, who the hell are you?

She says, Stanley. You're Stanley, right?

Who the hell wants to know? What the hell do you think you're doing hammering on my door like that? You're lucky you're a woman, lady, else you and me, we'd be having words.

A word is just what I want, Mr Stanley. A word with you and your son.

Donnie. What about Donnie? I'm gonna ask you one more time. Who the hell are you?

She says her name. She says it but Christ knows if I can tell you what it was. It was some nignog name. African or whatever. She's one of them, see. A coloured.

Barry. You're not supposed to call them that.

Then what the hell am I supposed to call em? Her skin, it's coloured, ain't it? In my book, that makes her a coloured.

They're African-American. You call them African-Americans.

American? What the hell's America got to do with anything? Look, the point is I don't know her name. Her accent's all right, I can understand what she's saying, but I couldn't tell you what she was called. Okay?

Right then.

So she tells me her name. I say, and?

And your son attacked my son.

Attacked. What are you talking about, attacked?

He attacked him, she says. On the bus. The school bus. Him and his friends, they pinned him down and they punched him and they kicked him and . . . and . . .

And what?

And she's crying now. That's the problem with women. You're having a conversation and halfway through they'll burst into tears. I dunno if it's the hormones or all the soap operas or what the hell it is.

I say again, and what?

And then she turns on me. When she answers, she spits. She shouts, like some fucking savage. They urinated on him, she says. He's twelve years old and they urinated on him. They beat him and they knocked him down and then they urinated on him. Your son did. Your bastard son!

Which is just too much. I'm like, hang on a minute. Just hang on a goddamn minute. That's my son you're talking about. That's my son you're accusing.

And she's like, there's no accusing about it. I'm telling you what happened. I'm saying to you how it is.

At this point I turn around. Karen, she's already lurking, and Donnie, I expect he was lurking too. But I yell for him. I shout, Donnie. Donovan! Get your arse down here. Now!

No one says nothing while we're waiting for him to appear. I hear his door shut. I mean, I know he's already on the landing. All he's done is, he's crept back along to his room and slammed the door like he's been in there the whole time. Like I said, he's canny. So when he gets to the stairs he's like, what? What do you want?

Just get down here, I tell him.

And when she sees him she goes off on one. She tries to get past me. She's reaching and lunging and spitting again and shouting. Then Karen here starts crying.

I wasn't crying.

Karen here starts crying and meanwhile Donnie's standing there halfway down the stairs and I've got this nut-job lunatic by the shoulders, trying to keep her out of my house.

Who the hell is this? says Donnie.

I don't answer him. I'm busy wrestling. I mean, she's a woman but she's not small. That lot: their women tend to be bigger, don't they?

Anyway, eventually she calms down. I say she calms down. What she does is she stops screaming. She wipes her mouth with the back of her hand and she's breathing in and out but in her eyes she's got that look, like she's willing Donnie to step just a little bit closer.

He doesn't. He hangs back. I told you, he's not stupid.

You, she says. What did you do?

Who is this, Dad? What's she been saying?

She says you attacked her son, I tell him. On the bus. Says you pissed on him. And I expect Donnie to laugh or something. You know, just cos it's so fucking ridiculous. But he doesn't. He doesn't laugh and he doesn't say anything. He looks at the floor.

Donnie, I say.

And the crazy woman, she's like, see! See! He did it, he admits it.

No! says Donnie. It wasn't me. I swear, Dad, it wasn't me.

I just look at him.

Honest, Dad, you got to believe me. I mean, I was there. I saw it happen. I saw what they did to him but it wasn't me.

He's lying! says the woman.

Shut up, I say. You, just shut up. Then, who did it Donnie? What did you see?

And Donnie goes shtum. Just clams up. Which makes it obvious, right? It was one of his mates. And it doesn't take a whatdyacallit, a whateverthefuckologist to work out which one.

Donnie, I say again. What did you see?

I can't, Dad. You know I can't.

It was him! My son told me it was!

It wasn't me. I swear to you it wasn't!

He saw him. He saw you!

Maybe he saw me but I didn't do it. There were lots of people there. Loads. Maybe he got confused. Maybe he only thought it was me.

He did not get confused! If he says it was you then—

You've got the wrong boy, I tell her. Do you hear me? You've got the wrong boy. Talk to the school. Tell the school what happened. Let them deal with it.

I spoke to the school, she says. I spoke to the headmaster. He said they can't do anything. Which means they won't do anything. So I'm talking to you. I talked to my son and now I'm talking to you!

Then Karen pipes up. There're cameras, she says. Aren't there? On the buses.

That's right, I say. Talk to the bus company. Look at the cameras.

They put tissue paper over the cameras! She's shouting again now. Your son did! He put wet tissue paper over the cameras! And she starts trying to get past me, to get at Donnie, and by that time I've had just about enough. So I do what I should of done in the first place. I grab her by the arms and shove her back. I tell her to piss off. I slam the door in her face. I go inside and finish my dinner.

That ends it. That's the end of it. I never see or hear from her again. Which just proves it, doesn't it? I mean, if she was so convinced it was Donnie there's no way she would of just crawled back into her hole, not after the way she was carrying on. What happened was, she went away and she spoke to her son again and her son was like, er ... well ... yeah ... maybe I was wrong. Maybe it wasn't Donovan. But do I get an apology? Does Donnie get an apology? Do we fuck.

So you can sit there insinuating all you like. I've heard it all before. I've heard it all before and not one word of it is true.

You know what, I don't know why I'm even bothering. You're like the rest of em, I can see it in your face. It doesn't matter what I say. I'm wasting my breath. Believe what the hell you want to believe. What the fuck does it matter now?

This is over. Right now.

Here, give me that thing.

How do you stop this?

Where the hell's the damn but—

I'm sorry about my husband, Inspector.

Don't worry. He wouldn't like me talking to you but he won't be back now, not till later. He'll come home when he gets hungry. My mum used to say, men are like dogs. They bark and sometimes they even bite but as long as you keep em fed they'll never stray far from home.

You mustn't think bad of him. He's upset, that's all. He gets angry – that's what he does when he's hurting inside. Sometimes I think it's the only way he has of expressing himself. I mean, he's passionate, that's his problem. He's a passionate man. And he misses his son. It's not right, is it, that a parent should outlive their child? I heard someone say that once, on the news I think it was, or *Corrie* maybe, and it stuck in my mind but I never thought it would . . . I mean, that we would . . . that . . .

Don't mind me. I'm okay. I'm not even crying. Look. See?

I'll tell you something I haven't told anyone else: I haven't cried. Not once. Not since Donnie died. I don't know why. I mean, it hurts, don't get me wrong. And I know they'll come. The tears. It was like this when my dad died. I was only seven but I remember. I remember not crying and trying to cry and worrying what everyone thought of me, that they thought I didn't love my dad, that they blamed me somehow for him dying. Then I worried that I was to blame, that he'd be alive if I'd of loved him more.

It was only after the funeral. Maybe two or three weeks after. I was shopping with my mum and we got home and Mum opened the door and she had all these bags and what would normally of happened was, Dad would of come out of the kitchen or the garden or from upstairs or wherever and he would of taken the bags from my mum and carried them through for her and all the time he would of been moaning about how heavy they were, about how much my mum must of spent. But he didn't come. Mum opened the door and it was just the empty house waiting. And she was puffing and struggling with the bags and it suddenly struck me as the saddest thing in the world. That my dad wasn't there to carry the bags. I cried then. I cried and I couldn't stop. My mum just held me. She left the shopping on the doorstep, with the peas defrosting and the butter melting, and she held me.

So it will be like that I expect. Except, well, Mum's not here now. And Donnie's not here now. And even when Barry's here, he's not always exactly in the moment, if you know what I mean. But I'll be all right. I'll manage.

I'm getting sidetracked. I don't mean to keep you. All I wanted to say was, what Barry said, he wasn't wrong. About Donnie. A lot of people said things that nobody could ever prove. And Gideon was definitely a bad influence. There's no question about that. It's just . . . I mean, the truth is . . .

The truth is, it wasn't easy for Donnie. His dad has certain expectations, certain rules. And Barry, I mean, he's not always around, like I said. He works and he has his friends and a man only has so much time, doesn't he? Particularly some men. Certain types of men. I mean, nappies, bedtime stories, football in the park. It's just not them. Do you know what I'm trying to say? So it wasn't easy for Donnie.

Because I work too, you see. I'm out most of the day. And we never had a brother for Donnie. We never gave him a sister. I would of liked to of done. I would of loved to of had a little girl, even two little girls, two little sisters for Donnie to protect. But Barry wasn't keen. So we didn't. Which means Donnie was on his own most of the time. Which isn't always good for a boy, is it? Boys, they need occupying, even the bright ones. Especially the bright ones. And Donnie was bright, just like Barry said. Although do you know what I think? I think he was ashamed of it. That's what I think. He was ashamed of being so bright. So he hid it. Either he hid it or if he let it show he let it show in ways that . . . Well. In ways that oughtn't to be encouraged.

Because that was the other problem with us not being around. A boy needs discipline, doesn't he? Not that Barry didn't give him discipline. But discipline, it's not just the bad stuff, is it? It's not just the shouting and, well, the rest of it. It's also the other things. Things like . . . I don't know. Like guidance, I suppose. Guidance is the word. I would try sometimes but it should come from the father, really, shouldn't it? I'm not saying it's Barry's fault. It's my fault, I know it's my fault. Because I remember what Barry was like when Donnie was younger, when we were having trouble with the schools and we had to move him, three times we had to move him, and I remember how Barry reacted. So since then, and because everything seemed to be all right at school, I didn't always tell Barry things. You know, like if Donnie had done something he shouldn't of. Because I was scared how Barry would react. And I thought, so long as he's settled at school, that's better than it was before.

I don't really know what I'm trying to say. It's complicated, that's all. I suppose all it is really is that Donnie had his problems. What Barry said, he wasn't wrong, but there were other things too. There was another side to things. And like I say, it's not Barry's fault and it's not Donnie's fault and if it's anyone's fault it's mine. It's just, I can't help wishing that I'd had a little help. Just sometimes, from someone. Because it's hard, being a parent. I mean, I had Barry. I wasn't all alone like some people.

So maybe it's just me but I have to be honest and say that I found it really hard. And now, after what's happened, well. This is about as hard as it gets.

The envelope was on her keyboard, wedged between two lines of keys so that it announced itself as soon as Lucia's desk came into view.

Her first thought was of the headmaster; that the envelope heralded some official censure. The envelope, though, did not look official. It was windowless, plain white, with her first name only printed in oversize capitals. And whereas formal correspondence was usually confined to a taut paragraph or two on a single sheet of A4, the envelope on Lucia's desk bulged.

Lucia looked about her. No one was paying her any notice. Walter was at his desk, leant back on his chair, his feet raised as usual and his keyboard on his lap. Charlie was on the phone, Harry was frowning at his computer screen and Rob was clutching a mug of coffee in one hand and excavating a nostril with the other.

Lucia dropped into her seat and let her bag slide from her shoulder. Her monitor blocked her view of the rest of the office but she leant sideways to check again whether anyone was

watching. Nobody had moved. Lucia turned her attention back
to the envelope. She picked it up.

It squished, like a Jiffy bag. The seal was taped shut, as though
the gum had not proved strong enough, and Lucia noticed with
distaste that there was a wiry black hair trapped at one end
under the Sellotape. She turned the envelope over and looked
again at the writing on the front. It said LUCIA – nothing
more, not an underline or even a full stop.

She shouldn't open it. She knew she shouldn't open it. But
there was an inevitability to events now. She shouldn't open it
but until she did her day was at a standstill. Probably Walter
or one of the others had left the envelope and their lives too
were in abeyance now until the trap they had set was sprung.
The sooner Lucia opened the envelope, the sooner they would
laugh and the sooner Lucia could tut, roll her eyes, throw the
contents into the bin and get back to pretending that this sort
of thing was beneath her, that it did not bother her, that in no
way did it make her feel small or vulnerable.

Or perhaps she was being paranoid. Perhaps the envelope
contained something of hers that she had lost or forgotten or
lent to someone and it was simply being returned. What that
thing might be she could not think but that did not in itself
rule out the possibility. She would open the envelope and
catch sight of what was inside and remember instantly what,
why, when and who. It would be such a trivial thing that she
would cast it, envelope and all, into her bottom drawer. Then
she would spend the rest of the morning trying to ignore the
voice in her head that mocked her insecurity, her cowardice,
her pervading sense of relief.

Lucia worked her finger under the seal. She wrenched the envelope open. As she did so its contents burst outwards and Lucia knew in that instant that she should have trusted her initial instinct and left the envelope alone.

Hair. The envelope was stuffed with hair. Short, black and coiled, like the single strand that had almost escaped. It fell in clumps on to Lucia's desk, her keyboard, her lap. It clung to her fingers. As Lucia recoiled, the envelope dropped and the last of its contents spilled out on to the carpet and vanished against the charcoal gloom.

'We all chipped in.'

Lucia held her fingers splayed in front of her. She blew, almost spat, at the hair that still coated them. She looked up.

'Me, Rob and Charlie. We didn't ask Harry because we didn't think he could grow any yet. Bless him.'

Lucia glanced over at Harry. At the sound of his name he raised his head.

'You know what it is, don't you?'

Walter had shifted so that he was leaning with both elbows on the filing cabinet that stood next to Lucia's desk. Rob and Charlie were on their feet now and carrying their grins closer.

'Lulu. Are you listening? I said, you know what it is, don't you?'

Lucia shook her head: not an answer, rather an expression of her incredulity.

'Like I said, we all chipped in.' Walter was leering now, playing to his audience. 'We just thought that, with everything that's happened, you were probably missing him. You know: your pal. Bumfluff.'

Rob and Charlie sniggered. Lucia looked again at her hands, at her desk, at the envelope on the floor. She opened her mouth. She shut it. She looked at Walter but Walter was silent now. He was grinning. He was waiting.

'You better be joking,' Lucia said at last. 'You better be fucking joking.'

Rob and Charlie laughed. They tapped palms.

'Don't you like it?' Walter said, feigning offence. 'I was sure you'd like it.'

Lucia could feel the curdled expression on her face. She swallowed, shut her eyes, tried to force herself to look less disgusted, less disgusting. As though they had been moulded from rubber, her features rebounded and settled into the same position: her brow creased, her nostrils flared, her teeth bared and her lips pulled taut.

'Hey, guys. What's going on?' Harry had moved to Charlie's side. He was smiling but warily.

Lucia looked at him but it was Walter who answered. 'Nothing for you to worry about, Harry my lad. We were just giving Lulu here a gift we prepared for her. She doesn't seem very grateful.'

Again Rob and Charlie guffawed.

'Gift? What kind of gift? Hey, Lucia. Is everything okay?'

Lucia heard Harry's words but could not think how to respond. She looked from Harry to the envelope on the floor and back to Harry. Harry edged forwards. He followed Lucia's gaze.

'What is it? What's wrong? Christ, Lucia, what's that? What is that?'

Lucia did not answer. She looked at Walter.

Harry turned. 'Walter? Jesus. What the hell is wrong with you?'

Walter laughed. 'Easy, Harry. It's just a little joke. Just some harmless fun.'

'Fun? This—' Harry gestured to the envelope, to Lucia '—this is your idea of fun?' He took a step towards Walter. Walter's expression hardened.

'Careful now, Harry. Don't start making trouble for yourself.'

'Harry,' said Lucia. 'Harry, please. It doesn't matter.'

'Lucia—'

'Please,' she said again. 'Please.'

Harry shook his head. He glared at Walter.

'That's a good lad, Harry. You listen to Lulu here. Mummy knows best.'

'Walter—' Lucia began but a holler from across the room cut her off.

'Is she in yet? Lucia!'

Cole was at his door, one hand on either side of the frame and leaning out into the office proper. 'Where the fuck have you been? Get in here!'

'Guv, I—'

'Now, dammit.' Cole turned away and disappeared behind the partition. With a glance at Harry, Lucia started towards the chief inspector's office. Walter, though, was blocking her path. She was about to tell him to move, to get out of her way, to shove him aside if it came to that but in the end there was no need. Walter took half a pace back and, with a dip of the head and a sweeping gesture with one arm, ceded the ground to Lucia. She noticed him wink at Charlie as she passed.

At the threshold to Cole's office, Lucia hesitated. She turned and saw the others still watching her. She stepped inside and shut the door behind her.

'Guv,' she said. Cole was facing the window, one hand on his hip, the other massaging the well-shined skin of his forehead. 'You wanted me, Guv.'

'Come in. Sit down.'

Lucia did not want to sit. She moved towards the only chair on her side of the desk and stood behind it. She gripped the cool metal frame and realised that her palms were sweaty. She let go of the chair and wiped her hands on her trouser legs.

'You're on suspension, Lucia. You're out. Collect what you need and go home.'

Lucia was silent. Gently, she nodded. Cole still had his back to her and rather than looking at him she looked at his desk. There was a tube of Colgate, she noticed, by the telephone. There were piles of paper and foolscap folders, and over these and what little surface of the desk was visible, there were fluorescent pink Post-it notes dotted like acne. Some were blank but most had on them a short note, invariably bracketed between question marks. Lucia found herself wondering what would happen to conviction rates in north-east London were the Post-it notes suddenly to become unstuck. Or perhaps more cases would come to court rather than growing stale in an atmosphere of indecision.

'That's it, Lucia. You know why. You don't need me to tell you why.' Cole turned to face her. He had not shaved, Lucia noticed. Either he had been running late that morning or he had been nervous about bringing a razor to the skin under his nose and around his lips, blotched as it still was with cold sores.

'No,' Lucia said. 'You don't need to tell me why. But you could tell me who.'

'Who. Who what?'

'Who it is that Travis can count on to be such a good friend to his cause.'

Cole shook his head. 'I told you before, Lucia: don't be naive.' He moved behind the desk.

'Come on, Guv. What am I going to do with it if you tell me?'

Cole sighed. He rubbed his head again. 'Then why do you need to know, Lucia? Why do you always need to know?'

Lucia almost laughed. She almost reminded the DCI what she did, what they both did. She resisted. She said instead, 'Elliot Samson's father told me that the school was changing status. He mentioned a government scheme, private funding, more autonomy. He said it was one of the first.'

Cole shrugged. 'I wouldn't know about that.'

'There's a lot of money involved in that sort of thing, I would imagine. A lot of commercial interests.'

'Probably. Possibly. Who the hell knows?'

'I don't suppose a public prosecution would look particularly good, would it? Chances are it would scare a few people the government wouldn't want to see scared.'

Cole sat down. He picked up one of the sheets of paper on his desk and peered under the Post-it note that was attached to it.

'Or is it more straightforward than that? Is it closer to home? The superintendent,' Lucia said. 'Your boss. I notice he's on the school's board of governors.'

Cole looked at Lucia without raising his head. 'Careful, Lucia.'

'I doubt he'd be too keen to be dragged into all of this, would he? I expect he would rather we left Mr Travis and his school well alone.'

Cole put down the paperwork he was holding. 'For an officer who has just mouthed her way into a suspension, Detective Inspector May, you seem remarkably reluctant to shut the fuck up.'

Lucia glared. She bit down on the retort that was wrestling for control of her tongue. Cole exhaled into the silence and returned his attention to his desk.

'So what happens now?' Lucia said at last.

'There'll be a hearing. You'll be reprimanded. Demoted maybe, at least for a while. You'll be advised to request a transfer.'

'A transfer? To where?' Lucia narrowed her eyes. 'Advised by whom?'

'To anywhere you like that's not CID. By the disciplinary board. By your colleagues probably. By me.'

'By you,' Lucia echoed. 'And if I don't?'

Cole's lips curled into a humourless smile. 'Then I expect that you will be transferred anyway.'

'You can't do that.'

'I can and I will. What's the big deal, Lucia? You and I both know it'd be doing you a favour.'

'A favour? In what way would it be doing me a favour?'

Cole reclined in his seat. He gestured with a nod towards the door. 'Before. Just now. What was going on out there?'

Lucia folded her arms. 'Why don't you tell me?'

'Watch your tone, Inspector.'

'Yes, sir. Sorry, sir. But I'd be interested in hearing what you think you saw. Sir.'

For a moment it seemed that Cole would not answer. He was glowering at Lucia and almost as she returned his stare she could see the skin on his face reddening.

'I saw trouble where before there was calm,' he said. 'I saw disruption and discord where before the officers in this department would have counted their colleagues as their closest friends. That's what I saw, Inspector.'

'Before. You mean before I joined.'

'Yes, Lucia. Before you joined.'

Lucia bobbed her head. 'And that's what you saw. That's all you saw.'

The DCI nodded.

Lucia pulled herself upright. 'You've spoken to Travis from what I understand,' she said. 'The two of you must have found you had plenty to discuss. You must have found yourselves getting along like sergeant majors at a reunion.'

'What the hell's that supposed to mean?' said Cole.

Lucia was on her way to the door. She stopped and turned before she answered. 'Nothing that will worry you, Chief Inspector. It just seems to me that you and Travis have in common a certain way of seeing things.' She made to move away and then checked herself again. 'Although, thinking about it, maybe seeing isn't quite the right word.'

Harry called out to Lucia as she strode from her desk towards the exit. She glanced towards him and half raised her hand but she did not slow. Walter said something as she passed his chair but Lucia ignored him. When she reached the door to the stair-well, she swung it harder than she had expected to. The handle hammered into the already cracked plaster and the sound of wood and glass and metal trembling fled down the stairs and into the depths of the building.

Lucia followed.

As she stepped on to the street she barely noticed the heat. She passed a newsagent, then turned back and went inside. From the stooped Bangladeshi man behind the counter, she bought twenty Marlboro reds and a box of matches and did not wait for her change. She found a bench. It was coated with graffiti and bird muck – like every bench in London, so it seemed – and smeared at one end with something that was probably but not necessarily banana. Lucia sat down anyway. The bench faced the road. Almost immediately a bus pulled up to the kerb. Its doors opened and the driver looked at Lucia and Lucia looked at the driver and the doors closed and the bus pulled away. Lucia took out a cigarette and with her third match managed to light it.

She smoked. Three buses later, she was still smoking. Four or five filters lay at her feet, two of them at least still smoul-dering. After using it to light another cigarette, she threw the one she was holding to the floor. The first drag of the new cigarette tasted even worse than the last one of the old. Each lungful, in fact, marked a steady decline; Lucia took no pleasure, no relief from what she was doing. She inhaled a second time, coaxing the flame towards the filter, but she drew too hard and she gagged. She coughed. She leant forwards and she retched. She was sick, and her sick splattered across her shoes and swamped the cigarette butts on the ground. Another bus pulled up but did not stop long enough even to open its doors. Lucia spat. She sat upright, wiped her mouth on her sleeve. She had tears in her eyes and though it was the shock of throwing up that had summoned them, she found herself unable to halt their flow. She buried her head in the crook of her elbow. She cleared her throat and spat again. The packet of cigarettes was clutched in her hand, she realised. It was squashed now, from where she had gripped it as a reflex to her stomach muscles contracting. She cast the packet on to the bench, into the banana, and stood up.

For some time Lucia walked. She realised she was drifting towards the school so she took a left and then another and found herself on the borders of Finsbury Park. It was a weekday, not yet lunchtime, and the sun was barely discernible, yet the grass was strewn with blankets and bodies and barbecues ready to be fired up. Lucia found a spot away from the crowd and lay back. She could taste tar and vomit. Her throat felt as though she had just woken up from sleeping all night with her mouth open. She craved water but now she had stopped moving the thought of getting to her feet once again and heading off in search of some filled her with lethargy. It was London and it was summer, Lucia reasoned; it would have to rain eventually. When it did, she would still be lying here. She would part her lips and angle her face to the sky and let the raindrops hit her face and run into her mouth.

But in the end she could not wait. She got to her feet, allowed a moment of dizziness to pass, then wandered towards the gates of the park. In a Sainsbury's Local she queued to buy some water. Even before she had left the shop she had drained half the bottle and immediately regretted having done so. The water, so cold it was barely fluid, made her head pound and her stomach ache. She was hungry, she realised. She had not eaten since yesterday evening and it was now almost . . . what? She asked a passer-by. Four. It was gone four. She should go home, she told herself. Except that she did not want to go home. Not to her flat, at least. Instead she walked again, and found a cafe she knew well, and sat by the window picking at a piece of chocolate cake and staring at the building opposite.

She drank tea. Three mugs of it, until the light outside began to fade and the owner of the cafe started to sweep up around her. When the cafe owner left so did Lucia. She lingered though, huddled in the doorway, pacing the length of the block and back again, leaning with one heel raised against the wall of the office block next door. All the time she watched the building opposite. The lights on the third floor were still off. The curtains were not yet drawn. There was no one at the entrance or visible in the stairwell. So Lucia waited, turned away, then turned back and checked again.

It was late when finally he came home. At first she was not sure it was him but when he dropped his keys and cursed and bent on to the balls of his feet to pick them up, she knew. Before she could reconsider she crossed the road. She stopped between two cars, just shy of the kerb. She said, hey, and the sound caught in her throat. She said it louder. And the figure in front of her turned and stepped out of the shadow towards her.

It will all be forgotten. Won't it? No one will remember. No one really cares. Even now, it is in the newspapers, but people buy the newspapers why? For the same reason they watch movies or read a novel. To be entertained. It is entertainment. They read the stories and they gasp and they tut – tut tut tut – but nothing is real to them. Not really real. They look at the pictures, the pictures of him, and they shudder and they say, just look at his eyes, you can tell, can't you, it is all in the eyes. And they will tut again and turn the page and move on to a story about fox-hunting or tax increases or a celebrity taking drugs. But if it were really real to them, they would not be entertained. If they cared, they would not turn the page. They could not. If what was in the newspapers seemed real, they would not buy the newspapers at all. They would lie awake at night, like I do. They would weep, like I do. They would despair, like I do. They would despair.

Even you. Why are you here? You do not care. Maybe you think you care but you do not. You are here because it is your job. Would you be here if it were not your job? And the questions you ask. Why do you ask them? How will what I tell you change things? It will not. Felix is dead. Felix was murdered. My son is gone and soon I will be the only person in the world who still remembers that he lived at all. He died in vain, Inspector. That is the phrase, is it not? He died in vain and that is the hardest thing of all for me to accept.

Do you know what Felix survived? You do not. I do not blame you for not knowing because how could you know? Even Felix did not know. He was not yet a baby and already he was as close to death as I am to you, here, now, in this room. Children that would have become his friends were dying. His relatives were dying: his aunt, my sister; his uncle, my brother; his grandmother and grandfather. His father, who did not even know he was a father, was dying. They died for no reason, just like Felix. They died because someone told them, believe in this God, He will save you. But it was the wrong God. Someone else, someone who had a gun and who had friends who had guns, decided it was the wrong God. And the real God, they said, was angry. The real God was vengeful. The real God, it turned out, was a devil.

But Felix survived. I survived, which means Felix survived. We came to England. We came to London. The Greatest City in the World. In London, they told us, only the old die. Only the sick die and usually not even then. Nobody dies for no reason. Nobody dies for a God that does not exist. There are no guns, they said. Not even the police have guns. To die from being shot, in London. Ha! Not unless a bullet finds its way over from Africa. So we felt safe. We thought we were being saved. We thought coming to England would save us.

He wanted to be a waiter. In a restaurant. That was his ambition. I laughed when he told me and he asked me why did I laugh? I stopped laughing. I said, Felix, you will be a waiter. You will be a waiter if that is what you choose to be. You could be a doctor too, you should consider becoming a doctor, but if you decide to become a waiter I will love you just the same. He told me he would think about it. He said, waiters get tips, Mother. Doctors do not get tips, do they? I had to agree with him. I had to say, no, Felix, they do not. He said, yesterday I was watching at the window and I saw a man in a restaurant give a waitress paper money. He folded it and he put it in her pocket, just here, in the pocket on her shirt. So on the whole I think I would rather be a waiter. But I will think about it. If you want me to think about it, I will. That is what he said.

He worked hard. He tried to work hard but his imagination interfered. He would dream. He would listen to a teacher and not know later at which point he had stopped listening. He would stare at the page of a book and come to a word and that word would carry him off, to somewhere other than the end of the sentence. He told me this. His teachers got angry with him and then they got angry at me so I spoke to Felix and that is what he told me. He said, Mother, what can I do? I want to learn. I know it is important that I learn. But I have so much thinking to do. I try to hold it off but sometimes I cannot stop it. It swallows me up, like it is thirsty and I am a glass of water. What can I do?

I could not get angry with him. How could I have got angry with him? I think, Inspector, that he would not have been a waiter. He would not have been a doctor either. He would have written stories or sung songs or painted pictures. He would have made something beautiful. He was beautiful already and everything he did was beautiful but others would have seen it just like I did. They would have seen it too.

Because they did not see it. Before he died, they did not see it. Felix was not popular. Partly it was because he dreamt so, I think, but mainly it was because he came from Africa. He was British, English, a Londoner, but he came from Africa. So the teachers complained about his attitude and the children, the other children, they complained about the colour of his skin. Even black children, Inspector. Especially black children. They said Felix was too black. They called him Africa as though the word itself were an insult. They beat him sometimes. They beat him and laughed and said, if it hurts so much then why don't you ever bruise, why do we never see a bruise?

This was in school, out of school, before school, after school. Felix would shrug. He would say to me, do not worry, Mother. Do not cry. It was my fault, it must have been my fault. Do not cry. And I would wish then that his father were alive and that he were here and that he were with us. Because that is what a father is for, do you not think? To protect his family. I tried but I failed and I failed and I failed. I would walk with him, to school, from school, but then we would both end up running. I would talk with parents and Felix would watch his mother get shouted at, spat on, laughed at and he would learn exactly the things I did not want him to learn, about what people thought of us, what they thought of where we had come from, what they thought we were worth. I would talk to the school and the people I spoke to, the teachers, the headmaster, they would nod and look concerned and tell me that boys brawl, Mrs Abe, it is the way of things in this country. This country. Like it was their country and not my country, not my son's country. The way of things. Like the way of things was fixed and decided and unchangeable. I have heard such words before, Inspector. Where I come from, such words are like medicine, they make it easier to cope with the pain. But not here. Not in the Greatest City in the World.

So I expect nothing. I have learnt to expect nothing. You seem nice. You look kind. But you know, I think, how this will end. It has ended already. Not for me, for me it will never end, but for everyone else it was over as soon as it began. Felix lived and now he is dead and already the world is forgetting his name. Tell me: will you remember his name? In a year. In a month. In a week. Will you remember his name?

A hand stroked her cheek and she twitched.

'Lulu.'

She turned away.

'Lulu. Wake up.'

The hand was on her shoulder now, prising her from the pillow's embrace.

'Lulu. I've got to go.'

This time the name he was using registered. She lifted her head, just a fraction. 'Don't call me that.' She tried opening her eyes but her eyelids resisted. The pillow drew her down; the blanket held her there.

Footsteps, the clinking of a set of keys. The muffled sound of water running, then more footsteps, almost to Lucia's side. She turned on to her back and forced her eyes open. She freed her hands from the covers and with her fingertips rubbed at the bridge of her nose.

'You snore, Lulu. You still snore.'

'I don't snore,' Lucia said. She sat up, so that only her legs remained under the blanket. 'And don't call me that.'

David shrugged on his jacket, adjusted his cuffs. 'Call you what?' He looked about him. 'Where's my phone? Have you seen my phone?'

'What you just called me. Don't call me that.'

'Lulu? I've always called you Lulu.'

'I know. But someone else does too. He heard you one time, I think.'

'Who does? Heard me what? Where the hell is my phone?'

Lucia's Nokia was on the coffee table. She reached for it and dialled the number she still knew by heart. 'Just someone I'd rather not be reminded of,' she said and lifted the phone to her ear. She heard the dialling tone and then, half a second later, the hollow echo of the soul tune that David had chosen as his ring tone. It was coming from his jacket pocket.

'That song,' said Lucia. 'That's our song.'

'You always said we didn't have a song. You always said having songs was corny.'

'I know. It is. But still.'

David disappeared into the kitchen. Lucia heard him open the fridge, lift out a bottle and take a swig of whatever was inside. He drifted back into the living room. 'I've got to go,' he said, yet he lingered just beyond the coffee table. He glanced towards the front door and then turned back to face Lucia. 'So,' he said. 'How does this work?'

'How does what work?'

'Well, do I kiss you goodbye or what?'

Lucia swung her legs from the couch and sat upright. 'What?' she said. 'No. Of course not. Why would you?'

David ran a palm from his crown to his forehead. His hair

had been cropped for as long as Lucia had known him but it seemed thinner now, the cut less a statement of fashion and more a muttered denial of the advancing years. It was no bad thing, Lucia thought. It made him look more vulnerable somehow. Less male. 'I don't know,' David said. 'You slept here. Usually when women sleep here I kiss them goodbye. Then I leave or they leave. More often they leave.'

'I didn't sleep *here*. I slept on your sofa. And what do you mean, when women sleep here? Who sleeps here? What women?'

David grinned. 'What's the matter, Lulu? Not jealous?'

Lucia laughed. In her head it sounded less than convincing. 'You and I both know that the only women who have ever spent the night in this flat are me, Barbarella over there—' she gestured to the poster on the wall '—and your mother. Oh, and Veronica. How could I forget about Veronica?'

'Victoria,' said David. 'It was Victoria, not Veronica.'

'Victoria, Veronica, Verucca. Whatever happened to her?'

David shifted, stroked his head again. 'She left. She got poached.'

'In boiling water?'

'By another firm. She got poached by another firm.'

'Well,' said Lucia. 'It was probably for the best. She wasn't your type, you know. Too hairy.'

'She wasn't hairy.'

'I saw her naked, David. She was hairy. She was downy.'

David shook his head. He made to leave, then stopped himself. 'What about you? Are you seeing anyone? Philip told me you weren't seeing anyone.'

'Philip's wrong,' said Lucia. 'I am seeing someone.'

'You're not seeing anyone.'

'I'm seeing someone. I am. His name is . . . '

'His name is?'

'His name's Harry. He's from work. We met at work.'

'Harry,' said David.

'Harry,' said Lucia.

David nodded. He grinned again. 'Right,' he said.

'What?' said Lucia.

'Nothing.'

'What? Nothing what?'

'Nothing nothing. It's just, well. If you're really seeing this Harry bloke, what are you doing here? On my sofa? Wearing one of my T-shirts and very little else?' His eyes slid below Lucia's waist. Lucia looked down and realised her legs, her thighs, were no longer under the blanket. She whipped the cover across.

'You have to go, David.'

'Huh? Oh shit. Shitshitshit.' David spun and darted from the room. Lucia heard shoes tumbling from the rack in the hallway. A moment later, David reappeared at the door. There was no trace now of his grin. 'Jesus Christ, Lucia. You're not . . . I mean, you aren't . . . '

This time when Lucia laughed it was with genuine amusement. 'How long has it been, David? Six months? Seven? I don't think even this T-shirt would have let me keep that quiet until morning.'

David's eyes closed. He breathed. He opened his eyes. 'Thank fuck,' he said. 'I mean, sorry, but . . . Thank fuck.'

Lucia tapped a finger against her wrist.

'Right,' said David and he disappeared again. He hollered to Lucia from the hallway. 'So what's up, Lulu? You turn up at my flat in the middle of the night—'

'It was nine-thirty, David.'

'—in the middle of the night, after six months in which you have basically refused even to talk to me. You eat three mouthfuls of the omelette I cook for you, then you fall asleep on my couch. If you're not pregnant, why are you here?' Again he poked his head around the doorframe. 'Do you need money? Is that it?'

'No! God no.'

'Because it's not a problem. I mean, I know it must be hard: with the flat, being on your own. I realise you don't get paid very much.'

'The flat's fine,' Lucia said. 'The money's fine.' Although as she spoke it occurred to her that it might not be fine for much longer. 'I just thought, I don't know. That we could have lunch or something.'

David was fiddling with his tie. He looked up. 'Lunch?'

Lucia nodded. 'Lunch. Just the two of us.' She realised immediately how this would have sounded. 'I mean, me and you. Not together, just alone. Not the two of us as in us.' She shut her eyes, waved a hand. 'Just lunch,' she said. 'Are you free?'

'For lunch?'

'That's right.'

'Just the two of us?'

Lucia sighed. 'Me and you, yes.'

David bobbed his head. 'Okay. Sure. I can do that. How about Ciullo's? On Charterhouse Street?'

'I'll find it. One o'clock?'

'One o'clock,' David echoed. He turned away, then reappeared at the door. 'You sure you're not pregnant?'

'I'm not pregnant, David. Cross my heart.'

'And you're sure about the kissing thing? Not even a peck on the cheek?'

'Not even that,' said Lucia.

It was the same apartment. The walls were still white, the carpet still green. The furniture was as it had been, in the same places, against the same walls, and looking only marginally more scuffed than it had before. Even Jane Fonda was a long-standing tenant, the result of a compromise Lucia and David had reached at the outset of their cohabitation and that Lucia had regretted for its duration: Lucia was granted veto on every other wall so long as Barbarella retained her position above the mantelpiece. She was framed, David had argued: that made her art. She was wearing rubber and squashing her tits together, Lucia had countered: that made her porn.

Much was the same then but everything seemed altered. There was the smell, for one thing. The bathroom, for instance, smelt of cleaning products, which meant it smelt like the toilets at work; the kitchen smelt of milk that had been spilt but not fully wiped up. In the living room, there was a new television. Flipped sideways it would have doubled as a dining table. There were speakers too. Dozens, it seemed, at random heights and angles. None was particularly large yet they loomed like security cameras in a lift. On the shelves, the space that had been vacated by Lucia's books had been infiltrated by the plastic boxes of DVDs, CDs and video games. There were bottles of spirits: Polish vodka, American bourbon, something yellow and Italian, all arranged like ornaments. And in various corners, cacti had been planted. Cacti were men's plants, Lucia had long ago decided: low maintenance, high bluster.

The sensation, Lucia thought, was of rediscovering a favourite jumper but realising, as you pulled it on, that it was actually a little tight, and it smelt musty, and the colour did not really suit you. As she readied herself to leave, she felt relief. She felt relief too that seeing David had not triggered in her the emotional relapse she had feared. She had loved him and for some time she had hated him but in the time that had passed since she had last seen him – and almost without her conscious self noticing – her feelings for him seemed to have settled between the two extremes. They were volatile still; they were treacherous. If he had insisted, for instance, and leant in to kiss her goodbye, she would not have stopped him. Some perfidious reflex might even have nudged her lips just a fraction closer to his. But he had not kissed her. As far as David was concerned, she had not let him. It felt like progress. Not victory, not quite that, but progress nonetheless.

She shut the door behind her. She slid her bag on to her shoulder and she Chubb-locked the door and she made her way to the stairwell. She allowed herself just a single glance back.

'David.'

'Lulu.'

'Please, David. Stop it.'

'Stop what? Oh.' He had been tapping a fingernail against his glass. He curled his fingers and slid his hand away.

'Not that. Stop . . . this. Stop smiling like that.'

'Like what?'

'Like you're on a date. You're not on a date.'

'It's not business.'

'It is. That's exactly what it is.'

David's smile broadened. 'Whatever you say, Lulu.'

'And stop calling me Lulu.' She turned her head away. 'You're not making this easy.'

The waiter arrived with the water Lucia had ordered. He made a fuss of placing it, clearing the wine glasses, presenting each of them with a menu. Lucia folded hers and set it to one side once the waiter had moved away. 'I need to talk to you,' she said. 'Am I going to be able to talk to you?'

'Sure,' David said. 'That's why we're here, right? To talk.' He leant in and reached for Lucia's hand. She let him take it, then snatched it back.

'David—'

'Lucia, look. I was wrong. Okay? I made a mistake and I've been paying for it ever since. Please, let me make things up to you.'

Lucia shook her head. She tucked her hands under the table. 'David. Listen to me.'

Before she could go any further, however, another waiter appeared beside them, pen and paper poised. Lucia picked up her menu and gestured for David to order first. He chose pasta. Lucia was looking for soup. When she found it, she changed her mind. 'Do you have chocolate cake?' she asked.

'We have a delightful Valrhona tart served with caramelised oranges.'

'Does it have chocolate in it?'

'It does, madam.'

'I'll have that,' Lucia said. 'Thank you.' She relinquished her menu.

The waiter retreated. Lucia looked back at David, who had his head slightly bowed and a hand on his forehead. She could not help but smile. Her order, she realised, had embarrassed him. It was a trait of his that she had forgotten: waiting staff intimidated him. A murderer, a rapist, even a crown court judge: none came close to having the same effect on David as a second-generation Italian in a bow tie bearing a notepad.

'David,' said Lucia. 'I need your help. That's why I'm here.'

'You said that already. You said that last night.'

'Yes. I know I did. But listen. It's the only reason I'm here.'

Doubt tugged at the edges of David's smile. 'But I thought you meant . . . I mean, when you said help, I thought you meant . . .'

'Sex.'

'No! Hell. Not sex.' A corner of his mouth twitched upwards. 'At least, not right away.'

Lucia rolled her eyes. 'I'm trying to be serious, David. I'm trying to have a serious conversation.'

'So am I, Lucia. I mean, what am I supposed to think? You can't deny that you've been giving me some mixed-up signals.'

'That's not true,' Lucia said. 'You know that's not true.'

'You hugged me. When you first saw me, you hugged me.'

'That was a reflex! It was platonic.'

'You were laughing at my jokes all evening. They weren't even that funny.'

'I was being polite, David. Your jokes are never particularly funny.'

'You let me kiss you goodnight.'

'You kissed me goodnight? When did you kiss me goodnight?'

'When you were lying down. On the couch.'

'Lying down? With my eyes closed? Sort of breathing heavily? That's called sleep, David. That's called being asleep. You may have kissed me but, trust me, there was no consent.'

David shifted. As he moved, the tablecloth twisted. He ran a hand across the surface to flatten it out. 'Well, anyway. The point is, you spent the night at my flat. Wearing just my T-shirt and a pair of knickers.'

Their table was tucked in one corner, against the bar and away from the entrance. Behind Lucia a Kentia palm loomed, close enough for her to feel the tips of its leaves against her hair. She felt prickles, too, of attention from the table across from theirs. When she spoke again, she kept her voice low. 'You need to get that image out of your head,' she said. 'Because it was a mistake. Clearly it was a mistake. I should have waited until morning. Maybe I shouldn't have come at all.' She made to stand. Before she could extricate herself from the palm, however, David reached across and put a hand on her forearm.

'Wait,' he said. 'Wait. Sit down, Lucia, please.'

The waiter arrived with their food, blocking Lucia's only path out of the restaurant. She hesitated. She glanced at David.

'Please,' he said. 'Please sit down.'

Lucia sat, on the edge of her chair, and the waiter set the plates in front of them. The tart was brown. As far as Lucia could tell, that was the only characteristic it shared with the chocolate cake she had pictured in her mind. She nudged her plate towards the centre of the table and watched as David prodded his pasta with his fork.

'Look, David. I'm sorry. If I gave you the wrong impression, I'm sorry. But surely you can't expect me . . . I mean, after what you did . . . '

David coughed. He gave the pasta another prod, then set down his fork and raised his head. 'What can I do, Lucia? You said you needed my help. What can I do?'

Lucia reached across the table and slid her fingers under his. She smiled. 'Thank you,' she said. 'Really.'

David shrugged. 'I haven't done anything yet. You haven't even told me what you want.'

'No,' said Lucia. She withdrew her hand. 'No, I haven't.'

'So? Tell me.'

'For the moment, all I need is information.'

'Information? What kind of information?'

Lucia propped her elbows in the space where her plate should have been. 'Start by telling me what you told Philip. After that . . . Well. After that, we'll just have to see.'

He showed me the gun.

Well, he didn't show me as such but I saw it. The week before the shooting, this was. We were in the staffroom and I was sitting next to him and I spotted it when he opened his briefcase.

I say *the* gun but I suppose it was just *a* gun. I'm only assuming it was the one he used. To be honest, it didn't even look like it would fire but that sort of tallies with what people have been saying. That it was an antique. A museum piece. From the war or something. That's what people are saying, isn't it?

So it was *the* gun, I suppose. It was wedged between a file and a stack of papers, like it was a Thermos flask or his lunch box or something. Like it was anything but what it was.

I say, Samuel, sort of laughing. That's not what I think it is, is it? He says, pardon me, and I nod. That, I say. In the case. It's not what I think it is.

Oh, says Samuel. Oh. You mean this?

And he lifts the lid of his case wide and picks up the gun by the handle. His finger finds the trigger and for a moment the barrel is pointing right at my head.

I sort of laugh again. I mean, I wouldn't make much of a policeman, would I? Someone points a gun at my head and all I can do is give a nervous giggle. But anyway, that's what I did. And I say, Samuel, I'd rather you . . . I mean if you could not please . . . So I giggle and I can't even finish a sentence.

Samuel says oh again. He says, no, no, no, don't worry. And he turns the barrel so it's pointing at the back of his case, at the upturned lid of his case, and beyond the lid, sitting opposite, is Terence, Terence Jones, TJ to those who know him, and Samuel's got the gun pointed right at him. And TJ can't see this because he's reading the newspaper and anyway the gun's still hidden by the briefcase. And Samuel, his finger's there on the trigger and I can tell he's about to squeeze. As in, fire. The gun. At TJ.

So what do I do?

I do nothing. I watch. It's all I can do. Like I say, you'd be happy to have me on the force.

But as it turns out the gun doesn't fire. Samuel pulls on the trigger but it sticks. It doesn't move. And Samuel looks up at me and he's not exactly smiling but he looks pretty pleased with himself nonetheless. Do you like cats, Inspector? I like cats. I have three. And Samuel looks like my tabby, Ingrid, when she's eaten her share of the giblets and Humphrey's and Bogart's too.

Samuel, I say. Really. And still I'm struggling to think what to say to him. Because it's not the type of situation you ever contemplate dealing with, is it? Not if you're someone like me. I'm interested, Inspector: how would you have reacted, do you think? If you had been me? Because you would have done what was right, I'm sure, and not just because of your training. Although I suppose it's perfectly obvious to me now. I should have wrestled the gun from him. I should have pinned him to the floor. I should have called for the headmaster, told the headmaster to call the police. That's what I should have done. That's what I wish I had done. Naturally that's what I wish.

But at the time I was waiting for an explanation. That's what rational human beings do, isn't it, when they're confronted with something beyond the scope of their everyday experience? They withhold judgement. They offer the benefit of the doubt. They fear the worst perhaps but they know deep down that there will be a perfectly reasonable explanation. That's the very phrase people use, in fact, isn't it? You'll see, they say. I'm sure there's a perfectly reasonable explanation.

And Samuel gave me one.

He drops the gun into the briefcase, rather carelessly. He clicks the briefcase shut. He says, it's real but it doesn't work. It hasn't worked since 1945. It was my grandfather's, he says. Or rather, it became my grandfather's. He stole it. Won it. However you want to look at it. He got it from a German, a Nazi. In Italy. My grandfather fought in Italy.

Which is fascinating, rather, isn't it? I teach religious studies but my subject and Samuel's are so intertwined that really the syllabuses should be merged. That's what I think anyway. Because what's the study of religion but social history? What's faith but an empathy with the past? But that's not why we teach religious studies, I'm told. My views, depending on who you talk to, are old-fashioned or avant-garde. Which is fine, I suppose. I'm not complaining. And I'm in danger of straying from the point. Which is, Inspector, that what Samuel said intrigued me. His explanation was logical and fascinating both. The gun was a relic from the war and he was, he told me, teaching his sixth-formers about Monte Cassino. He wanted to engage them, he said. Show them something that would bring them forwards on to their elbows rather than send them back on to their heels. Which is just the sort of thing Samuel would say because there was nothing he wanted more than to get his kids interested. I mean, all teachers, regardless of their subject, can empathise with the sentiment but for Samuel it had turned into a mission. He was committed. He was determined. He must have been, mustn't he? To put up with what he did. To keep coming into work after everything that happened.

So I'm convinced but still I manage to keep some sense about me.

Do you think that's wise? I ask him. It's a gun after all. And this is a school.

He shrugs.

I say, I mean it, Samuel. I really think you should be careful. The parents, the headmaster, the pupils for heaven's sake . . . Just imagine how they might react.

Now Samuel does smile and I don't like that smile at all. But it's a flicker, a spark that catches and then goes out, and after it fades it's hard to tell if it was even a spark at all. Maybe you're right, Samuel says. Maybe you're right.

I'm glad you think so, I say, because I really think . . . But then the bell goes and everyone gets up because it's the last double period before lunch. And neither one of us says anything more.

This would have been the Wednesday so it was exactly a week before. After that, I watched him fairly closely. As closely as I could, at any rate. It was hard, though, because we taught in different wings and neither one of us spent a great deal of time in the staffroom. We each had our reasons. He was a fairly solitary figure and I suppose I've always been one too. But I like to think that I am happy in my own company. There are moments, naturally, when I crave companionship and usually they coincide with times when there is none on offer. What's that – Murphy's law? Anyway, at school when I go to the staffroom it's usually to hear adult voices. Even TJ, for all his shortcomings, can seem a calming presence after you have been floundering all day amid the shrillness of youth. But Samuel: he was never happy in his own company. If this doesn't sound too self-important, Inspector, I've always seen myself as something of a spiritual barometer in this school. It's not a role anyone else would recognise, naturally, more an extension of my particular specialisation. Not even that, really. I'm just interested in people. That's all. I'm nosy, you might say. I like to know how people cope. Within themselves. What drives them. What undermines them. There's no great skill involved. You just have to listen more than you talk. You seem to listen well, Inspector, so I'm sure you know exactly what I mean. And with Samuel, it was obvious from the very start. Not that he would do what he did. Heavens. How could a balanced individual expect that of anyone? It was obvious, rather, that he was troubled. Sad. Sad is the word. Sad and lonely and unable to break from the mould into which his life had settled.

So he was vulnerable. Extraordinarily so. And he was having a difficult time, as you probably know. But though the gun worried me, I'm not sure that even then, at the time I saw it, he had decided he was going to use it. You're going to ask me why he was carrying it then, aren't you? Before the shooting I would have repeated to you his story. I believed him, mainly because I wanted to. Obviously, though, he was lying about it not working. Maybe the safety catch was on when he squeezed the trigger or something and that's why it didn't depress. I mean, is that how guns work? I'm not an expert on these things. He didn't show the gun to his sixth-formers either. I know he didn't because I asked – subtly of course – Alex Mills, one of the pupils that Samuel and I shared, when he was helping me clear away after class. At the time I was relieved. I assumed Samuel had seen sense and that the matter was at an end. It didn't occur to me that he'd never had any intention of show-ing the gun in class.

So why did he have it? I'll tell you what I think. You heard about TJ's behaviour, am I right? You heard about the children and how they treated him. Most important, I think, you heard about the football match. They broke his leg, Inspector. Delib-erately. Oh I know, I know, they claimed it was an accident and the headmaster believed them but he must have been the only one in the school who did. If indeed he really did. But can you imagine? These thugs had been hounding him for months and for a while Samuel might have been able to convince himself that it was all harmless – traumatic but physically harmless – but then they snap his fibula.

Have you ever broken your leg, Inspector?

A bone then? An arm perhaps?

Well, I have and let me tell you that it hurts. It's agony. I don't handle pain very well – I'd not make a very good woman, I'm afraid! – and Samuel didn't strike me as the stoical type either. So he was scared, Inspector. That's what I'm trying to say. Maybe the gun . . . I mean, he said it was his grandfather's. So just having it, carrying it with him, maybe it made him feel better. Safer. Less vulnerable. For all I know, he'd been carrying it since the football match. But like I say, that doesn't mean he intended to use it.

Something changed though. I was watching him, like I said, and at the beginning of the next week, the week of the shooting, something most definitely changed. I told you that I thought he was scared but I also think he kept it fairly well hidden. Like it was simmering. You know, like a pan on a gentle heat. But then, come Monday. Well. All of a sudden it was bubbling over. There was no hiding it any more. You only had to talk to him. You only had to watch him for a moment. Although, saying that, no one did. No one spoke to him. No one paid him any attention. He was Samuel, after all. The only person the teachers of this school go further out of their way to avoid is Mr Travis, and in the headmaster's case it is for entirely different reasons.

I spoke to him though. I was watching him. I noticed that the clothes he was wearing on the Monday were the ones he'd gone home in on the Friday. He had two suits, from what I could tell, one beige, one brown, and he never wore the same suit two days in a row. He changed his shirt every day too. And his tie. You wouldn't notice unless, well, unless you'd noticed but he had a strict rotation. Mondays it was one combination, Tuesdays it was another. There was no great diversity of style. I suspect the shirts had come five in a pack. The ties likewise. Not that I'm snobbish about such things. The clothes maketh the man, that's what they say, isn't it? Well Al Capone wore spats and Jesus Christ dressed in rags, which pretty much settles that argument in my mind. But I know how important such things are to other people, to the younger generation in particular. Just look at TJ, for instance. If he's not in a track-suit, he's wearing an Italian-made sports jacket and a tie with a knot the size of my fist. Like the footballers do when they're giving interviews after a game. So that's why I noticed it with Samuel. He was particular about such things, it seemed to me, but not for aesthetic reasons. It was as though he had estab-lished a system in order that he would no longer have to think about that system. On Mondays he wore suit A with shirt B and tie C. He just did.

So I realised immediately on the Monday. He was wearing Friday's outfit and Friday's wrinkles. Saturday's and Sunday's too, by the look of things. There were rings around his eyes, like a cartoonist would draw on a character who's just been beaten in a fight, and a web of red lines stretching across the white. What with the state of his clothes, I'd say he'd slept – if he'd slept at all – slouched in a chair or on the sofa or in the seat of his car.

It's the end of first break and he's drifting out of the

staffroom when I put my hand on his shoulder. As he turns, he spins and steps backwards. He stumbles on a chair leg and almost falls. TJ sees it happen and gives a snort. He makes some comment, some crack about having a good trip, and then he's gone and Samuel and I are the only ones left in the room.

Is everything okay? I ask him. Samuel, I say. He's watching the doorway, you see. Samuel, I say again. Is everything okay? You seem . . . well . . . I don't finish the sentence.

What? he says. Oh. Yes fine. Excuse me. And he tries to slip by but I take his arm. Again he flinches. Again he pulls away. What? he says. What is it?

Nothing, I say. I'm startled by his tone. It's aggressive. Defensive. Not like Samuel at all. I mean, usually when he spoke he was never anything but polite. To a fault really. He was courteous but courteous like a waiter in a fancy restaurant, one who doesn't necessarily own the place but certainly wouldn't offer you a table if he did.

Nothing, I say again. I just wondered, that's all. Whether everything was all right.

He laughs. A snort, really, like TJ's. Oh yes, he says. Everything's fine. Everything's wonderful. And he tries to get past me again.

I don't let him. I don't know why but it seems incredibly important all of a sudden that I talk to him, that I find out what's bothering him. So I reach and place an arm across the doorway.

Samuel looks at me. He glares at me. He says excuse me again but in a way that means you better had.

Samuel, please, I say. If there's something the matter you should talk about it.

And he laughs again, that same derisive grunt. He says, that's reasonable. I mean, you'd think that talking would help, wouldn't you?

I say, sorry?

But he doesn't elaborate. He just says excuse me again and this time I let him go. There doesn't seem to be any other choice.

It was only afterwards that I remembered about the gun. I'm walking to my classroom and my innards give a sudden lurch, like it's just occurred to me I've left something burning in the oven back home. I stop and I think and I tell myself there's nothing to worry about. He was upset about something, that was all. Something personal that wasn't any of my business. I had no right to pry and he had every right to be angry with me. And he'd explained about the gun. He'd demonstrated to me that it didn't even work. But when I thought about that, I thought about the expression I'd caught on his face after he had pointed the gun at TJ, that little flash of jubilation, and I grew anxious in spite of myself.

I asked around. Other teachers, even one or two of the pupils I trusted not to make a fuss. But no one had noticed anything strange. Like I said before, most of them barely noticed Samuel at all as a rule. No, nothing odd, they told me if they had seen him. No odder than usual. And they would laugh and I would smile and that would be the end of that.

In the afternoon, Samuel and I shared a free period. I knew we did but I checked the timetable just to be sure. So I went looking for him again. I would talk to him properly this time, I told myself. I would find out what was troubling him. I would ask him again about the gun. I would insist, if it came to it, that he hand it over to me, museum piece or not. But I couldn't find him. I looked in every classroom, in the staffroom, in the playground, in the girls' changing rooms for heaven's sake. I ended up in the secretary's office – you know, the room next to the headmaster's office, where Janet has her desk and where we keep all the registers and the staff rotas and that sort of thing – even though I knew he wouldn't be there. It was the last place I looked and when I didn't find him there I lingered. For no particular reason other than I didn't know where else to go. I leant against one of the filing cabinets and started to click my tongue against the roof of my mouth. It's a habit I have. Most annoying to those around me, I would imagine.

Everything okay, George? You look as stressed as I feel. This from Janet. She's seated at her desk.

I don't reply. I give a grunt maybe.

George? she says again. I look at her and she's smiling. She's waiting.

Yes, Janet. Thanks. Everything's fine. I push myself away from the filing cabinet and I'm about to leave. Then I say, you haven't seen Samuel have you, Janet?

Samuel? she says.

Samuel. Samuel Szajkowski.

No, she says. Then, yes. That is, he's gone home, she says. The headmaster sent him home. I ... um ... don't think he was feeling very well.

Oh, I say. Oh. And I'm pondering this as I make to leave.

With one word, though, Janet stops me. She asks me why. And I don't really notice at the time but it's a suspicious why. A defensive why. Like you'd say to a friend who's just asked you how much money you have in your wallet.

No reason, I say. It's not important. And this time I do leave. And do you know what, Inspector? I wish now that I hadn't. Given what has happened. The benefit of hindsight and all that. Because there was something more to it. I know there was and I realise now that Janet knew there was. And it doesn't take much to get Janet talking. That's why I left, in fact. She can trap you, just with her eyes and her tongue, from the opposite corner of a room. She would have told me what she knew if only I had asked. I wouldn't even have had to ask, come to that. All I would have needed to do was provide her with an opening.

Instead I spent the rest of my free period trying to concentrate on marking papers. After that I had classes. The next day, the Tuesday, Samuel didn't come to school at all. He was still ill, that was all I could find out. Then, on Wednesday morning, I saw him. I was in the staffroom and I must admit I had almost forgotten why I was so desperate to find him. Not forgotten exactly. My unease, rather, had become more like idle curiosity. Only when he walked through the door, just as everyone else was filing out, did that sense of urgency reassert itself.

He's still wearing the same suit, the same shirt, the same tie. This time there's no doubting that his clothes are unwashed, stained, crumpled. Also, he smells. I can tell he smells even from the distance I am away from him because the teachers he passes wince, they wrinkle their noses, they pull back so as not to brush against him. It's time for assembly – it's time for *the* assembly – but I hang back anyway to try and talk to him. Vicky Long, though – she grabs my arm. She starts walking and talking and dragging me towards the door. I try to extricate myself but before I know it I'm in the corridor and Samuel's left alone in the staffroom. Vicky's talking to me about the musical she's directing. An end-of-term performance of *Oklahoma!* She's short a cowboy and she's hoping I'll agree to step in. There are only a few lines, she tells me, and practically no singing. There's a dance or two but nothing complicated. A jig. A two-step. I'd have them down in fifteen minutes. Thirty minutes maybe – fifteen minutes a dance. So what do I say? Will I do it? It will be such fun, she promises me. Will I do it then? What do I say?

I don't say anything. I'm in the assembly hall now, climbing the steps to the stage. I'm taking my seat and something or someone catches Vicky's attention and she drifts towards the seats on the other side of the lectern. I look down at the rows in front of me. The children are already seated. Some are whispering, one or two are laughing, giggling really, but most are sombre. They've caught on to the mood that the headmaster's summons sought to convey. They know that there has been trouble. They know that the headmaster is about to put on a show.

I'm still looking for Samuel when Mr Travis walks in. He closes the rear set of doors behind him, with a click that is more ominous somehow than if he had slammed them shut. Silence. The children stare ahead, at their hands in their laps, at their feet. A few affect nonchalance, bravado. There are two empty seats on the stage: one behind the lectern, the other at the lectern end of Vicky's row. None of the other teachers seem to notice, however. They are watching the headmaster as he strides the length of the hall. He's wearing a grey suit and a black tie. His shoes are polished to a military sheen. His footsteps are not loud but they resonate. They are as relentless and as purposeful as a countdown.

The rest, Inspector, I believe you know. I did not get a chance to talk to Samuel. I did not make that chance. Whether I would have been able to change anything anyway, I'll never know. Possibly I would have. Probably what happened next would still have found a way to happen.

It's not much of a consolation, is it? It's not much of a consolation at all.

At the gate, Lucia paused. David had already stepped through and was several paces closer to the door. He turned when he realised Lucia was no longer at his shoulder.

'What is it?' he said.

Lucia looked up at the house. It seemed empty. Abandoned almost. There was no movement at any of the windows. All the upstairs curtains were drawn, in fact, including those in Elliot's room. Through the bay window downstairs Lucia could see an empty sofa, a coffee table bearing a stack of coasters and nothing else, a carpet devoid of toys, magazines, rogue shoes or slippers: anything that would suggest the house was still inhabited. The television in the corner was switched off.

She stepped through the gate and refastened the latch. She sensed David watching her as she passed him. 'Second thoughts?' he said but she ignored him.

A freesheet protruded from the letterbox. From its pages, a clutch of flyers had fallen on to the doormat. Lucia looked for a doorbell but could not find one. She glanced at David, then turned back to the door and twice tapped her knuckles against one of the frosted-glass panels.

'No one's going to hear that,' David said.

But a moment later they registered footsteps. Someone was coming down the stairs, in a hurry it seemed. The steps ended with a thump and for a second or two there was silence. Then a chain rattled and a lock clicked and the door unstuck itself from its frame as whoever was inside tugged it inwards. A girl's face appeared, level with Lucia's midriff.

She did not look like Elliot. Her hair was so blonde it might almost have been bleached. If she had freckles, they would have been the kind that only came out in the sun. And her eyes were blue, whereas Elliot's had been a muddy grey. Her nose, slightly squashed, may have resembled her brother's; the worry lines on her forehead too. It was the girl's expression, though, that most reminded Lucia of Elliot. In the set of her features she seemed apprehensive, almost fearful.

When she spoke, however, there was no trace of Elliot's timidity. 'Yes?' she said.

'Hi,' Lucia replied. 'You must be Sophie.'

The girl frowned. She turned to look at David and her frown deepened. 'Who are you?'

'This is David. My name's Lucia. Is your father home, honey? Your mother?'

'Are you reporters?'

Lucia shook her head. 'No. We're not reporters.'

The girl's eyes narrowed. 'What's the password?'

Lucia looked at David. David looked at Lucia.

'Password?' Lucia said. 'I don't think we know the password. If you could just—'

The door closed. Lucia was left staring at the flaking mustard paintwork.

'So,' David said. 'What now?'

Lucia hesitated, then knocked once more, louder than she had the first time. Even as she withdrew her hand, however, there was a rattle and the door was pulled wide. Elliot's father stood just across the threshold. His daughter was seated at the bottom of the stairs in the hallway, her chin in her upturned palms, her eyes fixed on Lucia and David: intruders.

'Detective Inspector May,' Samson said. He seemed barely to notice David. Even as Lucia introduced her companion, Samson's handshake was cursory, mechanical, uninterested. 'Come in,' he said. 'Fetch your mother, Sophie. And clear away your things.'

There was a book lying face down to the side of one of the stairs. Sophie snatched it up and stomped her way to the landing.

'Sorry about that,' Samson muttered and gestured them into the lounge. David thanked him. Lucia led the way.

'Have a seat,' said Samson and they sat, side by side on the pale-green sofa Lucia had seen through the window from the porch. She found herself sinking back into the upholstery but resisted, shifting herself forwards until she was perched on the edge of the seat, her feet drawn in beneath her and her hands clasped together in her lap. David mimicked her pose.

'Excuse the mess,' Samson said but there was no mess. He was referring, Lucia assumed, to the boxes piled in the dining area at the far end of the room. Lucia could not tell what was packed inside them but the lounge itself had been stripped of adornments. Only the furniture, a few pictures and, tucked between cushion and arm on Lucia's end of the sofa, a copy of that day's *Times* remained. Lucia recalled the dishevelment she had spied the last time she had been in the house: the piles of books, the coats and shoes in the hall, Sophie's bike, the remnants of breakfast scattered like crumbs; all the trappings, in short, of a family home straining to accommodate its occupants.

'You're moving?' Lucia said but Samson shook his head.

'Just having a clear-out. Getting rid of a few things. Junk. Kids' stuff mainly. I should offer you tea. Or coffee?'

David looked to Lucia. Lucia shook her head. 'We're fine. Thank you.'

The room fell silent. Samson lingered by the door, one hand gripping the handle. He glanced at the chair opposite the sofa and moved towards it, reaching as he did so like a toddler wary of a fall. He lowered himself on to the arm, his knees still pointing towards the door.

They waited. David cleared his throat.

When Elliot's mother entered the lounge, Lucia and David stood. Like her husband, Frances Samson looked tired. She looked, too, like she had been crying. There was a handkerchief barely concealed in one of her fists. Her hair was combed but bunched back in an unglamorous knot. She wore jeans and a shirt, untucked, that might once have belonged to her husband.

Lucia took a step forwards but Elliot's mother merely

nodded and slid away, until she was barricaded behind the armchair. Samson remained perched on the arm. To an observer, they would have seemed the reluctant callers, Lucia and David the uneasy hosts. Sophie remained out of sight but Lucia had the impression that she was lurking at the top of the stairs.

'Thank you for seeing us,' Lucia said. 'I realise you're probably both very busy.'

To Lucia's surprise, Samson laughed. The sound was bitter, almost derisive. 'Not that busy, Inspector. Not busy enough, if you want the truth.'

Samson's wife put a hand on his shoulder. 'Paul,' she said. Samson did not turn around and her hand dropped away.

'What do you want, Inspector? Why are you here? Forgive me for being so blunt but your call – it was somewhat unexpected.'

Lucia nodded. 'This is David Wells,' she said, looking at Samson's wife. 'He's a solicitor. A very good solicitor.'

David mumbled something. He tugged at one of his trouser legs, fiddled with a cufflink.

'David's firm was involved in a case some time back. It was several years ago now but it's relevant. To your situation. To what happened to your son.'

Now Samson began to fidget. He said nothing.

'There was a boy,' Lucia continued, addressing Elliot's father again. 'He had problems at school, just like Elliot.'

'Elliot didn't have problems, Inspector. He was bullied. The problems weren't his. They were forced upon him.'

Again Lucia nodded. 'What I mean to say is, this boy was

bullied too. He was persecuted, just like your son. In different ways perhaps. Through different means. But he suffered.'

'That's very sad, Inspector. What's your point?'

'Call me Lucia, please. This isn't exactly an official visit.'

'Lucia then. What's your point?'

'Perhaps it would be best if David explained.'

David coughed. He shuffled. 'I should say,' he began, 'that I wasn't involved in the case myself. This was before my time. Before my time at Blake, Henry and Lorne, I mean. But I'd heard about it. And after Lucia here came calling, I did some reading. So I'm pretty much up to speed.'

Samson frowned. His wife too.

'Anyway,' said David. 'Basically what happened is this. There's a boy, Leo Martin, he's sixteen, he takes his GCSEs and he fails, I suppose, about half of them. Which no one expects him to do because he's a bright kid. Very bright, as in he should be getting straight As or A stars or whatever it was in 2002. So his parents kick up a fuss, start by blaming the exam board, and there's this whole hullabaloo, and after the parents and the school dig a little deeper, it turns out that the reason Leo failed is that the time his parents thought he was spending studying for his exams in the school library, he was actually doing coursework for a bunch of kids in the year below him. I mean, they're younger but they're bigger and they're meaner. And for some time they've been tormenting this kid, terroris- ing him, threatening him. They threatened his sister too, who's ten or eleven or younger anyway, and the only way Leo can get them to leave her alone is to play their little pet. You know, doing the dares they set, stealing the stuff they tell him to steal, putting up with their beatings and, eventually, doing their schoolwork for them when it looks like they're about to fail themselves.'

Samson's eyes drifted into the hallway, searching for his daughter, Lucia assumed. David noticed and paused. 'I should say allegedly. I mean, all of this, it's what the parents claimed. Later, in court. They sued, you see. They sued the school.'

'Why?'

David turned to Elliot's mother. 'Pardon me?'

'I said, why? Why did they sue the school? If they had to sue anyone, why not the parents of the kids who did this to him?'

'Their argument – my firm's argument – was that it was the school's responsibility to protect the children under its charge. The bullying, for the most part, happened on school premises, during school hours, when the school, effectively, assumed the role of parent in monitoring the behaviour and the well-being of its students. Our position was, what could the parents of these kids have done, even if they had known what was going on? They weren't there.'

Elliot's mother shook her head. 'I don't agree. The parents are responsible. The parents are always responsible.'

'I think,' said Lucia, 'I think the point David's firm was making is that the school had a duty of care. Just like businesses have a duty to their employees, to their customers, but all the more so because schools are in a unique position of trust.'

Elliot's mother did not respond. Her lips drew tight. She looked down at her hands and poked a protruding corner of handkerchief back behind her knuckles.

'Right,' said David. 'That's right. So that's what we said. The school was neglectful. The school was negligent. The school, through its inaction, directly contributed to the physical and mental distress suffered by Leo Martin, and to the otherwise unaccountable dip in his academic performance. Which, needless to say, would have a tangible impact on his future earning potential.'

'So it was about money?' said Elliot's mother. 'For this boy's parents, it was about money?'

David held her eye. 'Yes,' he said. 'Essentially.'

'In this case,' Lucia added. 'In this case it was about money.'

'And in our case?' said Elliot's father. 'In our case, what would it be about? I mean, I assume that's why you're here. You, you're touting for business. And you.' He glowered at Lucia. 'You're working on commission, am I right?'

'Now wait a minute—' David said but Lucia, returning Samson's gaze, put a hand on David's arm.

'That's not why we're here, Mr Samson. I promise you that's not why we're here.'

'But you just said—'

'I said in Leo Martin's case, money came into it. The important thing – the reason we're telling you this – is because of the precedent.'

Samson was shaking his head. 'I don't buy that. What else is this about, if it's not about the money?'

Lucia sighed. 'The school,' she said. 'It's not as innocent as you think. It's not innocent full stop. The bullying there is endemic. It's not just Elliot. It's not even just the pupils. And the school ignores it. The school averts its eyes like it was some obscenity scrawled on a wall.' She was leaning forwards now. Her knees were pressed against the coffee table. 'You told me yourself, Mr Samson. They're in the process of arranging private funding. What do you think would happen to that funding if the truth were to come out?'

'You're wrong,' said Elliot's mother. 'The school's been good to us. The school's been supportive. They sent us flowers. The headmaster, he wrote a letter.' She was close to tears, Lucia realised. Her handkerchief was unfurled. 'And what about Sophie?' Frances Samson continued. 'Sophie's due to start there the September after next. What kind of parents would we be to put the prospect of a financial settlement above the education of our daughter?'

'Right,' said her husband. 'Quite right. And what about you?' He turned to David. 'What's in it for you? I mean, you're a solicitor, right? Why are you here if not for your twenty per cent?'

David's back straightened. 'I'm here because Lucia asked me to be here. I can leave. If you want me to, I can leave. Believe me, there are other things I could be doing with my time.' He stood. Lucia rose too.

'Please,' she said. 'David, please sit down. Mr Samson, Mrs Samson: this was my idea, not David's. David is here as a courtesy. He doesn't stand to gain from this at all.'

Elliot's father scoffed.

'My firm doesn't even know I'm here,' said David, still standing. 'Probably they wouldn't want to get involved. I don't know. If you decided to go ahead, I'd have to talk to them. Possibly they would see an upside in the publicity. It never hurts being on the victim's side. Even if it is a losing side.'

Lucia's head sank. She found herself unable to watch the Samsons' reactions.

'A losing side?' said Elliot's father. 'You mean we wouldn't win? Even if we agreed to this, you're saying we wouldn't win?'

'It's unlikely,' Lucia conceded.

'It's a virtual certainty, I'm afraid, that you would lose.'

Lucia raised her head. 'Sit down, David, for Christ's sake.' She looked across at Elliot's father. He was smiling an incredulous smile.

'So this boy,' he said. 'This boy whose parents sued. He lost. He lost and the school won.'

David finally sat back down, so far forward on the seat that he was in danger of sliding off. He regarded Samson for a moment, then he nodded.

'So the jury—'

'The judge.'

'The judge, then. Whatever. The judge agreed with us. He said what we said.'

David did not answer. He glanced at Lucia, ceding the floor to her.

'It wasn't entirely straightforward,' Lucia said. 'Things came out in the hearing. Not about the boy, not about the school – as far as we know, everything happened just as David said it did. But the parents. There were question marks. They'd spent some time in the States and brought back with them a certain . . . That is, they had a tendency . . . '

'They liked to sue,' David said. 'It didn't reflect well.'

'So what would be the point? Why bother? My wife and I, my family, we're moving on.' Samson noticed Lucia's eyes dart to the pile of boxes and his expression became rigid. 'We're trying. All right? We're doing our best. Why would we want to jeopardise that?'

'Mr Samson,' Lucia replied, 'the last thing I would ask you to do is jeopardise your family's welfare. What I'm asking is that you do just the opposite. I'm asking you to protect your daughter, your daughter's friends. I'm asking you to create such a stink that the school has to do something. It has to accept responsibility and act to make sure that what happened to Elliot doesn't happen to anyone else's child.'

Now Samson stood. 'Listen to me, Inspector. We've said this before but clearly you need it repeated. What happened to Elliot, what happened to our son – it wasn't the school's fault. What the hell could they have done? If you have some scheme that would allow us to punish the idiots – the animals – who are responsible for Elliot's death, then maybe we'll listen. If not, if this is the best that you can come up with, then, well. I suggest you and your friend here show yourselves out.'

Samson took a step forwards. He was not a big man but he loomed over Lucia where she sat. Lucia, though, did not move. 'Remind me, Mr Samson,' she said. 'Why was it that nothing was done after Elliot was attacked? Why were the boys who beat him – the boys who bit him and cut him – why were they allowed to walk free?'

'Because no one saw, Inspector. No one saw them do it. That's what you told us, remember? That's what your colleagues told us.'

'That's right. That's what we said. We spoke to everyone we could and everyone told us the same thing. Elliot's friends.

Elliot's teachers. Even Elliot's headmaster. They all told us that no one saw.' Lucia reached down to her ankles and into her bag.

'What's that?' said Samson. 'What have you got there? Is that a tape recorder? You're not recording this, are you?'

Lucia placed the tape recorder on the table in front of her. 'Just listen,' she said. 'Please.'

Samson hesitated. He turned to his wife, who shrugged. Lucia waited until he had lowered himself again on to the arm of the chair. She pressed play.

Repeat what? Which bit? You mean what he said? I saw them. Something like that. He said, I saw them and they saw me.

But really, Inspector, it was just Samuel being Samuel, just like I said to the headmaster. I'll tell you what happened, of course I will, but with Samuel it was always the same. The headmaster, he came to despair of him. History teachers, he would mutter, and it's true: we never did have much luck with history teachers. Amelia Evans, for example. She taught history before Samuel. And oh dear. What a shock she had. She came to us from a grammar school. An all-girls grammar school. She told the headmaster she wanted a challenge. She used those very words. I was sitting right here, a bit closer to the door maybe, and I heard her use those very words in her interview. Well. A challenge I suppose is one word for what the children gave her. A nervous breakdown is another. So there was Amelia and before her there was Colin Thomas, who it turned out was on a list that meant he shouldn't even have been within shouting distance of the children, and before that there was Erica, Erica something or other, a nice enough girl, I thought, until one day she just didn't turn up. Not a phone call, not a letter and not a sign of her ever since. And of course there was Samuel himself.

He was too polite, that was the problem. It seems a ridiculous thing to say now, given what he did, but I could have told you at the start that there would be trouble, I could have told you that there would be tears.

Although not this kind of trouble. I mean, how could anyone have predicted this? I'm sitting here and we're talking about what happened and I know that Samuel did it, that a hundred people say he did it, they saw him do it, but still I just don't believe it. I suppose it's one of those things you'll never quite believe unless you've seen it happen with your own eyes. And I didn't. Thank heavens. Thank heavens I didn't because something like that, I don't know what I would have done. I don't know how it would have affected me. I have such trouble sleeping these days as it is. It's the pressure of work. All this work. I have trouble just switching off. I take these tablets, my Jessica gave them to me. Jessica's the middle one, the brightest one really – not the best presented, that would be Chloe, my youngest – but the brightest. And I don't want to seem ungrateful but they're not proper tablets. They're what do you call it. Complementary. Which means they're about as much use to me as a goldfish in a pillowcase. Jessica, she works for Holland & Barrett. Katie, my eldest, got her the job and she's deputy assistant manager now, which is wonderful. But the things she brings home. The rubbish she gives me to take. I tell you, you can keep your herbal Nytol. Give me half a diazepam and a large glass of something French any night of the week.

But Samuel. We were talking about Samuel. He was always so very polite, you see. Not like some of the teachers we've had here. Some of the teachers we have here. Really, it's no wonder that children these days are turning out the way they do when you look at the example they're being set. Terence is a tease, he makes me smile sometimes in spite of myself. But some of the language he comes out with. Honestly. And it's not just Terence. Vicky's as bad. Christina's as bad. And George. George Roth. He's a nice enough fellow and I've never heard him swear but I'm still not sure that it's right. He's a homosexual, you see. Which I don't have a problem with. Live and let live, that's what I always say. But a homosexual teaching Christian values. To children. I don't know. Maybe it's just my upbringing. Maybe I'm old before my time. But that, to me, does not seem right.

So I worried about Samuel. I really did. He never seemed quite cut out for it. He never seemed quite tough enough. I hear things, you see, Inspector. I don't listen out for things but being in my position, being as close to the headmaster as I am – emotionally, it goes without saying, but also with my office being where it is – it's not always easy not to hear things, even when you do your best not to listen. And not a month after he started, Samuel was in with the headmaster. I didn't catch every word of what was said. The headmaster, he has such a clear voice, such an authoritative voice – a newsreader's voice I always tell him – but Samuel, it used to sound through the door like he was talking into his sleeve. Still, I heard enough to know that he was finding it difficult. I heard enough to make me wonder whether teaching was really for him.

And it was more than once. It got to the point I had to make up excuses, tell Samuel that the headmaster was in a meeting, on a call, out of his office even though he's hardly ever out of his office, I mean he's so committed to this school. He's another one, you see. We're very similar, he and I. He can't help it either but he really shouldn't be working himself so hard. And I tell him that. I say to him, you've earned a break, Headmaster. Let someone else shoulder some of the responsibility. And he tells me not to nag, not to make a fuss but if I don't make a fuss then . . . Well. Who will?

He'd speak to Samuel more often than not of course but what could he do? I'm finding it hard, Samuel would say, like he was expecting the headmaster to wave some magic wand. Thinking about it, though, this was mainly in the autumn term, Samuel's first. After that, Samuel stopped being such a nuisance. He seemed to understand that there were certain things he should really have been able to sort out for himself. He came when he was summoned of course. He came to discuss lesson plans and the syllabus and exam results and the like. Just like every teacher really. But otherwise he became a rare visitor to our little corner of the school. He kept himself to himself. That's why it was such a surprise when I found him here on the Monday morning, the Monday before the shooting.

First thing, this was, like I was saying. The headmaster wasn't even in yet. I was just arriving and invariably I'm about the first. Not that I get paid for coming in early but I have to if I'm to make it home at a respectable hour. But Samuel was waiting. He was sitting just out there on the floor, his back against my door, his knees tucked up against his chest. When he sees me he jumps right up. He says, I need to see the headmaster. No good morning, no hello, Janet, how was your weekend? Just that: I need to see the headmaster. So I say to him, good morning, Samuel. What are you doing here so early? And he says, is he in? The headmaster: is he in? And I say, it's only just seven o'clock. The headmaster arrives at fifteen minutes past. I'll tell him you were here, shall I? Because I'm thinking, I've just arrived and I've a pile of things to sort through and I don't really have time to sit and natter. Particularly with someone like Samuel, who was always very courteous as I say but not really one for a natter. He seemed to be missing the gene.

Samuel looks at his watch. He frowns and looks around him, like he's worried someone's been sneaking up on him while his attention's been on me. He says, I'll wait. I'll just wait here. And I say, really, Samuel, the headmaster has a lot on his plate this morning. I think it would be better if you came back later. But he just slides to the floor. He doesn't say anything else. He just sits there, like people used to do in the sixties.

When the headmaster arrives I'm at my desk. Every morning he comes through my office to get to his so I can give him the morning's post and his newspaper and his cup of coffee. He has it black, with sugar just up to the rim of the spoon. So I get to my feet when I hear him and I'm trying to think what I can say to make it plain that I did my best but Samuel, he just wouldn't leave. But I'm looking at the door and it doesn't open. I hear them talking outside, both at once it seems to me, but the walls are thicker between here and the corridor so I hardly catch a word. All of a sudden, though, they're in the headmaster's room next door and this wall, it's only a partition.

I saw them. That's when he said it. I saw them and they saw me. And he's not talking in his usual tone of voice, I mean there's nothing muffled about it now so I can tell he's got himself all in a fluster. And I'm standing there with the headmaster's coffee and I roll my eyes and I'm debating whether to knock or instead to just leave them to it. I leave them to it.

Who? the headmaster says. Who did you see? Calm down, for pity's sake, man.

You have to help me, says Samuel. You have to do something. They'll come after me, I know they will.

The poor headmaster, I can tell he's losing his patience. What are you talking about? he says. Who did you see?

Who? says Samuel. You know who. Donovan. Gideon. The two of them and their mates.

Donovan Stanley, Inspector. One of the boys who was shot, as things turned out. I assume that's who Samuel meant. Donovan and his best friend Gideon. Always causing mischief, those two. Just silly stuff, usually, just boys' stuff, nothing for Samuel to make such a fuss about. I mean this was exactly the type of thing Samuel and the headmaster had been through before. This was exactly the type of thing. And I thought Samuel had got a grip on things but clearly he hadn't. He was out of his depth: that's the plain truth of it. Working in a school: it's not as easy as people assume.

I don't have time for this, Mr Szajkowski, the headmaster says and he didn't. I could vouch for the fact that he didn't. There was a big meeting that morning, you see. With the governors and some special guests. A very important meeting for the future of the school. The headmaster was excited. Truly,

I've never seen him so excited. So it was very reasonable, really, that the headmaster should show Samuel to the door.

Samuel says, please, Headmaster. Please.

Mr Szajkowski, the headmaster says. Get a grip on yourself. You can't go behaving like this in front of the children. You're a teacher, man. Set an example.

And now it sounds like the headmaster is over by the door, and Samuel, Samuel's shuffling around in front of the headmaster's desk. Then there's silence for a moment, neither one of them says anything. Until the headmaster speaks again. He says, well, Mr Szajkowski, I really must be getting on. And Samuel doesn't reply. He doesn't say anything, nothing that I can hear. He leaves, I suppose. I don't hear him leave but I suppose that's what he does because the door clicks and there's quiet again and then the headmaster appears in my office.

So that's it. I mean it's not very helpful, I don't suppose but, yes, that's just about it. That was the last time I saw Samuel.

No. Wait a minute. I saw him later. Of course I saw him later. How silly of me. I saw him later to send him home. The headmaster asked me to, you see. After the police arrived. After they left, actually; after they'd told us about Elliot Samson.

Elliot's a first-year here. Year seven we call them now. He was attacked, Inspector. Beaten up quite badly, by all accounts. It happened after school on the Friday but we didn't hear about it until the Monday morning. Your colleagues arrived at about ten. Price, one of them was called. I didn't catch the other one's name. That's when they told the headmaster. That's when he and I found out. This was after the business with

Samuel but before the governors' meeting, although in the end that had to be postponed.

The headmaster and I are in my office. The police have just left, as I say. We're both a little shocked, I suppose. I mean the headmaster, he looks dreadfully pale. And I say to the headmaster, what a terrible thing to have happened. Because it was. Terrible, just terrible. And the headmaster nods and doesn't say anything and we're both just looking at the floor.

Then the headmaster says, Janet. Have you heard any more from Samuel?

I say, no, Headmaster, not a thing. Nothing since first thing.

And the headmaster looks at me. He says, first thing? You mean you heard all that this morning? He's looking at me like suddenly I've done something awful but I could hardly help overhearing, could I? And I'm standing there not knowing what to say and I say, no, well, yes, I mean the walls are very thin. And he sort of frowns. He says, what did you hear? What did you make of it?

I say, make of it, Headmaster? I couldn't very well make anything of it. It was just Samuel. Just Samuel being Samuel.

And the headmaster says, yes. Well. Quite. Still, he says, and then he's thinking. He says, Janet. Do me a favour, would you?

Of course, Headmaster. What is it?

He says, send Samuel home.

I say, home, Headmaster, and he says, home. Let's see, he says. It's almost lunchtime. He should be in the new wing, classroom three or four. Catch him there and send him home. Tell him to take some time off. The police, they'll be back this afternoon to follow up on this Samson business. They want to talk to the children. To the staff too. I don't think Samuel's really up to that. Not in the state he's in.

I say, no, Headmaster. You're probably right.

Good, he says. Good. Oh, and Janet.

Yes, Headmaster?

What did you tell the governors? Did you reschedule?

I told them something urgent had come up. I told them I was waiting to talk to you.

See if you can set it up for tomorrow morning. Send my apologies and tell them what's happened but make it clear that the assault took place outside of school. I don't want them worrying. I don't want them distracted.

Yes, Headmaster. I'll do it right away, Headmaster.

After you've dealt with Samuel, he says.

I say, of course. After I've dealt with Samuel.

One more thing, he says. I suppose we should schedule an assembly. Better make it Wednesday. First thing. All the pupils are to be there. All the staff too. No exceptions, Janet.

And I say, yes, Headmaster. Will there be anything else, Headmaster?

But there isn't anything else so that's when I go looking for Samuel. He's in classroom three, just as the headmaster said he would be. Although I could have found him without directions because the classroom, it's utter chaos. The new wing – we call it the new wing but really it's not so new any more, it must be ten years old at least – the new wing is right at the northern end of the building but I can hear Samuel's class from the dining hall. He's teaching year sevens. I say teaching but when I look through the glass he doesn't seem to be doing very much of anything. He's at his desk. He's leant forwards on his elbows and he's got one hand on his head. The children, they seem to be doing whatever they feel like doing: just chatting, most of them, but one or two are running about and there's even one little girl standing on a chair, over by the window, I mean she's virtually falling out. And I probably should have interrupted but I don't. I just wait outside until the bell.

After a minute or two it goes and it's barely finished ringing before the children are out the door. The ruckus seems to nudge Samuel from his daydream and slowly he gets to his feet. I'm waiting for him by the door.

I smile at him but he doesn't smile back. He would have walked right past me if I hadn't said his name.

Janet, he says. What do you want?

Which is not the way to talk to someone, is it? It's not the way to talk to one of your colleagues and not what I would have expected of him. So I was rather brusque, I'm afraid. I say, the headmaster says to go home. He says to take some rest. He doesn't expect you here this afternoon, nor tomorrow I assume.

Is that all? says Samuel and he's already walking away.

I say, yes. I'm rather taken aback. I say, yes, then I say, no. Because I forgot to tell him about the assembly. So then I say, you're to be here on Wednesday morning. The headmaster will be addressing the school, to talk about what happened to Elliot Samson. And Samuel can't know what I'm talking about but he doesn't even wait for me to explain. He just leaves. He looks at me, he looks me in the eye, and then he leaves.

And that, Inspector, was the last I saw of him. It was the

very last time I saw him. I don't suppose I've been very helpful but I don't know what else I can tell you. I saw Samuel in
the morning and he was upset about something but I couldn't
say what. It was unusual, his behaviour, but not that unusual,
not for Samuel. Then the police arrived and there was this
business about Elliot, which was terrible of course, truly dread-
ful. Although he is getting better, so I'm told. He's in hospital
but he's doing fine, which is one piece of good news at least.
But yes, the police arrived and then I spoke to the headmaster
and we agreed it would be best if we sent Samuel home. So I
found him and I did. And that's it. That's everything. I mean,
if there's anything else, I can't think of it. Because I'd tell
you if there was, of course I would. Because I do tend to talk,
Inspector. I do tend to prattle on. You've probably realised that
for yourself. Most people have to stop me. It's not always easy
once I get going but most people have to stop me from saying
too much.

It was the hottest day.

Ever, said the headlines. Since records began, ran the small print. It was like labouring up an incline, Lucia thought, and finally reaching the summit. Although it occurred to her too that it in fact felt no hotter than yesterday, than any other day since the heatwave had begun.

She entered the lobby and nodded a greeting to the staff at the desk. A facilities worker wheeled up a trolley beside her as she waited for the lift, and when the doors to the elevator shuddered open, she gestured him in ahead of her before squeezing in behind. Lucia pressed button three. The facilities worker pressed six. The doors closed and a motor whined and the winch strained audibly to hoist them upwards. Lucia focused on her distorted reflection in the chipped brass panelling of the doors, her thigh pressing against the metal handle of the trolley and the aroma of coffee from the urn on top making the air seem thicker and more humid than it already was.

The whole cast was assembled. Harry was there, Walter was there, his two goons huddled beside him. No court appear-

284

ances today. No suspects to interrogate, no crime to solve. No reason to be anywhere but as close to centre stage as possible.

Lucia caught Harry's eye and offered him a glimpse of a smile. She crossed the office and stopped at Cole's door. It was closed so she knocked and she waited. She tucked a loose strand of hair behind her ear. She breathed.

'Come in,' a voice called.

Lucia glanced at Harry again, then levered down the handle and stepped inside.

'Lucia,' said Cole. He was behind his desk, half standing, his weight on the heels of his hands. He was smiling. She had not expected him to be smiling.

'Guv,' Lucia said. She closed the door behind her.

'Come. Sit. Coffee? You don't want coffee. It's too damn hot for coffee. Water?'

'Thank you,' Lucia said. 'I'm fine.' She crossed the office and lowered herself into the chair her boss had indicated. Across from her, Cole sat down too. He was still smiling.

'This isn't formal,' he said. 'This isn't official.'

'No. I realise that. But before you say anything—'

Cole held up a hand. 'I need some help, Lucia. I need your help.'

'Guv—'

'Please, Lucia. Give me a moment.'

Lucia fell silent. Cole reclined in his chair. His hand drifted to his upper lip but stopped short when he noticed Lucia watching.

'The toothpaste,' he said. 'It didn't work. It burnt like hell, if you want the truth.'

Lucia shifted. The chair, plastic and unyielding, was scraping the backs of her knees. The rest of her felt sticky, starved of air. 'I'm sorry,' she said. 'It was just something I read. I shouldn't have mentioned it.'

Cole waved a hand. He leant forwards, folding his arms and propping his elbows on the desk.

'Mr Travis,' he said. 'The headmaster. He received a letter.'

Lucia had not intended to allow the conversation to get this far. Now that it had, she found herself curious about where it might go. 'Yes,' she said. 'I know he did.'

'And you know too, presumably, what that letter contained?'

Lucia held Cole's gaze. She nodded.

The chief inspector studied Lucia. He drummed his fingers against the surface of the desk. Behind a bulging cheek, his tongue occupied itself with something that had caught in his teeth.

'It's a problem,' he said. 'You can see, can't you, that it's a problem?'

'I would say that it was a problem for Mr Travis, Chief Inspector. Wouldn't you?'

Cole bobbed his head. 'Certainly,' he said. 'Certainly it's a problem for Mr Travis. But I'm hoping that you and I might find a way to make that problem disappear.'

'I see,' Lucia said. 'And that's why I'm here. That's why you think I'm here.'

Cole did not reply. Instead he hoisted his smile, as though mindful suddenly that he had allowed it to droop. He stood up and crossed to the water cooler. 'You're sure you're okay?' he said. When Lucia did not respond, he drew himself a cup, then returned to his position behind the desk. He did not sit down.

'A court case,' he said. 'A civil prosecution. Perhaps you'd explain to me, Lucia, just what it is you are hoping to achieve.'

'That's not for me to say, Chief Inspector. It's not my business, after all.'

Cole laughed. He laughed and for the first time betrayed his impatience. 'I think we're past pretending, Inspector. Don't you?'

Lucia made to stand. 'I'm not sure this conversation is going to accomplish anything, Guv. If you don't mind—'

'Sit down, Inspector,' said Cole.

Lucia held still.

'Please,' Cole said. 'Sit down, Lucia.'

Lucia sat. She folded her arms.

'From what I understand, the Samsons have a grievance. They are lashing out, it seems to me, in the only way they can.'

'No,' said Lucia. 'That's not—'

Cole cut her off. 'They are lashing out at the school and they are lashing out at its headmaster. Wait, Lucia. Just wait a minute.' He smiled again. The smile did not reach his eyes. 'It's understandable,' he said. 'Of course it is. They lost their son. Elliot, isn't it? That was his name, am I right? They lost their son and no one was punished. Why wouldn't they be angry?'

'They are angry,' Lucia said, struggling now to keep her voice steady. 'They're furious. And they're not alone.'

'It's understandable,' Cole said again. 'I sympathise. We all do. Even Mr Travis, as hard as you may find that to believe.'

Again Lucia tried to interrupt. Cole spoke over her. 'But

what if something could be arranged? I mean, that's what this is really all about, isn't it? Retribution. Revenge. Payback for what happened to Elliot.'

Cole finally granted Lucia the opportunity to speak. She found that her throat was clogged with words.

'Arranged?' she managed to say. 'What do you mean, arranged?'

Cole gave a shrug. He prodded at the edges of a pile of papers on his desk. 'Gideon, isn't that his name? His friends. The ones who attacked Elliot. There's nothing we could do, obviously. The investigation is closed. But Mr Travis . . . Well. It's his school, after all.'

'Forgive me, Chief Inspector, but I thought our position – I thought the headmaster's position – was that no one had witnessed the attack. Isn't that what the Samsons were told?'

'We're talking openly, Lucia. I thought we were talking openly.'

Lucia shook her head. She found herself smiling in spite of herself.

'This case,' said Cole, his tone more abrupt now. 'No one wants it. I know you've got a problem with Travis and maybe you can live with ruining one man's career but what about the school? What about the other teachers, the other pupils?'

'You're missing the point. You're completely missing the point. It's because of the teachers and it's because of the other pupils that the Samsons are doing what they're doing.'

'And the force, Lucia? What about the force? Don't think this won't touch us. Don't think we won't be implicated too. Because your friends are going to be standing up in court and telling the world that the police failed them. That the police failed their son. Do you think that's going to make our job any easier next time? Do you think that's going to make this country safer? Because I don't. I do not.'

Lucia stood. 'I've heard enough,' she said. 'I really think I've heard enough.' She turned away and took a step towards the door.

'Okay, Lucia. Okay.'

Lucia glanced behind her. Cole was standing with his arms raised, less a gesture of surrender, more an indication that Lucia had forced on herself whatever was coming.

'Forget the school,' Cole said. 'Forget Travis. Forget about your own fucking colleagues. What about you? What do you think is going happen to you if you decide to go ahead with this?'

'I told you. It's not my decision. The Samsons have made their own choice. All I've done is give them the information that no one else would. The information they deserve.'

'Exactly, Inspector. Exactly. You're already on suspension. What good do you think all of this is going to do for your career?'

'My career,' Lucia echoed. She turned back to face her boss. 'I almost forgot.' She took an envelope from her bag and held it out. 'This is for you. This is the reason I came. It's only a line or two but you'll find it covers the important points.'

Cole frowned. He took the envelope from Lucia and checked each side, as though unsure of what it was he was holding. 'You're resigning?'

'I'm resigning.'

'You're giving up. You're quitting.'

'Call it what you like. This job isn't what I thought it was. It isn't what it should be.'

'That's crap, Lucia. That's idealistic crap. And this,' he said, brandishing the envelope, 'doesn't get you off the hook.' He tossed Lucia's letter on to the desk. It skidded across the surface and off the other side. 'What you did,' he said. 'What you've done. You could face charges. Criminal charges. You used privileged information from the Szajkowski investigation to incite Elliot Samson's parents into launching a civil prosecution against the school. It's abuse of office, Lucia. Mr Travis has every right to go straight to the IPCC.'

'Mr Travis may go wherever he wishes,' Lucia said. 'If you like, I could even come up with a few suggestions myself.'

'For Christ's sake, Lucia! You're not even going to win!'

Lucia shrugged. 'Like I say, it's not my business. I would assume, though, that winning hardly mattered. It's not usually the court's judgement that counts in a case like this.'

'So what's the point? What the hell is the point?'

'Remember Samuel Szajkowski, Guv? He wasn't tried but he was judged. Travis allowed him to be judged. And Leo Martin. Try mentioning Leo Martin's name to Mr Travis. See what colour he turns.'

'Leo Martin? Who the hell is Leo Martin?'

'Just a boy. Just another boy who didn't win. He won the argument though. The press made sure of that.'

Cole scoffed. 'You're talking in riddles, Lucia. You're talking yourself into a shit heap of trouble, that's what you're doing.'

'Tell me, Guv: why are we even having this conversation? If

winning were all that mattered, why not just let the Samsons lose?' Lucia took a step towards the desk. 'You know as well as I do that even if their case comes to nothing, they will have achieved what they set out to achieve. Because, for Travis, there'll be no hiding. There'll be no vested interests to use as cover. You, your boss, whoever else is on the headmaster's side: none of you will be able to help. You might even find yourself trapped in the same corner as the man you seem so eager to protect.'

Cole was shaking his head. 'I told them you would be reasonable. I told them there wouldn't be any need for threats. But it'll happen, Lucia. If your friends go ahead with this, you'll face the consequences. I won't do anything to protect you.'

'I wouldn't ask you to. I wouldn't dream of it.'

'It's worth it then. The cost, the personal cost, all for an inch or two buried at the bottom of page nine – it's worth it to you?'

Lucia stooped and picked up the envelope from the floor. She placed it on Cole's desk. 'Samuel Szajkowski,' she said. 'He shot Donovan and then he fired at the stage. He was aiming at Travis, Guv. Not at the woman who betrayed him or the man who tormented him. He was aiming at Travis.'

'I don't care, Lucia. Travis doesn't care.'

'No. I'm sure he doesn't. I'm sure, right now, he has other things on his mind. But he'll have plenty of time to think about what it means once he's settled into his retirement.'

Outside, they were waiting. They did not look like they were waiting but their lack of interest was unequivocal. Only Harry was openly watching for Lucia as she emerged. He raised his eyebrows. Lucia returned a grimace.

Heads lifted and tracked Lucia's path across the office. She would have made her way straight to the stairwell had Harry not caught up with her first.

'Lucia,' he said. His hand on her shoulder guided her around. 'I realise this may not be the best time . . . '

Lucia looked beyond Harry's shoulder. Cole's door was still shut but Walter, seated at his desk, was regarding them with an expression somewhere between incredulity and delight. Rob and Charlie loitered, their leers cocked and at the ready. 'It's not a great time, Harry.'

'No,' he said. He glanced behind him. 'No. But if you did in there what I imagine you went in to do . . . Well. I suppose we might not be seeing each other for a while.'

Lucia found herself smiling at Harry's turn of phrase. 'What's up?' she said.

'Nothing. Nothing important. I just wanted to ask you something, that's all.' His voice was quieter now, though the others were still listening. They would still be able to hear. 'I wanted to ask you whether you fancied going for a drink? Just to a pub or something. Not now obviously. At some point. Just whenever. Or not,' Harry added. 'You know, whatever.'

'Whatever?' Lucia echoed.

Harry's fingers rubbed at his forehead. 'Not whatever. I didn't mean whatever. All I meant was . . . Jesus Christ, Lucia. You're not making this easy. All I meant was—' he began again but Lucia placed her fingertips on his arm.

'I know what you meant, Harry. I'd like that. I'd like to get a drink sometime. You know, whenever.'

Harry beamed. 'Great,' he said. 'I'll call you.'

'Do,' said Lucia. Smiling again, she made to turn away.

The sound of flesh slapping flesh stopped her. Walter was beating out a sluggish applause. He was grinning, Lucia saw, but not at her. Harry was his target now. Harry, who was moving eyes down towards his desk.

'Bravo, Harry my lad. It looks like you've got yourself a date. And here we all were thinking you were a shitepoke.' Rob and Charlie laughed. Walter looked across at them, affecting a puzzled expression. 'Although thinking about it,' he said, 'does it really count if the bird you shag is a dyke?'

Harry was passing Walter's chair. He stopped abruptly. 'Watch your mouth, Walter. Watch your fucking mouth.'

Walter stood and Harry inched towards him.

'Why do you do it, Walter?' At the sound of Lucia's voice, the two men turned to face her. 'The jokes like that. This front you have. Why do you do it?'

Walter readied himself to reply but Lucia did not allow him the chance. 'Is it because you don't like women? Is that it?' She was closing the distance between them. Walter leant back against his desk.

'It all depends on the woman,' said Walter. He laughed but the sound was hollow. Lucia was suddenly very close. When she spoke again, she spoke in his ear.

'Is it that you don't like women?' she said again. 'Or is it because it's not women that you like?'

Walter recoiled. He tried to move away but Lucia held him

still. 'Because it's hard, this job, for a woman. For someone like you, it must be so much harder.'

This time Walter pulled free. Lucia stepped away, ceding the ground.

'What did she say?' said Charlie. 'Hey, Walter. What did she say?'

Walter kept his eyes on Lucia. His grin became a growl. 'She didn't say anything. She didn't say fucking anything.'

Lucia faced Harry. Her lips found the corner of his mouth. Before Harry could react, Lucia was moving away, across the office and back towards the stairwell. When she reached it, she turned, and could not help but catch sight again of Walter. He was watching her with an expression of resentment she had only ever seen before through the grille of a cell door. Lucia, though, felt none back.

Acknowledgements

Thanks and love to my wife, Sarah, above all, and to my family: Mum, Dad, Katja, Matt, Galina, Ekaterina, Sue, Les, Kate, Nij, and of course to our budding football team. Also to Sandra Higgison, Richard Marsh, Jason Schofield, Kirsty Langton, Christian Francis, John Lewis, Darryl Hobden and Anna South for their support, guidance and advice. Any errors appear in spite of their help and are my responsibility alone. Thank you, finally, to all at Picador and Felicity Bryan, in particular to Maria Rejt and Caroline Wood.

A Reader's Guide to *Rupture*

Points for discussion

1. Over the course of the novel the author increasingly presents Samuel as a sympathetic character. Is this process entirely successful?

2. *'You have a murder weapon, a motive, a room full of witnesses . . . I've got an hour before I'm due to go home. I could write your report and still knock off twenty minutes early.'*
— DCI Cole, p. 25

The school shooting incident seems an open-and-shut case. What do you think motivates Lucia into continuing her investigation?

3. *'What happened to our son – it wasn't the school's fault. What the hell could they have done?'*
— Elliot Samson's father, p. 271

To what extent do you agree with this assertion? Is, as Lucia claims, the school culpable, or should blame be apportioned elsewhere?

4. Much of the story takes place in oppressive heat during one summer in London. Do you believe there is any symbolism in this? What effect might the heat have on events?

5. *'You're twenty-seven. A fair age. Not a mature age but an adult one. You are an adult, Mr Szajkowski?'*
— Mr Travis, p. 101

Does the novel present Samuel as an adult? In what ways does *Rupture* portray other individuals acting in a manner counter to their age?

6. *'The parents are responsible. The parents are always responsible.'*
— Elliot Samson's mother, p. 267

Parental figures loom large in the novel, either through their presence or their absence. How are they variously portrayed and how important are they to the events that unfold?

7. *'How can I say I loved him after what he did? How can I admit that to myself? I tell myself now that I never loved him and I pray that what I tell myself is true.'*
— Maggie, p. 51

Each narrator gives their interview after the shooting. How reliable are their accounts likely to be? To what extent might their words be influenced by hindsight?

8. '*No one really cares . . . They read the stories and they gasp and they tut . . . But if it were really real to them, they would not be entertained. If they cared, they would not turn the page.*'
— Felix's father, p.231

How accurate do you think this view is? Do you feel it correctly reflects society's behaviour towards certain tragedies? Can you think of any other incidents that have been exploited by the media for mass consumption?

9. '*It was monstrous, what he did, but he was not a monster.*'
— Lucia, p. 83

By the novel's end Samuel appears well intentioned but misguided. What do you think pushed him to take matters into his own hands rather than leave it to the proper authorities?

10. '*So what is it, Lulu? If you don't have a thing for him . . . Why are you so desperate to defend him?*'
— Walter, p. 125

Both Lucia and Samuel experience severe bullying in their workplace. What other experiences do they share?

11. '*Lucia dear. You're no fun any more. No cigarettes, no alcohol before midday. I mean, really. Is this what they've been teaching you in the Met?*'
— Philip, p. 85

Throughout the novel, what details emerge of Lucia's past? What sort of character does she appear to be prior to the school shooting?

12. *'It's always easier to deal with the pain if you can twist that pain into anger.'*
— Sarah's stepfather, p. 120

Is this how Samuel behaves in the novel? Do any other characters behave in a similar manner?

13. *'This job isn't what I thought it was. It isn't what it should be.'*
— Lucia, p. 290

How does *Rupture* portray the police force? Do you feel this is a fair representation?

14. *'I don't know what Samuel did. Probably he just went on being Samuel. Probably he assumed it had gone okay. He was a man after all.'*
— Maggie's friend, p. 135

Maggie's friend implies men and women perceive things differently. Do the female and male accounts in *Rupture* differ significantly? If so, in what ways?

15. *'When we looked at the alternatives, Inspector. The other schools. Some of them . . . You just wouldn't. You just couldn't. And there was Sophie of course. We had to think of Sophie.'*
— Elliot Samson's father, p. 186

In the above lines Elliot's father implies that bullying, or the threat of bullying, is potentially a price worth paying for an improved education. How far do you agree with this view?

A conversation with Simon Lelic

How would you sum up *Rupture* in one line?

A teacher kills three pupils and a colleague in a school before turning the gun on himself, but in the aftermath it becomes clear that the man who pulled the trigger is not the only one responsible for the crime.

What inspired you to write this particular story?

Some time before I started writing *Rupture*, I came across a short item in the newspaper about an American college professor who shot and killed one of his colleagues. There were few details in the article, but it immediately started me wondering what could have driven such an obviously intelligent and, you would have assumed, emotionally mature man to commit such a desperate act. I was reminded of incidents from my own time at school – teachers, for instance, being subject to victimisation that was often more vicious than anything I had witnessed in the playground. From there, the story that turned into *Rupture* began to grow. I became fascinated by the idea that the experience of teaching in a school could never be entirely distanced from that of being a pupil there.

What can readers look forward to next from you?

My next novel is entitled *The Facility*. It is a somewhat dystopian depiction of the UK several years hence, in which civil liberties have been undermined to the point that the government is free to incarcerate members of the public when an epidemic of a previously unknown disease threatens. The story is told from three perspectives: that of one of the men imprisoned, of a journalist trying to help free him, and of the official charged with running the government facility.

What do you enjoy reading?

Anything that is well written. I worship Cormac McCarthy but have to stop myself reading his books when I am writing so that I don't subconsciously try (and fail, inevitably) to ape his style. Other writers I particularly admire are Nabokov, Don DeLillo, Hilary Mantel and John Fowles. Also David Mitchell, Jon McGregor and Sarah Waters, plus Rupert Thomson, who uses similes and metaphors with an imagination and fluidity unmatched by any contemporary writer I have read.

What advice would you give to aspiring authors?

I am not sure I have earned the right yet to dispense advice but, if pushed, I would tell aspiring authors to be selective about what advice they follow! I know from experience how tempting it is to latch on to every utterance you come across concerning 'how to write', to the point where you are frantically trying to accommodate conflicting, contradictory counsel. Find what works for you; forget about how other writers do it.

Tell us something unusual about yourself.

I have a black belt in karate. Also, grade 1a playing the organ – a grade my wife (a grade-eight flautist) maintains does not exist. But I have the certificate, dating to about 1986, to prove it, as well as a distant memory of being able to play the *Ski Sunday* theme tune. And that's about as unusual as I get, I'm afraid.

If you enjoyed RUPTURE,
you will love

THE FACILITY

the astounding second novel from Simon Lelic

Out January 2011

Henry Graves has dedicated his life to the prison service, losing his marriage and sacrificing his relationship with his daughter in the process. He is used to being uprooted, to dealing with angry and embittered prisoners, but he is unprepared for the challenge his new and secret assignment brings. Tasked with managing a government facility hidden deep in the country-side, Henry finds himself tested as never before: by the confused and frightened prisoners, by the sinister Dr Silk and, above all, by his conscience.

Tom Clarke, a precocious but naive journalist, has his own problems, meanwhile. His career – and his life – is turned upside down by the arrival of Julia Priestley, who seeks his help in finding her estranged husband, Arthur, an innocent dentist who has been arrested under severe new anti-terrorism legis-lation. The authorities admit they have taken him but will not say where he is being held – or why.

Discovering a trail that implicates those at the very top of government, Tom and Julia begin a quest to find Arthur, and the truth about his incarceration. But some people will stop at nothing to keep the facility's secret hidden, and soon the couple find themselves fighting for their lives.

A fast-paced and gripping read that raises complex moral questions, *The Facility* is a terrifying portrait of a society obsessed with security at whatever cost.

An excerpt follows here.

Henry Graves watches through the doorway as the man from the Home Office surveys the room. There is little to see – two bunks, two piles of bedding, a toilet, a sink, a narrow window with wire-mesh glass – yet Jenkins inspects what there is, as though considering whether to make an offer. He taps a wall and seems satisfied, then taps again and gives a frown when his knuckle yields a thud. He peers in the toilet and behind it. He fiddles with a tap and turns it on and the ferocity of the water takes him by surprise. He arches his groin to avoid being sprayed and turns the tap off again. He moves to a bunk and presses a palm to the mattress. He sits.

'I'm no prude, Graves,' he says, after a moment. His attention is on the bunk opposite. 'But two bunks. In each cell.' He turns to face the corridor. 'Do you think that's wise?'

He is not the first to make the point. Graves's assistant, John Burrows, asked too, though in less delicate terms. 'The inmates will eat together, minister, and they will exercise together but they will only be required to share a room with a member of their own sex.'

'Quite,' says Jenkins. 'That's precisely my point. I'm not concerned so much about the women but the men . . . I mean, aren't most of them . . . That is, aren't they all . . .'

'They are not all homosexual, minister. And besides,' Graves adds, 'I do not see the harm. The harm, I would say, has already been done.'

Jenkins's lips give a twitch: not quite a smile but not far off it. He casts around once more. He stands. 'Good. More than adequate. So: is that everything?'

'Except for the grounds.'

Jenkins checks his watch. He squints behind him at the cell window. 'Is it still raining?'

Graves looks where the minister is looking. Through the wire and the dappled glass, he can make out only a pervading greyness. 'There is cover. We shan't get wet.'

Jenkins checks his watch again. 'Just quickly then. I've another appointment and then a long journey back.' He steps from the room and turns in the wrong direction. 'This way?'

'This way, minister,' says Graves. He gestures with an open palm towards the opposite end of the corridor, then follows at his guest's shoulder.

'You shan't be staying for lunch?' Graves says. 'We were told you would require lunch.'

'Perhaps next time.' Jenkins is scanning the walls around him as he walks. 'Could do with a lick of paint down here, Graves.' He pauses for a moment and points. 'Is that damp? You should get that seen to. The longer you leave it, the worse it'll get.'

Graves peers. 'Indeed. It does look like damp. I will ensure it is seen to, just as soon as the budget allows.'

'Do it sooner rather than later,' says Jenkins, walking on. 'You have a budget, naturally, but it's a question of priorities. It's all very well having a forty-inch plasma screen in the recreational area but if that damp spreads any further, you won't have any power to run it.'

'Power, minister?'

'Power, Graves. I've seen it happen. The damp gets to the cabling and the whole damn fuse board ends up fried, especially in an old building like this. Where will your budget be then?' Jenkins turns his raised eyebrows towards his host but Graves has stopped three steps behind. He stands at the door to the stairwell.

'This way, minister,' Graves says. Jenkins retraces his steps and rumbles his thanks as he passes through.

'You are sure about lunch?' says Graves, returning to Jenkins's side in the corridor below. 'It would not be any trouble. In fact, I believe it has already been prepared.'

'Hm? What's that?'

'Lunch, minister. It's all prepared.'

Jenkins shakes his head. His jowls wobble. 'Thank you, no. I'm due to meet my sister. She lives in a village not far from here, as it happens. Although it's all relative, I suppose, in country like this. I say not far but it's forty miles at least.'

'Very sensible, minister. Combining business with a little pleasure.'

Jenkins glances at Graves as though to gauge his tone. Graves keeps his face expressionless and the minister gives a grunt. 'There'll not be much pleasure, Graves, I assure you. Aside from the company, I don't suppose the cuisine at the local

311

brasserie is up to much. Given the choice, I would rather suffer the delights of your canteen.'

Graves inclines his head. 'I shall pass on the message,' he says. 'Our chef, I am sure, will appreciate the compliment.' He has gone too far this time but he pretends not to notice the minister's scowl. 'The door is just ahead. Please, allow me.'

The rain has indeed stopped. The clouds seem to have followed its descent, however, turning the courtyard into a basin of mist. Even from the edge of the covered walkway, they can barely see across to the arches opposite. Above them, the ragged line of the second-floor windows is visible, but the pitched roof and corner turrets are nothing more than shadows.

Jenkins jabs his chin towards the centrepiece of the quad: a fountain, depicting Neptune in a chariot behind three horses. 'A touch extravagant, would you not say?'

'It is hideous, I know. The whole building, really, is an architectural chimera. His Majesty, for one, would not approve. There's Gothic here, Romanesque there, Palladian and Tudor in the outbuildings. None of it original, of course. Except for the staff quarters, which were built in the fifties.'

'You got it working, though. You left the damp but fixed the fountain.'

'It was no great expense, minister. We felt it would be beneficial. The sound of running water, a place for the men and women to gather. You understand, I am sure.'

'They are prisoners, Graves.'

'They will be imprisoned, minister. It is perhaps not quite the same thing.'

'Guff,' says Jenkins. 'Of course it's the same thing.'

Graves gestures to an opening in the grey-stone wall. 'We can pass around and through the gateway if you would like to see the rest. There is no shelter past the main building but from the passageway you will be able to see the layout of the grounds beyond.'

'No need.' Jenkins wipes a thumb across the face of his watch. 'I am sure it is satisfactory. Everything seems more than satisfactory. Except for that damp,' he adds, raising a finger. 'Be sure to see about that damp.'

'Indeed, minister. I will ensure it is attended to. And lunch. You are adamant I cannot persuade you?'

'Just my things, if you please. My overcoat is in your office. This way, is it?' Jenkins points the way he is facing.

'If you'll follow me,' says Graves and he leads off in the opposite direction.

Burrows is behind him, his pimpled nose pressed to the glass. He snorts periodically, a prompt for Graves to solicit his opinion. Graves is careful not to. He keeps his attention on the papers spread across his desk.

'Thirty minutes, would you say? Thirty-five?'

'He was here a good hour,' says Graves. He stacks a folder in the pile to his right, picks another from the pile to his left and opens it in the space between.

'Not including the time he spent on the phone, I mean. Thirty-five minutes, by my reckoning, at the very most. And we've been preparing, what? Six weeks if you count the renovations.'

'It's his prerogative.' Graves uncaps his pen, makes a note of a name in his pad. He closes the folder he has in front of him and sets it on the right-hand pile.

'We bought steak. Howard did. It's not as though they've given us money to waste.'

'It will not go to waste, I am sure.'

'You asked him, though? You told him Howard had prepared lunch?'

'Twice,' says Graves. 'Three times, in fact. It was beginning to sound suspicious.'

Burrows turns back to the window, though Jenkins's car is long gone. Graves glances at his assistant. There is a haze of condensation on the pane in front of him, thickening with each outward breath, ebbing as he inhales.

'Satisfactory,' says Burrows, still staring at the gravel drive. 'That's the word he used?'

'He said more than satisfactory, John. More than.'

'Did he mention anything else?'

Graves sighs. He shuts the folder in front of him and sets it on the pile to his right. He puts down his pen. 'Like what?'

'I don't know. Anything. There must have been something that made an impression.'

'The water pressure. In the accommodation wing.'

'What about it?'

'It made an impression.'

'What about the fountain? Did you show him the fountain?'

'I did.'

'And? What did he say?'

'He wondered whether it might be a touch extravagant.'

'Extravagant?' Burrows spins from the window. 'What's that

supposed to mean? It's running water! Did you say to him it was running water?'

Graves nods.

'And he understood the connotations? He understood the subtlety?'

'It's a fountain, John. It's a naked god, ten feet high. It's not subtle.'

'I meant the calming effect!'

'I know what you meant,' Graves says. 'And you are right to be proud of the idea. Let's leave it at that, shall we?'

Burrows frowns, turns away. He mutters something Graves does not catch. Graves can feel himself becoming infected with his assistant's irritation, though it is Burrows's petulance that grates the most.

'Really, John,' he says, knowing he should resist. 'What did you expect? A ribbon and some oversized scissors?'

'No,' says Burrows. 'Of course not.'

'What then?'

'Some recognition. That's all. We've done what they asked us to do and we've done it on time, on budget and without a single leak.'

'Which means we've done what we're getting paid to do. Nothing more. You knew the terms when you accepted this post. You knew and you accepted it anyway.'

'They barely gave me a choice.'

'One always has a choice, John.'

Burrows makes to answer back but Graves cuts him off. 'Enough,' he says. 'You've made your point. We have work to do.'

Burrows moves away from the window. He slumps into his boss's reading chair and tucks his outsized hands between his knees. His feet turn inwards and meet toe to toe. 'Everything's ready. What more is there to do?'

There are two more folders for Graves to check. He opens them in turn, content to let Burrows wait while he works. He adds one of the names to the list in his notebook, then straightens the pile of folders by his right hand and taps it with the pen in his left. 'These names,' he says. 'They will all be in the first batch?'

Burrows shrugs. 'I think so.'

Graves snaps before he can stop himself. 'Sit up straight, man. Answer properly. Talk to me properly.'

Burrows slides upright in the leather chair.

'These names,' Graves repeats. 'Will they all be in the first batch?'

Burrows nods once, rather precisely. 'Yes, sir. That's what they told me.'

'How many exactly?'

'Fifty-seven. Mostly men, a handful of women.'

'And how many to follow after that?'

'Twenty-nine, they said. But that may change.'

There are twelve names on Graves's list: ten men and two women. He tears the page from his notebook and slides it across the desk. 'Bunk these people separately. Just for the time being.'

'Separate from each other or separate from the rest of the prisoners?'

'Give them their own rooms. Keep them in the main wing but I don't want them sharing.'

'All right,' says Burrows. He stands and takes the list and checks the names but does not ask his boss's reasoning. Possibly he does not need to; more likely he is wallowing still in his sulk.

'Also,' Graves says, 'have someone take a look at the plastering outside room twelve. Probably there's a drain overflowing somewhere. Fix it, paint it. Check the rest of the corridor too.'

'Yes, sir. Is that everything, sir?'

There is a note to his assistant's tone that Graves does not appreciate. 'No, John, it is not. This project, this facility: it is not a game.'

Burrows draws back his shoulders. 'I realise that.'

'Well, then,' says Graves. 'I hope you realise too that when these people arrive here, they will be angry. We cannot afford to let their anger get out of hand— '

'The staff are well equipped. They are well trained.'

'We cannot afford to let their anger get out of hand but we must respond with equanimity too.'

Burrows narrows his eyes. 'I'm not sure I follow.'

'Talk to the staff, John. Remind them that the men and women in our charge are human beings. They are not criminals. I would like everyone to remember that.'

'Yes, sir. I am sure it will not be a problem.' Burrows folds the list and sharpens the crease. He makes to leave.

'One more thing,' Graves says. 'They are dying, John. The people who will arrive here: they are dying. They might not know it yet but that's the truth of it.' He takes the lid off his pen and turns to a fresh sheet in his notebook. 'Please,' he says. 'Remember that too.'

picador.com

blog
videos
interviews
extracts